PERFEKT CONTROL

THE ÆRE SAGA: BOOK TWO

S.T. BENDE

The Ære Saga

Perfekt Control

Copyright © 2015, S.T. Bende

Edited by: Lauren McKellar

Cover Art by: Alerim

First publication: 2016, S.T. Bende

This book is a work of fiction. Names, characters, places, and incidents either are products of the author's imagination or are used fictitiously. Any resemblance to actual persons, living or dead, events, or locales is entirely coincidental.

DEDICATION

To my perfekt gentlemen. I thank God for you.

"Love all, trust a few, do wrong to none; be able for thine enemy rather in power than use, and keep thy friend under thy own life's key."
-Countess of Rousillon, *All's Well That Ends Well*

CHAPTER 1

"STUFF IT, BRYNN," TYR muttered as he pulled a smoking pan from the oven. The God of War stood in our open kitchen. His girlfriend's frilly pink apron popped against his standard uniform of jeans and a Henley. He glared at me as he dumped the blackened contents of the pan into the sink, where it blended with a sea of similarly situated peers. Our kitchen had morphed into a veritable cake graveyard.

"I didn't say anything." I held up my hands.

"Didn't have to." Tyr threw the empty cake pans at the stovetop, where they clattered loudly in protest. "Your obnoxious little laugh speaks volumes."

I forced my face into a neutral position and tilted my head at the lacy fabric tied around Tyr's waist. "Your cooking attire took me by surprise. That's all."

Tyr pulled the oven mitts from his hands and threw them at me. Hard. My fingertips stung as I plucked them from the air.

"Was that really necessary?" I asked.

"Was cackling like a caffeinated hyena necessary?" Tyr countered with an eyebrow raise.

Harrumph.

"The apron's Mia's. I thought if I wore it while I cooked, maybe this time I wouldn't burn her *förbaskat* birthday cake."

I waited in silence while Tyr scrubbed the big silver bowl clean, pulled a box of cake mix out of the cupboard, and turned to me. With his narrowed eyes and tight-lipped frown, he was the picture of resignation. "Apparently, this apron's not the reason my girlfriend's such a great cook."

"No, it's not." I bounded across the kitchen to rescue the cake box from Tyr's hand. He was squeezing it so hard, I thought it might need saving. "Fred's going to make the packet explode," I pointed out.

Tyr clung tighter to the box with his prosthetic right arm. Mia, Henrik and I had developed it under the guise of an Engineering project, and it had saved his life when the homicidal wolf Fenrir bit his original arm clean off. Now, Fred served proudly as Tyr's right forearm, attached by biomechanical medicine, Asgardian magic, and just a touch of fairy dust.

When poor Mia discovered her freshman lab project was actually the saving grace for an Asgardian deity, she thought we'd led her straight to the psych ward. But crazy was the name of the game when you were tasked with protecting the God of War.

Apparently, diplomacy was the name of the game when you were trying to help him bake.

"Okay, fine. Kill the poor mix." My tone softened when Tyr's shoulders drooped. "Look, Mia's a great cook because she loves it. She likes taking care of us. She especially likes taking care of *you*. And the last thing she'd want on her birthday is for you to beat yourself up over something as silly as a birthday cake. You can always order one from the bakery. Want me to call them?"

"No, Brynn. I'm making my girlfriend a *förbaskat* cake. If you're not going to help, then get out of my kitchen."

"I share kitchen custody, you know." I elbowed past him and opened the refrigerator. I pulled out the carton of eggs and set them on the counter, then closed the door behind me. "When Mia started spending weekends here, her bodyguard did, too. Remember?"

When Asgard's resident war god fell for Redwood State University Engineering undergrad Mia Ahlström, I'd been reassigned from my valkyrie post to protect the sweetest mortal this side of Midgard. And when the wolf Fenrir made a hit on Tyr's life, Mia and her newly christened bodyguard started spending a lot more time at War's impeccably decorated cabin in Arcata, California. Instead of collecting fallen soldiers for Odin and Freya as I'd done as a battle valkyrie, these days I attended Engineering classes, workouts, and study sessions with my charge. I also got to weekend with the uber-uptight war god, and the hottest bodyguard in the history of the realms, Henrik Andersson.

Immortal life was looking good.

"*Ja*, you stay here sometimes." Tyr ran his hands through his dark blond hair. The normally tousled strands now looked downright disheveled. "But you're useless in the kitchen. I need someone who can fix this. Where's *my* bodyguard?"

As if he'd heard Tyr's summons, the front door slammed, and Henrik's footsteps sounded in the hall. A moment later, the tall frame of the guy I'd had the hots for since kindergarten filled the kitchen doorway. I bounced on my toes—the movement usually distracted me from the unavoidable stomach flutters I got whenever I looked at Henrik's wavy hair, easy smile, and thick, muscled arms. But there was no avoiding the twinkle in his grey-blue eyes as he looked around the kitchen.

He grinned at the brooding war god stewing over the stove. "Having trouble, mate?"

Tyr let out a growl that echoed across the cavernous kitchen.

"He's trying to make a birthday cake for Mia." I pointed to the sink, now overflowing with blackened culinary rejects. "But it's not going so well."

"Well, did you offer to help him?" Henrik asked.

"We all know Brynn can't cook," Tyr retorted.

"I can too cook!" I threw a nearby dishtowel at Tyr. He plucked it out of the air before it could smack him in his surly face.

4

"She can cook," Henrik agreed. He walked around the big island in the center of the room and slung an easy arm around my shoulders. An army of angsty butterflies took flight somewhere beneath abs two and three. If I hadn't had *my whole entire life* to get used to hiding my emotions, I probably would have giggled.

"Thank you, Henrik." I stuck my tongue out at Tyr. "Henrik says I can cook."

"Your cooking's fine. It's the baking you're lousy at." Henrik pulled his arm away and moved to inspect the oven. When his back was to us, Tyr turned to me with a smirk.

"Shut up, Tyr." I scowled as I shoved him. Hard.

"Well, there's your problem." Henrik adjusted the dial on the stove. "Your temperature's off."

Tyr's brow furrowed as he scrutinized the box on the counter. "No, it's not. The thingy's at three hundred and fifty. The directions say three hundred and fifty."

"*Ja.*" Henrik walked to the sink and washed his hands. "But you've got the broiler turned on. It's overriding the temperature control and frying your cake." He turned off the water and dried his hands. "You want to keep at it alone, or do you want some help? I don't mind pitching in, but if I'm doing this we're chucking that lousy cake mix and doing it from scratch."

A small wrinkle appeared between Tyr's eyebrows as he weighed his options. Mia would be home from class soon. He'd obviously started early enough, judging by the sea of slaughtered cakes, but now he was down to the wire. He let out a long-suffering sigh. "I'll

5

take the help," Tyr acquiesced. "But I am decorating it myself."

"Whatever you say, *kille*." Henrik pulled milk, flour, cocoa powder and sugar onto the counter. Without even glancing at a recipe, he added ingredients to the standing mixer. "Brynn, grab me the red food coloring, would you?"

"Um, sure." I glanced around the kitchen, my eyes darting from cabinet to cabinet until they fell on Tyr. He gave me a wicked grin.

"You wanted to help, remember?" Tyr said.

"Oh, like you know where it is, Captain Cake Killer." I glared.

"To the left of the stove, just above the spice rack," Henrik offered without turning around. His back flexed as he reached for the oil, the corded muscles straining against his thin grey T-shirt. I sighed. Loudly.

"Uh, okay. Thanks." I crossed to the cabinet, wishing I could wipe the smirk off Tyr's face. My indiscreet ogling hadn't escaped his notice.

It never did.

I handed the food coloring to Henrik then situated myself next to Tyr. Backs against the stove, arms across our chests, we kept ourselves safely out of Henrik's path. It was better for everyone this way.

It was particularly better for Mia's birthday cake.

"Anything we can do?" Tyr asked.

"Somebody want to flour the pans?" Henrik glanced over his shoulder. Tyr and I stared blankly. "Wipe the cake pans with butter," Henrik explained slowly, as if he were talking to a pair of preschoolers, "then dust them lightly with flour. You two master chefs think you can pull that off?"

It took an enormous deal of self-control to *not* roll my eyes as I picked up the butter. "Sometimes you can be a real know-it-all, Henrik Andersson."

"Ah, you love me, Brynnie." Henrik shot me a wink and turned off the mixer. My overworked heart clattered violently against my ribcage. *Bounce, bounce, bounce.* Henrik pulled the bowl from the stand and raised an eyebrow. "Where's my pan?"

Oh. Right. Tyr grabbed the butter out of my hands and rubbed a generous amount into each of the cake pans. I snatched a handful of flour and sprinkled it over the tops. "How'd we do?"

"*Perfekt.*" Henrik gave his easy smile as he divided the batter between the pans. He placed them in the oven and checked the temperature controls. "Now we wait. If we put them into the fridge when they're done, they should be cool enough to decorate about an hour after Mia gets home."

"Not soon enough." Tyr frowned. "I wanted to give it to her when she walked in the door."

"We'll do our best." Henrik patted Tyr's arm. "But a cake needs to cool *completely* before you layer it, or decorate it. So it'll probably be good to go by—"

"It's her birthday." Tyr glared.

"Then you should have asked for my help sooner." Henrik shrugged. "Now if you two can stay out of trouble for the next hour or so, I've got a stabilizer I need to reattach to some grounding cords.

"What are you working on now?" I followed Henrik out of the kitchen.

"There's been some weird activity in the portal behind Elsa's cottage."

"Oh my gods, why didn't you say anything?" I skidded to a stop. "The one Fenrir got in through?"

"One and the same." Henrik kept walking, so I forced my feet to move.

"Why aren't we out there right now making sure nothing gets through?"

"Because I only just noticed it this afternoon. Don't worry, I'm already on it. I've got a halter lock in place, but I'm working on a little something extra to make sure the portal's dog proof. Not that Fenrir could come back or anything; a certain shiny pink ribbon and a little thing called the prison chamber have him on lockdown. This will just be a little bonus security—an early Christmas present for our prince of preparedness." Henrik cocked his finger toward the kitchen.

"Much as I love to make fun of Tyr, this isn't a good time, Henrik." I grabbed him by the arm and spun him around. His biceps were hard against my palm. "Wh-wha..." I stamped my foot and forced myself to focus. "What are we going to do if Hymir or one of his minions get through? We all know he's madder than a wet fire giant that we captured Fenrir. And with that vindictive streak, Odin only knows what he's plotting as his revenge." I tightened my grip around Henrik's muscles. "And what about Loki? He's been awfully quiet lately. Hasn't delivered any of us to the jotuns or stolen a treasure in a really long time. Isn't it about time he had an episode?"

"That's the thing." Henrik scratched his chin, where a smattering of stubble testified to his long hours in the upstairs lab.

"What's the thing?" I tore my eyes away from Henrik's insanely sexy, stubble-strewn chin. The days he sported facial hair seriously tested my *perfekt* control.

"Loki hasn't created a disturbance in... it's been a few decades now. It's possible everything's hunky-dory with him."

"Mia's little sayings rubbing off on you, too?" I snickered.

"They are catchy." Henrik paused at the bottom of the stairs with a chuckle. The noise resonated along the hallway, and the space filled with his easy laughter. My lips curved up at the contagious sound. "Point is, whatever he's up to, if it's anything at all, he's not showing his hand. And Hymir's been quiet since Fenrir's capture. If he's got anything to do with the disturbance around the Arcata portal, he's doing it behind the scenes. We just have to make sure whoever's working for him doesn't develop better tech than we do."

"Nobody develops better tech than we do. We're the *perfekt* team." The words were out of my mouth before I realized how they sounded. Henrik's mercifully dense Y-chromosome kept him from picking up on my double meaning. "I mean, our technology's *perfekt*—always way ahead of the game. 'Cause we're so smart. Um, yeah. Listen, if you need anything, I have some of that titanium alloy left over from the robotics backup we started in case Fred didn't perform to specs. If we combined it with some of the *älva* dust we've got left over, we might be able to develop an auto-return glitch to attach to the portal."

"We're out of *älva* dust; used the last of it on Fred," Henrik reminded me.

"Oh. Right."

"We'll figure something out, *sötnos*. I'll give a holler if I get stuck. You might not be able to bake, but you're one Helheim of an engineering mastermind." Henrik pinched the tip of my braid, and my breath caught. I was having a *really* hard time controlling myself today. Muspelheim must be in retrograde. *Stay calm, Brynn. He's just a guy...*

Liar. Henrik Andersson had never been just a guy to me. And he probably never would be. I'd been head over heels for the boy next door since he defended my honor in the kindergarten playground roughly six hundred years ago, and my feelings hadn't changed in... ever. But it didn't matter. Asgard had survived for millennia thanks to an unchallenged system of rules and structure. Henrik was a seasoned warrior, and I was a junior valkyrie. And our sole priority, for as long as Odin commanded it, was to protect Asgard's first line of defense—the God of War. And on *his* order, we were to protect Tyr's girlfriend, Mia. Personal feelings, and even more so a relationship, would be an enormous liability, notwithstanding the fact that valkyrie code stipulated I wasn't allowed to date until I made captain rank. Besides, my seat in Henrik's life was planted firmly in the friend zone. I was his colleague, his little brother's classmate, and while we were stationed in Arcata, his occasional flat mate. That was as far as our relationship could go.

It didn't stop the uninvited battalion of butterflies springing to attention every time he looked at me. I might have been an immortal battle goddess, but I was still a girl.

Henrik let go of my hair, and turned around with a small smile. He jogged up to the second floor. The muscles of his backside flexed as he ran, and I permitted myself a solitary inward sigh as I watched pure denim-clad perfection ascend the staircase. When I tore my eyes away from the spot where Henrik had disappeared, I noticed the six-foot, six-inch deity smirking in the kitchen doorway.

"Shut up, Tyr." I grabbed my keys off the key hook Mia had installed in the entry, and ripped the front door open. "If anyone needs me, I'm going to the gym."

"You forgot your yoga mat." Tyr chuckled from inside.

"You know I don't do yoga." I glared at my insufferable friend. "There's a kickboxing class in ten minutes, and my gym bag's in the car. And I need some *space* from *this*." I waved my hands in front of me, outlining Tyr's irritating form.

"Don't be late for Mia's birthday dinner," Tyr warned.

My glare softened. "I wouldn't miss it. She's my friend, too, remember?"

"She's special to all of us," Henrik called as he ran down the stairs and out to the garage. He returned seconds later with a small transistor. "Forgot this in the garage lab." Before we could comment, he'd blurred up the stairs in a display of Asgardian speed.

Tyr nodded to the door. "Have a good workout then." He glanced up the stairs with a half-smile. "I'd imagine you have a lot of frustration to work off."

"Shut *up!*" My glare returned in full force, and I slammed the front door behind me. He might have been my charge, and one of my oldest friends, but if Tyr Fredriksen made one more innuendo about my feelings for Henrik, I might have to kill the troll-face.

"Happy birthday dear Mia, happy birthday to you!"

Tyr's adorable mortal girlfriend grinned, her blush spreading to the roots of her chocolate brown hair. She tucked one loose lock behind her ear and leaned over the coffee table to blow out eighteen symmetrically placed birthday candles. Tyr was as predictable as he was bossy, and he conducted his life with the control typical of most warriors, from his impeccable housekeeping habits to his perfectly organized garage. I, on the other hand, could barely wrangle my nightmare hair into submission, never mind keep my room clean.

"What did you wish for? More time with your *favorite* roommates?" Henrik slung an arm around my shoulder and pulled me back onto the couch. Benefit number one of the friend zone: Henrik didn't think twice about physical contact. I honestly believed he forgot I was a girl.

So long as he kept on touching me, I was *totally* okay with that.

"Watch it, Henrik," Heather warned. "If you guys didn't have Captain Beefcake all up in here, you know Mia would spend more time at her 'official' residence—you know, the one her mail still goes to. I doubt *you're* sticking to her cleaning schedule."

Mia's blush deepened.

"Captain Beefcake, eh?" Tyr scratched the stubble along his jawline. "I could get on board with that. What do you say, *prinsessa*? Want to call me that from now on?"

Charlotte patted Mia's flaming cheek, then turned to Tyr. "Sorry about Heather. We don't let her out much these days. Her internship's keeping her busy."

"How's it going at the clinic?" Mia diverted the subject as she cut the cake. Heather passed out slices, and I tried not to be too obvious about sniffing Henrik's chest as I turned to watch her. *Mmm. Laundry detergent and sunshine and calm...*

"It's okay. I'm having a hard time balancing this unit's Chemistry load with the volunteer hours,

13

though. I might need you to tweak my study schedule." Heather handed plates to Henrik and me. I reluctantly sat up, breaking the blissful contact.

"Consider it done. Anything for my roomie." Mia sliced the final pieces of cake, and curled up on the loveseat with Tyr. She handed him a plate before digging into her own frosting. "Mmm." She licked the cream cheese icing off her fork with a contented moan. "Meemaw's Red Velvet. Tyr, you made it just right!"

Henrik pushed his fake eyeglasses up his nose. Asgardians had *perfekt* eyesight, but he liked to wear the glasses around mortals. He thought it made him blend in. *Snort.* I guessed he wore them for Charlotte and Heather's benefit tonight. "Actually," Henrik began. But he stopped short when I elbowed him in the stomach. Hard.

"Let him have this one," I hissed, trying to erase the mental picture of Henrik's pristine abdomen walking shirtless to the shower *every single weekend*. Why couldn't his room have an en suite bathroom?

Henrik leaned close enough that his beachy smell enveloped my space. Fresh air, and sunshine, and a tang of lime. "Brynnie." He frowned. "I worked my butt off perfecting her Meemaw's recipe."

"And I'm sure Tyr will thank you in the morning," I whispered back. I raised an eyebrow at our friend, who had one hand on his plate and one hand on his girl-friend's behind. The look in his eyes was undeniably possessive.

"Fair enough." Henrik sighed.

"Sorry your sister couldn't make it, Tyr." Charlotte looked up from her cake. "I was looking forward to meeting her."

"You still haven't met Elsa?" Mia shook her head. "You're going to love her. Her friend Forse, too."

"They're still just friends, huh?" I asked.

"Apparently." Tyr shrugged.

"Yeah, we've got a whole lot of stubborn people around here." Mia shot me a pointed look. I snorted. My dating life was not mine to control. Not yet, anyway.

We ate in contented silence, and when the last fork scraped the last crumb of red velvet, Tyr shifted Mia in his lap. "Well, *mitt hjårta*, looks like your birthday is drawing to a close. And I have a gift for you that's not fit for public viewing."

I buried my face in Henrik's chest to stifle my laughter. Beside us, Heather let out a muffled guffaw.

"Well, it's getting late. We'd better get home." Charlotte took Tyr's hint. She stood, carried her plate to the kitchen, and stared at Heather until she did the same.

"Uh, right." Heather scurried to the kitchen and back, then grabbed two jackets from the hall closet. She threw one at Charlotte, then stuffed her arms through the other. "Homework waits for no woman."

"Y'all don't have to go." Mia gave Tyr a pointed look. She gently removed his hand from her backside and stood up. "We have more cake. Anybody want seconds?"

Heather looked like she was about to say yes, but

15

Charlotte grabbed her by the arm and dragged her toward the front door. Mia followed. "Thanks, Mia, but we really should let you, erm, *enjoy* the rest of your birthday. Come *on*, Heather."

As Heather begrudgingly followed her roommate out the front door, she turned with a sparkle in her eye. "Glad to see you finally *glowing*, Mia." With a naughty wink, Heather closed the door behind her, leaving Mia standing in the hallway with flaming red cheeks and a gaping mouth. She stayed very still as the lights of the girls' car flashed through the windows, sweeping across the drive. After a long moment, she pivoted on one riding boot, and returned to the living area. Her eyes darted around the room as she bit her bottom lip.

"Yep. We heard it." Henrik let out a hoot, and I hit him over the head with a couch pillow. His glasses fell off, and he picked them up and set them on the coffee table. "What? We're all thinking it. You want us to clear out so you two can have the house to yourselves?"

"Henrik!" Mia shrieked.

Tyr looked like he was considering the offer.

"No." Mia glared at Tyr. "No, we do not."

Tyr chuckled as he stood and crossed to Mia. He pulled her into his arms and nibbled on her crimson ear. "You're hot when you're embarrassed."

"Hush your mouth, Fredriksen," Mia protested. But after a minute she leaned into his touch.

"Before you get too into this," I interrupted, "we need to talk about the time freezer."

"Now?" Mia wrinkled her brow. "Is everything okay?"

"Not sure." I paused as Elsa and Forse opened the front door.

"Sorry we're late. Happy birthday, Mia!" Elsa ran to Mia and threw her arms around our friend. Mia beamed, while Tyr tousled his sister's blond waves. Hers were smooth and loose, and not the least bit unruly. Mine took a half-hour to blow-dry straight, and even then they frizzed at the slightest sign of moisture.

Some goddesses got all the luck...

"*Hei*, Elsa. Forse." Tyr held out a fist. Forse closed the front door, before walking into the living room and bumping Tyr's knuckles in the universal male sign of greeting. "You're late."

"Don't be rude." Mia swatted Tyr's shoulder and pointed to the coffee table. "We've got plenty of cake left. Would you like some?"

Forse ran a hand through his hair while Elsa wrung her fingers together.

"What's going on?" Henrik rested his arm on the back of the couch as he studied Forse's face. "It's never good when your jaw twitches."

"Wait." Elsa held up her hand. "First we need to wish Mia a happy birthday. Forse?"

"Right." Forse pulled a small wrapped package out of his back pocket and handed it to Mia. She took it with a smile.

"You didn't have to get me a present."

"Of course we did. You're a part of the crew now. And we want to bribe you not to leave us. Odin knows we're a lot to put up with." Forse crossed his arms and tilted his head at Tyr. "Especially this *kille*."

"Shove it, Justice." Tyr growled at Forse, using our nickname for the peacekeeping god. Forse just laughed.

"Open it." Elsa clapped her hands. With a grin, Mia tore open the paper.

"You guys!" Mia squealed, holding up the sporting store gift card. "Thank you! I totally need new running shoes. How'd you know?"

"Hmm, maybe because my brother literally runs you into the ground?" Elsa tossed her hair over her shoulder. "How many miles do you two cover in a week, anyway?"

Mia glanced up at Tyr. "I don't know. Maybe thirty?"

"Closer to forty." Tyr rested his hand on Mia's lower back.

"Mother Frigga." Elsa shook her head. "Cut her a break, will you Tyr?"

"It's me," Mia corrected. "I don't want to be the helpless human you guys lock in the house if something attacks us. Again." She shot me a pointed look.

"I didn't lock you in anywhere!" I protested.

"No, but your boss did. And she's not here, so I'm blaming you." Mia looked around. "Where is Freya, anyway? I saved her a piece of cake with extra frosting."

I couldn't help but smile. Mia and Freya got off to a rocky start, since Mia was under the misconception

18

that Freya and Tyr were an item. But the girl and the goddess spent a chunk of time together on our last lockdown at the safe house, and they bonded over their shared loves of fashion and cooking. Now Mia was just as enamored with the Goddess of Love as the rest of us were... and the feeling was mutual.

"That's why we're late." Elsa rubbed her hands on her leggings, nervously. "There's a teensy situation at the portal."

Every god in the room snapped to immediate attention. The mortal simply stopped breathing.

"What do you mean 'a situation?'" Henrik pushed off the couch and stepped slightly in front of me. I jumped up and moved around him so we stood side by side.

"What's happening?" I asked.

"We're not exactly sure." A *V* formed between Forse's brows. "It's been sparking for the last hour. Tiny electric currents are shooting off the outline of the portal, traveling roughly three meters on due south, then disappearing before they hit the ground. We don't understand what's absorbing the energy. We would have come over sooner, but we didn't want to ruin the party."

"Disappearing?" Henrik's frown matched Forse's. "That's not right. If the portal's being activated, the current should flow to the dirt and ground itself. At least, that's what it did last time."

"I know. I wouldn't believe it unless I saw it." Forse shifted in the entryway.

I tapped Henrik's exceedingly firm shoulder. Great Odin's ravens, how much was he benching these days? "Um, could your blocker be doing it?"

"Huh? Oh! Right." Recognition dawned in Henrik's eyes. "I installed the prototype of a new blocker that should provide an extra level of security." Henrik glanced at Tyr. "But I haven't locked down the tech. Maybe it's short circuiting because of the rain?"

"It's not raining yet," Elsa countered. "Forecast says tomorrow. You sure that's it?"

"No." Henrik paused. "We should go check it out."

The front door burst open, knocking Forse out of the way. He caught his footing and turned, shielding Elsa with his body. Tyr, Henrik and I leapt into action. I threw myself in front of Mia and herded her back into the living room, while Henrik opened the weapons closet and threw a sword at Tyr. Tyr plucked it out of the air and stood *en garde*, while Henrik aimed the crossbow he'd chosen at the intruder.

Oh, skit. Here we go again.

CHAPTER 2

"**Y**OU'LL **NEED THE WEAPONS**. But not for me." The Goddess of Love burst into the hallway in a whirl of strawberry-blond and freesia. Freya's eyes were wide as her ponytail whipped back and forth. "There's a new portal next to the original one, and something's on the other side. We have to move."

"Brynn. Follow protocol," Tyr barked.

"On it. Mia, upstairs. Now." I wrapped my fingers around my charge's wrist and dragged her away from the door.

She dug in her heels. "You are *not* locking me up again. You know I'm a better shot than all y'all."

"Not the time, love." Tyr placed his hands on her shoulders and stared her in the eyes. Her rigid posture relaxed at his touch. "I have no doubt that you'll fight at my side at some point, but today is not the day."

With that he kissed the top of Mia's forehead and gave me a nod. I tugged her up the stairs while Henrik flung weapons at Forse and Freya. "Move out. Brynn, Elsa, if we don't report back in ten, call the big guy to send backup."

"Odin's on speed dial, got it. Elsa will send the bird. Henrik, grab your earpiece. We'll run communication." I caught Henrik's eye as he tucked a nano-molecular particle accelerator in his back pocket. It looked like a regular gun, but our innovative—and slightly unorthodox—minds had tweaked the technology to create the perfect implosive.

We *so* worked well together.

"Consider it done." Henrik grabbed another small item from the closet and pocketed it.

"You might want to take one of the vacuums, too. Just in case you need to contain the dark matter," I suggested.

Henrik nodded. He reached into the closet one more time and pulled out a small metal box, depositing it in the side pocket of his cargos.

Be careful, I mouthed.

You too, he mouthed back. And with a nod, he followed Tyr, Freya, and Forse outside, closing the door behind him.

Elsa locked the door and followed me up the stairs. "Let's go to the man cave," she suggested. "I can get a feed from there."

"A feed for what?" Mia questioned. A shout from outside prompted me to nudge her ahead of me. "Stop pushing me, Brynn!"

"Sorry," I said, not sorry. "You know the protocol."

Mia recited Tyr's rule as I hurried her along the upstairs hall. "In the event of an attack, secure the mortal in the panic room. Or, as we refer to it in front of company, the man cave."

"Asgardians believe in efficiency." I shrugged. "No reason one room can't have multiple functions."

"True," Elsa agreed as she followed us into the Arcata cabin's technologically endowed hideaway. "But would it kill you guys to decorate it a little? I get that the boys need a place for their surveillance equipment, and that the *Brynnrik* mini-lab lives over there." She gestured to the cluttered workspace while I snorted at our friends' nickname for the tech-oriented brain they claimed Henrik and I shared. "But the rest of the house is so nice. This is just... sparse. And it's such a big room, you could put some paintings on that empty wall, or maybe hang some curtains..."

She wasn't exactly wrong. Our technological paradise might have looked bland from a decorator's standpoint, but functionally it was a work of art. We'd taken down a wall that separated two large bedrooms, portioning one section off for surveillance equipment, video screens, gadgets, and the requisite lounger and gaming system, and leaving the remainder of the work space for tables littered with beakers, burners, soldering irons, robotics gear, and the odds and ends we needed to develop our occasionally unorthodox tech. We kept any tools we couldn't fit upstairs in our larger lab space out in the garage

"I'll let you approach Tyr with your plans for a man

cave makeover." I closed the door once the three of us were safely ensconced in the room and slid the dead-bolt across the jam. I keyed the code into the pad on the wall, and heavy black shutters slid over the bullet-proof windows. The alloy was fire resistant, bomb resistant, and most importantly, deflected every form of magic Henrik and I had thrown at it during beta tests, dark magic included. We'd recently insulated the house itself with the same material, ensuring that in the event of an attack, nothing, not even a homicidal devil-spawn wolf, could get through.

Tyr wasn't taking *any* chances with Mia.

"Hold on." Mia walked to the blacked-out window. "If you do that, how are we going to see what's happening?"

"A little birdie will show us. Elsa?" I crossed to a flat screen and turned it on. Elsa closed her eyes and held out her hands, one facing the window and one facing the TV. After a minute, the screen flickered to life, showing a high-def image of the tracking party.

"That's you? You're a... a *human video camera*? How is that even possible?" Mia's voice was high enough to make me check the windows. Good thing Henrik insisted we reinforce them. Mia had a set of lungs that could rival a berserker.

"Technically, I'm a *goddess*video camera, not a human one." Elsa's voice carried the joy of a thousand pinwheels. She absolutely oozed calm, even under the most stressful circumstance. "I'm telekinetically manipulating a pre-positioned mobile visual recorder, and transmitting its feed to a surveillance station—in this case, to the man cave."

"So you guys leave cameras lying around the forest, just in case you need to spy on someone?" Mia's tone hadn't lowered one note.

"Tyr's *extremely* thorough about security." Elsa nodded. "But in case we didn't have a mobile unit handy, I could pull one from the closet downstairs and send it to any location within the nine realms via the Bifrost."

"Amazing," Mia muttered.

"Can you pan out so we can watch for hostiles?" I asked our in-house drone. Elsa tilted her hand. Now the screen showed an overhead view of Henrik, Tyr, Freya, and Forse moving past the trees bordering Elsa's cottage, roughly fifty meters from the cabin. They banked right and headed into a thick cluster of sequoias. Northern California's redwoods were gorgeous to look at, but they were one massive pain when it came to surveillance. Unless, of course, you were the one looking for cover.

"I have a lock on the viewer." Elsa opened her eyes. She kept one hand pointed out the window, the other at the flat screen. As she spoke, the image on screen swooped down—she must have sent the camera beneath the tree-cover. "If you see anything suspicious, call out coordinates and I'll redirect the birdie."

"Will do." I typed a message into my phone and pressed *send*. On screen Henrik appeared, and pulled his cell out of his pocket. He read my text, nodded, and placed his earpiece in his left ear.

"What'd you tell him?" Mia looked back and forth between me and the screen.

"Just that we're watching. And that I'll communicate verbally if we see anything out of the ordinary," I explained.

Mia dropped into the wide leather chair. Her hair framed her face with characteristic perfection, but tiny fissures lined her eyes. The stress of spending the bulk of her free time with the God of War and two body-guards was bound to catch up eventually.

"You okay?" I asked.

"Peachy as a summer pie." She closed her eyes. "Does it ever slow down around here?"

"We had a few calm weeks. It was great to have your brother visit for Thanksgiving—especially the part where he sat Tyr down for the 'if you ever hurt my baby sister I will crush you' talk. I wish I had a video of *that*." I stared at the screen. "Henrik, there's static along the northern edge of that cluster of trees—approximately one hundred meters from Elsa's cottage."

Henrik gave a small nod, then said something to Tyr, Forse, and Freya.

"I can't hear him." I shook my phone and turned the speaker feature on and off. "Why can't I hear him?"

"I don't know." Elsa bent her fingers. "Is that better?"

"It's not the viewer, though now that you mention it, sound should have come through those speakers too." I adjusted the volume level on the monitor. On screen, Henrik spoke to Tyr, who nodded. But the only things I could hear were Mia's shallow breaths and Elsa's soft chant as she tried to strengthen her abilities.

"Still nothing?" Elsa asked after a moment.

"Nothing. It's really weird." I watched as Freya and Forse jumped to attention. They turned and ran into the darkest part of the forest.

"My powers can't *see* in there!" Elsa groaned. "It's too dense. Why don't they go the other way?"

"What happened? Did they see something?" Mia leaned forward on the edge of the chair.

"I don't know!" I brought my fist down on the desk. "I can't hear *anything*."

Elsa and I froze simultaneously. If our sight and hearing were rendered useless, it all but debilitated our vantage point. Oh, *skit. Skit, skit, skit, skit. Skit.*

"Henrik!" This time I shouted into my phone. "Grab Tyr, and go after Freya and Forse. Then get out of there. It's an ambush!"

Henrik looked left and right, his lips moving the whole time. I tried to make out the words since *I couldn't hear*, but I knew Henrik relayed my message when Tyr drew his weapon and took off after our friends.

"What's happening?" Mia sounded relaxed enough, but she knitted her fingers together in worry.

Whatever you bloody well do, keep Mia calm. I could practically hear Tyr's angry instructions. Given the visual feed and our need to diffuse the situation on the ground, it was going to be a tall order.

"Mia, our first priority is to keep you safe. Whatever you do, do *not* leave this room unless I tell you to. Got it?" I jumped up to check the locks on the door and the windows. I'd already set the supernatural protections around the house, but they'd only been programmed to keep things *out*. We were still free to leave—we needed to be able to call for the Bifrost and flee if absolutely necessary. "Elsa, that goes for you too. Stay in here unless I order us out. The realm can't afford to lose our High Healer/interim Unifier."

"It can't afford to lose any of us," Elsa corrected through closed eyes.

"Brynn, what's happening?" Mia asked again. "And how can I help?"

"I don't know what's happening," I said. Elsa's viewer dropped to ground level and followed Tyr and Henrik as they bolted through the redwoods. The thick foliage seriously impeded visibility, and the viewer briefly lost sight of them as it flew through the trees.

"Elsa!" I exclaimed. "Find them!"

"Sorry." She shook her head. "It's having a really hard time following their movements."

"I know, but you have to try. Can it see Freya or Forse at all?" I asked.

"No." Elsa scrunched her face up in concentration. Tiny beads of sweat appeared at her brow line as Henrik's back appeared on the TV. "Got him."

Henrik moved slowly, so his back was against Tyr's.

They turned in a quick circle, and I knew from experience they were evaluating the environment for the most immediate threat. My eyes took in every inch of the screen, and I verbalized my assessment for Henrik's benefit.

"I can't see Freya or Forse from this angle, but there are footprints five meters due south of your twelve o'clock that could belong to them." I squinted. "Women's size seven, men's size... twelve? Dang, girl. Your man has big feet." I nudged Elsa with my elbow, and her cheeks turned pink.

"He's not my man," she demurred. "Just do your job, Brynn."

"Pan out," I countered. The viewer pulled back and Henrik and Tyr shrank as the screen expanded to include more of the forest. "Footsteps head south for six meters, then turn due west and... Ground team! Get down!"

Henrik dropped to the ground, pulling Tyr with him. Something dark swooped across the screen, passing over our friends and tracing the path of the footprints.

"What was that?" Mia blurted.

"Follow it! It's stalking Freya and Forse. Elsa, pan out as much as you can without compromising visibility." The birdie had to stay below the canopy or the trees would block out everything, but my current vantage point wasn't enough to let me see where the *thing* had gone. And I still couldn't see the rest of the tracking party. The screen flickered with static. I could barely see *anything*.

"Brynn." Elsa sounded strained. "Something's trying to block it. I don't know how much longer I can hold the feed."

"Just stick with Henrik. He's moving."

Elsa nodded. Her brow furrowed, and she pressed her lips into a thin line. The image on the screen cleared. Now we watched Henrik's back as he and Tyr tore through the forest. The dark thing swooped down on them again, and Henrik loaded his crossbow and took aim. Two shots sailed to the north, but the boys didn't break their stride to check their target. The big black thing dove again, and this time Tyr swung his broadsword. The weapon was so big it should have been totally impractical, but Tyr was half giant, and he held it as if it were nothing more than a basic training dagger. The boys kept running as the shadow continued to attack. They alternated turns trying to bring it down, but nothing worked.

"Henrik, can you hear me?" I spoke into my phone. The back of his head nodded in response. "Good. We still don't have audio on you guys, but whatever that thing is, it's circling back. It looks like it's running a figure-eight pattern overhead. I'm assuming it doesn't want you to reach wherever you're going, which I also assume means you're heading in the right direction. I'm going to have Elsa run the bird up ahead to see if we can find Freya and Forse."

The shadow dove. This time it came so close to Tyr

his sword made contact. A thick black liquid splattered against the screen, oozing downward in a slow trickle.

"Can you clear it?" I asked Elsa.

"No," she replied. "But they can."

"Henrik, wipe the lens of the viewer," I ordered. "Your seven o'clock, two paces behind. Tyr struck the attacker, and it emitted a black goo that's covering the birdie."

Henrik reached behind him to wipe the lens clear. He held the camera to his face and gave a disarming wink, then took aim with his crossbow and fired at his attacker just as it dove for Tyr again. His weapon made contact, sending a trail of black ooze pooling onto the dirt. The shadow quivered, and disappeared. Henrik raced to Tyr's side, nudging him in the direction of the footprints.

"Elsa, send it ahead," I ordered.

She nodded, and the images on the screen flew by. Reddish trunks of sequoia trees, thick green ferns, more trees, and then...

My breath caught in my throat. *No. Not again.*

I zeroed in on the four shapeless black blurs herding Freya toward a tall, indigo door. This wasn't like any portal we'd seen before. It was twice the size of its predecessors, with a wrought-iron frame that emitted sparks I could only imagine were curses, and a door the purplish color of a fire giant's boil. The four blurs slammed against Freya from each direction. Her body convulsed at each contact, like she was being shocked, the frequency of the attacks creating the illusion of a prolonged seizure. The whites of her eyes flashed as she endured the pain, biting her bottom lip so hard she drew blood. The blurs swarmed at the red liquid, ramming her backward with renewed frenzy. A few more meters and the door would suck her into another realm.

When I finally found my voice, it sounded hollow. "Henrik, they're trying to abduct Freya. It's a new portal, six meters north of the previous location. Four black things, like the one that attacked you and Tyr but smaller, are trying to get her through. I don't see Forse, but... oh, *skit.*"

Elsa pulled the viewer back. Forse's prone body appeared onscreen just as Tyr and Henrik skidded into view. The horde of black blurs battering Forse into unconsciousness rose and merged into one thick mass before charging straight at Tyr. Elsa gasped, and I reached out to squeeze her arm. Running intel during a skirmish sucked. It was like watching your worst nightmare play out, and knowing there was nothing you could do to stop it.

"He'll be okay, Else," I assured her.

Elsa sniffled behind me.

Forse lay on the ground, twitching violently, while Henrik took aim with his crossbow and fired. The blurs had merged into a single massive black entity, and while the arrow struck the darkness, the trickle of liquid that oozed from the point of impact didn't slow it in the slightest. It converged on Tyr, covering him in a dense fog before cinching into a vise at Tyr's throat.

Two strangled cries let out behind me, but I didn't turn to comfort the girls. Instead I kept my focus on the screen where Tyr swung his sword through the mist as his face morphed from tan, to red, to purple. The *thing* was squeezing the air from his lungs.

Gods were immortal, sure. But for the Aesir of Asgard, immortality didn't mean we could live forever. It meant we lived until we were taken out. An object laced with dark magic could debilitate a full-blooded god faster than Mia could whip up her Meemaw's Mississippi Mud Pie. And since Tyr was only fifty percent Asgardian, his survival odds decreased by half.

The pieces clicked into place. This wasn't an abduction, or even an invasion. This was an assassination attempt. Whatever those black things were, they were using Freya as the bait to lure Tyr into the open. They knew he'd fight for her, and they knew at some point he'd be vulnerable. Freya and Forse were out of commission. Henrik was scrambling to load his bow. The only thing standing between that *thing* and the extinction of Asgard's first line of defense was… was…

"Henrik, drop the bow. Use the vacuum," I barked. The vacuum was the name Mia and I gave our newest experiment. It looked like a small metal box, but it suctioned repulsive forces that counteracted gravity, aka 'dark energy,' and compressed them within a small chamber. It was equally effective on dark matter—the unseen, highly reactive particles generated from the harshest elements of our cosmos. The vacuum would contain the dark elements for up to seventy-two hours before destroying itself and its contents—plenty of time to deliver perps to the prison chamber for questioning.

Henrik threw his crossbow on the ground and dug into the pocket of his cargo pants. He whipped out a small box and turned so his back was to the viewer. I couldn't see his hands, but I knew the moment he activated the vacuum. He charged at the shadow, arms held high. As he ran, the black mass loosened its hold on Tyr's neck, allowing the war god to suck in a breath. Henrik reached up to pull the shadow off our friend and it cinched around Tyr again. Its four individual forms retained their singular body as they battled Henrik for dominance. Henrik thrust the vacuum at the shadow, and it shook violently, wrenching Tyr off the ground and jerking him back and forth. Tyr kept his fingers locked around the blackness squeezing his throat. The defensive measure stabilized his spinal cord, and at the same time it constricted the darkness trying to choke him. His strength must have been the breaking point; with a flash of light the singular black mass broke apart into four individual shadows. Each member was sucked down into the vacuum. The device rattled violently as it absorbed its charges and Henrik opened his hands, letting the box fall to the dirt. Tyr dropped to the ground and stayed very still.

"*Skit*," I swore again. "I've never seen anything like that. What the Hel did that thing do to Tyr? Elsa, do you think you can heal him? If not, I'm calling Odin for reinforcements, and telling Heimdall to Bifrost Tyr back to the healing unit."

"I can try." She exhaled. "No doubt those shadows are filled with dark magic, but I've expunged it before."

"They'd have to be, in order for the vacuum to work. We programmed it so it would only attract the bad stuff. We didn't want to trap anything with it the dark energy could feed off." I waited while Henrik ran to Tyr's side. Freya might have been in more immediate danger, but protocol dictated we ensure the safety of our primary charge before pursuing any secondary threats. Henrik checked Tyr's vitals, then looked at the birdie with a nod.

"Oh, thank Odin." I exhaled. "He's alive. Elsa, turn the birdie on Freya so we can strategize her extraction. Henrik, you're the only conscious god in the field. Stay with Tyr while Elsa evaluates Freya's situation."

A ragged breath reminded me I was failing at my *other* responsibility.

"Oh, Mia." I turned around and wrapped my arms around my friend. "I'm sorry. But he's going to be fine. They didn't kill him, and Elsa should be able to withdraw the lingering dark magic that's keeping him from insta-healing."

"Insta-healing?" Mia's quivering lip totally undermined the projected brave face.

"Hey, I know it's scary after last time. But I swear, we're not going to let anything happen to him. Trust us?" I squatted down so we were eye to eye.

Mia nodded. "I'm trying. Now what's insta-healing?"

I could always count on her analytical mind to override her emotions. She was *so* Tyr's *perfekt* match. Before I answered her question, I turned to Elsa. "Freya's not on the screen."

"No, she's not," she murmured. Her brow was furrowed in concentration.

I bit back my panic. "Did those things take her through the portal?"

Elsa shook her head. "If the portal opened I would have felt the energy surge. They must have moved her somewhere within the forest. Give me a minute to sweep the area."

Oh, thank Odin. Freya's still in the realm.

While Elsa waved her hand to redirect the camera, I turned back to Mia and called up my best calm voice. "So, insta-healing. You know how our bodies just sort of instantly heal? The process is slowed, or even debilitated by the presence of darkness. But Elsa can remove the darkness. The perks of having a healer for a friend, *ja?*"

"I'm going to have to ask you how being a healer works." Mia pulled her fingers away from her mouth. Poor thing would be all kinds of furious when she realized she'd shredded her nails.

"I'll explain everything." Elsa kept her eyes on the screen, studying the panoramic shot of Tyr, Henrik, and the forest surrounding the portal. "It's mostly energy based—some chakra cleansing, some flower extracts. Oh, no. Brynn, look!" Elsa pointed to the monitor and concrete walls slammed against both sides of my heart.

"Henrik!" I shrieked. "Stop them!"

But it was too late. As Henrik jumped up from Tyr's side, two new shadows flung Freya into view. They rammed her back and forth between them, driving her toward the portal as they delivered one final blow. Freya's legs flew out from under her and the shadows swept in, whirling around her in a funnel and pulling her through the indigo door. The door shimmered and disappeared in a burst of smoke.

And just like that, the Goddess of Love was gone.

CHAPTER 3

W HATEVER BLOCKED OUR POWERS lifted when Freya disappeared. The sounds of grunting gods and combat boots pounding dirt flooded the man cave as Forse pushed himself to his feet and loped unsteadily to Henrik. The boys each shouldered one of Tyr's arms, and dragged him back toward the cabin.

"Audio's back. Henrik, are you and Forse okay?" I asked.

"Yeah. But Tyr's still out of it. You saw what happened with Freya?"

"*Ja*. She's gone. And I'd imagine any trace of the magic left with her. At least you have the shadows that attacked Tyr in the vacuum. We can send them back to Asgard with Heimdall, and Odin or Thor can assess their origin." I glanced at Mia. She sat perfectly still, drawing shallow breaths. "It's okay," I reminded her. "Elsa can heal him."

"Uh, Brynn?" Henrik's voice shook. When I looked back at the screen he'd shifted Tyr onto Forse, and was frantically searching the ground. "The vacuum's gone. There's no trace of it. They must have taken it through the portal."

"How? I had my eyes on the shadows nearly the entire time. Hold on." I swiped the screen, turning back the footage, then running through it frame by frame. Sure enough, one of the shadows swept low to the ground in the exact spot Henrik had dropped the vacuum, before it flew through the indigo door. *Skit*. "Yeah, they took it. Good thing we made more than one, but still…"

"Now we have no leads." Henrik tromped back to Forse, and took his share of Tyr's weight. "We're going to get him back to the cabin. Have Elsa prep the healing box."

"Already on it," Elsa said. She set the birdie to auto-pilot, and keyed a code into Tyr's laptop. A drawer popped out of the desk, and Elsa extracted a small silver box. "Brynn, can I move you over there?"

"'Course." I stepped to the side and watched as Elsa activated the box. It unfolded itself, becoming a fully stocked healer's table, complete with flower essences and the all-important vitals rectangle. Elsa used her magic to raise the rectangle over Mia's chair, then looked at our friend apologetically.

"I'm really sorry to have to do this, but I'm going to need that seat."

"Of course." Mia jumped to her feet and fell to the

ground in one swift movement. "Sorry," she muttered. I reached down to pull her up, and she shook her head. "I'm a little nervous after last time."

"I know." I wrapped my fingers around her arm and squeezed gently. "If it helps, it gets easier. You get desensitized to the attacks."

"I wish I could say that was helpful." Mia sighed as Elsa manipulated the chair into a reclining position. Now it resembled something of a bed. Tyr's legs would hang off the end, but it would get the job done. "Thanks for trying, Brynn."

"What are friends for?" I shrugged.

"Okay. I'm ready for them." Elsa stepped back to admire her handiwork. The leather seat had transitioned to a pull-out bed, with the requisite vitals monitor hovering above. The healing table stood at the ready, offering all the standard Asgardian remedies. An uncorked vial rested on its side, ready to trap any lingering dark magic. Elsa would dispose of it in her own way.

"Good. Henrik, we're shutting down now. What's your ETA?" I spoke to the screen.

"I'm circling the perimeter to confirm no additional active portals. I'll be there in three minutes. Keep Mia and Elsa on lockdown," Henrik answered.

"Affirmative." Three minutes would have to be enough. I turned to Elsa and Mia. "I've got to do something before they get back. Can I have a second?"

Elsa blinked in confirmation and touched Mia's elbow.

"Come on, Mia. Let's pack your things. Tyr's going to want you at the safe house for a while."

Mia nodded, but I could see the resignation in her eyes. "What's my excuse for skipping class this time? Strep throat? Mono?"

Elsa smiled, despite herself. "The kissing disease would seem appropriate, *ja?*"

Mia squeezed my arm as she passed through the door. "Should I pack a suitcase for you or Tyr? Which one of you is stuck on human-sitting duty?"

"Stop it. And I'm not sure," I admitted. My teeth worried my bottom lip. "This only happened once before; we don't exactly have a protocol for it. But don't stress about me, I'll pack for myself."

Mia gave a single nod and pushed through the door. She was back to her composed self. "Well then, I'll throw some things together for Tyr. I'd imagine things are going to move very fast once they get back. And nobody wants to be caught with unwhipped meringue."

I loved our human, but sometimes the things she said made less sense than troll talk.

Mia and Elsa rushed out of the room in a blur of glossy waves and lavender and vanilla perfumes. I sank onto the floor as I picked up my phone and dialed. My stomach turned exactly once at the thought of delivering this news, but I forced it to still. With deliberate effort I closed my eyes, inhaled through my nose, and willed my stomach to settle. After five seconds that felt like a lifetime, I regained command of my body.

Perfekt control was one of the first things they taught in valkyrie school.

"Brynn." My mother's warm voice came through the phone after only three rings. "How are you? Are you eating enough? Your dad and I saw those photos of you with that mortal girl you're looking after—she looks lovely but both of you could use a good meal. Why don't you come home for the weekend and—"

"Mom," I interrupted. "I don't have much time."

Knuckles cracked as my mom clamped down on the phone. "What now?"

"Freya's been abducted," I whispered.

The strangled cry that came across the line made it clear my mother knew what this meant. Not that she'd ever forget.

"Again?"

"Again," I confirmed. "Tyr's going to formulate a strategy and get everyone situated. He'll probably contact Odin in the next hour or so. Don't worry."

"Don't..." My mother trailed off.

"I just didn't want you to hear it from someone else first. Tyr, Henrik, and Forse are on their way back to the house right now. We'll work out a plan, and I'll let you know who's going after her and who's running intel from the compound."

"Please volunteer for intel," Mom wheedled. "I can't lose you."

"It doesn't work like that," I reminded her. "And you're not losing me. I'm great at my job, remember?"

Mom sighed. "Your job. Why couldn't you be a

healer? Or a fight choreographer? Or a Norn..." The sadness seeped into her voice.

"Nobody's immune, Mom. You know that."

"Yes, but... you don't have to go *looking* for trouble."

To distract myself from losing control, I loosened my braid and used my fingers to comb through my unruly waves. I focused on the texture of the strands and the tug on my scalp as I crafted a low ponytail. *Control regained. One minute left.* "I'm not looking for trouble, Mom. I'm looking for Freya. Or, I will be, if that's Tyr's order. This is his call. I just wanted to let you know."

"Is Henrik with you?" she asked.

"He's on his way back right now."

"Okay." Mom sounded relieved. "I'm so glad the two of you have each other. He's always looked after you. I still remember the night he stepped in to take you to your Fall Ball in high school, when that horrible boy stood you up. Henrik saw you sitting on the porch steps in your beautiful dress, crying, and ran next door to put on his suit and—"

"Not the time, Mom," I muttered.

"Right. Sorry. Be careful, sweetheart." This time, the tension in Mom's voice was tempered with love.

"I always am. And I promise we'll get Freya back before things go too far. It won't be like last time." My breath caught on the words.

"I know you miss her, too," Mom whispered.

"*Ja.*" I pressed the heels of my hands to my eyes to stop the tears threatening to escape. "I'll let you know when I've got my assignment. We'll find Freya before the realms notice the absence of love," I promised.

"Please hurry," Mom urged.

"We will," I murmured in agreement. There would be no time to lose. Freya represented all that was good in the realms. The love she instilled upon beings of all species begat kindness. And that kindness was infectious, spreading like a ripple across the calm waters of a pond at sunrise. We needed her love like we needed air—it was our life force, the energy that gave us strength to fight for *ære*—for honor—even in the face of total defeat.

Without it, there would be only chaos.

"Please be careful," Mom urged again.

Before I could answer, the front door clicked. Heavy male footsteps pounded up the stairs. They sounded angrier than footsteps had any right to. Not without good reason...

"Gotta run. Give Dad a hug for me." I hung up and shoved the phone into my back pocket. I raced into the hallway and nearly collided with an angry deity.

"As God of War, I wholeheartedly object. Sending my guards in my place is a display of cowardice, and a gross misuse of resources that will lead to—" Tyr stopped shouting into his phone, presumably to hear whoever was on the other end of the line. After a moment, his eyes narrowed. "You can't issue an order that will compromise Freya's rescue. I'm the most effective tracker we have. I should be on the ground for this."

"What's going on?" I whispered to Henrik, who flanked Tyr.

"Odin's telling Tyr how to run the recon. And apparently he's not telling him what he wants to hear." Henrik raised an eyebrow.

"You're setting them up to die, and you know it!" Tyr yelled. "This is obviously some kind of trap."

He fell silent as Odin explained something we couldn't hear. After a moment Tyr's shoulders dropped. A command was a command, and Odin was the only god who outranked Tyr.

"Well, if it is me they're after, you don't need to hand them my bodyguards first. They'll find a way to get to me eventually, and—" Tyr broke off. As he listened, his free hand made a fist. "Fine," he snapped. "But my objection is on record. And if anything goes down, I'm going in after them. Nobody else is dying because of me."

With that, Tyr turned off his phone and shoved it in his back pocket. He let out a growl and stared me down with angry eyes. I held his gaze, barely ruffled by his outburst. We could handle any death trap Tyr thought we'd be walking into. Odds were good we'd seen far worse.

"Where is she?" Tyr barked.

"You're awake. And walking. How do you feel?"

"Where is Mia?" he repeated.

"I'm here!" Mia flew down the hall and threw herself at Tyr. "Oh, thank god you're okay. The last thing I saw was... well, you're here. And you're standing." She pulled back just enough to take in his features. "And you're angry, but you're not bleeding, so that's a good sign. Right?"

Tyr kissed the top of her head, and set her on her feet. "I need you to pack a bag. We're taking you to the safe house."

"Already on it. I'm packing one for you, too." Mia squeezed Tyr's arm.

"*Takk*. Go finish, and be back here in five." Tyr was all business.

"Okay." Mia scurried back into Tyr's room, shooting a worried glance over her shoulder as she ran.

"So we *are* taking Mia to the safe house," I confirmed. I'd guessed correctly.

"*Förbaskat* right, she's going to the safe house." Tyr glowered. "Along with my sister, and..." He glanced between Forse, Henrik, and me. With a furious growl, he ran his fingers through his messy blond hair. "Living room. Now. The trail's lost; we can't waste any more time."

"Elsa needs to heal you, Tyr. She's got the room prepped," I said.

"I don't need a healing. I'm fine. Living room."

I opened my mouth, but Henrik shot me a look that said *not now*. If the fire emanating from his normally cool grey-blue stare was any indication, he was every bit as furious about Freya's abduction as Tyr.

Well, honestly. Who wasn't?

The boys turned in unison and filed down the stairs. The door to Tyr's room was cracked open, and inside Mia stuffed shirts and shoes into a bag. Without giving myself a chance to think, I jogged after the guys.

"Okay, what's the plan?" I sat gingerly on the edge of the couch. The tension radiating off three sets of male shoulders was palpable. Whoever took our friend would have some *serious* testosterone to contend with. Tyr paced furiously in front of the fireplace, his footsteps landing with heavy thuds as he placed each heel on the ground. Henrik stood in front of the window, his arms crossed, angry sweat beading in the crook of his beautifully sculpted biceps.

I cleared my throat. Forse looked up from his seat beside me on the couch. His hands were clenched so tight, I was surprised his fingernails hadn't drawn blood.

Boys could do anger like no other, but they had nothing on the wrath of me. I'd lived through this once already. And I knew the casualties it could bring.

"The plan?" I ground out through gritted teeth.

Henrik's face softened. "Brynn."

"Later." I held up a hand. "Tyr, what are our orders? You *do* have a plan to get her back, *ja?*"

Tyr stopped pacing long enough to stare me down. "Before I decide, are you fit to proceed on this mission? Be honest with me, Brynn. I can't have a weak link in this chain."

"I am plenty fit, *thank you very much.*" I tried to keep the indignation out of my voice. I might have had the highest stakes in the room but Freya had trained me to be a warrior first.

Tyr stared at my jutted jaw, blazing eyes, and fingers tightly gripping each other. "You sure about that, hotshot?"

"Stuff it, Fredriksen. I said I'm good, so I'm good." I loosened my grip on my knuckles to prove my point.

"Fair enough. Odin thinks this is a trap to get to me, and he doesn't want Love and War incapacitated simultaneously. So against my advisement, the Alfödr has ordered the two of you to go after Freya." Tyr crossed his arms over his chest. "Henrik, you're the most efficient assassin in the corps at the moment, and Brynn, for whatever reason, you temper his destructive energy with an impulse for creation. We don't know who's taken Freya or why, so innovation is going to be the name of the game on this one. But the second you feel like this mission exceeds the standard level of danger, *the second*, call me in and I'll be your backup. Odin can just deal." Tyr's eyes moved to my right. "Forse, you're going to stay behind and run intel with me. We're transferring the girls to the northwest compound."

"Is taking Mia and Elsa to the beach house the safest idea?" I questioned. "Are you sure the location is secure after... you know..."

After Fenrir attacked the shield barrier. After Hel's guard, Garm—a dragon, not a dog, for the record—attacked Henrik. After Tyr lost his arm and nearly died...

"It's safe. Henrik beefed up security last week, and I cast a holographic enchantment along the barrier so the entire region looks like an uninhabited forest. The

Oregon coast lost a good twenty square miles of cove, but they can spare it."

Forse stood up. "Do I have time to pack or are we evacuating right now?"

"You have five minutes." Tyr pulled his phone out of his pocket and checked the time. "I want to touch down at the safe house and have Heimdall's remote surveillance operational in ten. Wherever Freya is, we need to get her back. We can't have a repeat of—" Tyr's gaze shifted to me and back to Forse so quickly, anyone else would have missed it. I pulled my shoulders back and rose from the couch. Anybody who thought I wasn't strong enough for this mission was dead wrong.

"Just be back here in five. I'll contact Heimdall." With that, Tyr stormed toward the hallway.

"You might want to tell Elsa her stubborn brother's refusing medical attention," I called after him.

"Shut up, Brynn," Tyr said back.

Henrik grabbed Tyr's arm as he passed the window. "Where do Brynn and I go?"

Tyr narrowed his eyes. "I don't know. Didn't you say you were working on a new device? Something that can freeze time?"

"We are. It's in the weapons closet, but it's unfinished. If only we'd been faster with development..." Henrik frowned, his arms again clenching his remarkable biceps. "We ran out of *älva* dust and we can't proceed to beta phase without it."

"Then I suggest you start in Alfheim." Tyr raised one eyebrow. "They took Freya right out from under three assassins, Henrik. Whoever they are, they're good. But if we'd had the advantage of stopping time..." Tyr shook his head. "I'll transfer the contents of the closet to the compound. Get the *älva* dust and report back to the safe house. We'll need to weapon up with every tool in our arsenal."

"Affirmative." Henrik pulled his shoulders back and stood with his fists at his sides while Tyr strode from the room. On the outside, he was the picture of determination. But I'd been obsessed with him for so long, I knew exactly what the twitch in his eye meant.

Henrik was nervous.

"What's the matter, Henrik? Not thrilled to go on a jotun hunt with me?" I furrowed my brow. "Troll hunt? Fire giant hunt?" My fingers framed my waist as I crossed to his side. "Do you have any idea who did this?"

"You were watching the monitors. Did *you* see who took her?"

"No. I slowed the images to micro when I tracked the vacuum disappearance, and those creatures are still nothing more than a black blur. I don't get it—we modified that camera so it would catch a hundred frames a second. *Nobody* moves that fast."

"Somebody does." Henrik scratched at the day-old stubble on his chin. "Unless those blobs are just shapeless energy."

"Gods, why couldn't we have had the time freezer ready for today?" I squeezed my stomach harder. "One of us could have activated it and she'd still be here. Ugh. I guess we're going to Alfheim."

Henrik's eye twitched again. *Gotcha.*

"Have you spent much time there?" I asked, innocently.

Henrik's knuckles turned white. "I haven't been there in a long time."

That *so* didn't answer my question. Unfortunately, my five prep minutes were closing in on four. "Well, if you've been reading Tyr's weekly state-of-the-realm compilations, you'll know it's still in a friendly state; one of the light elves or meadow elves or fairies will show us where the newest coffee shops have popped up." I nudged Henrik with my elbow, and he gave a thin smile. Enough digging. Time to lighten his mood or I'd have a seriously crabby traveling companion on my hands. "Well, you heard the commandant. We're down to four minutes to pack whatever we might need for Odin knows how long of a trip. And I, for one, have got a slew of hair products to wade through."

Henrik raised an eyebrow. "We're on the brink of war and you're worried about your hair?"

"*Hei.* I'm kidding." I darted into the hallway. At the foot of the stairs, I turned and gave him a brilliant smile. "I know *exactly* which products to pack."

Henrik chuckled. Mission completed. I darted into my room and threw on my black cargo pants and matching V-neck t-shirt, then tossed a change of clothes, the bare minimum toiletries, and my warm jacket into a backpack. My dagger fit neatly into the side of one combat boot, and I sheathed my rapier at my belt. It was a friendly realm; no need to go in with weapons drawn.

Though I did throw a second dagger in my other boot, just in case the climate shifted.

I was at the foot of the stairs in less than two minutes. Tyr joined me sixty seconds later, followed by Henrik, who passed me one of our extra vacuums. I shoved the little box into my backpack as Forse flew through the front door carrying two bags.

"Elsa keeps emergency bags packed ever since… you know." He shrugged.

"She packing for you too, these days?" I teased.

"Uh…" Forse's blush stretched from the crew neck of his T-shirt all the way to the roots of his hair.

"Where are the girls?" Tyr growled. "Elsa, Mia. Get down here. It's time to go."

"We're coming. I had to make sure I had all my school books. And enough clothes to get me through the season change—you didn't say how long we'd be gone." Mia appeared at the top of the stairs, struggling to pull an enormous suitcase.

Elsa stood behind her, two of Mia's monogrammed bags in each arm. "Why do you torture me, Tyr? I had to repack the healing box because you couldn't wait a few extra minutes and let me do my job. You know I'm giving you an exam when we get to the safe house."

"Whatever. Fine." Tyr tapped his foot.

"Are you relocating permanently?" Henrik stared at

the sheer volume of items Mia carried with her. His eyes shifted to my single backpack.

You're welcome, I mouthed.

Tyr blurred up the stairs and back down, bringing Mia in one arm and the bulk of the luggage in the other. Elsa followed at a more dignified pace, carrying the rest of the bags.

"Everybody outside," Tyr ordered. "The Bifrost drops in one minute."

We hurried through the front door, along the porch and into the wooded grove that shielded the cabin from curious eyes. When we stood a safe distance from the main structure, I hugged my friends.

"Be safe," I whispered to Mia as I pulled her close. "Don't let him boss you around more than usual."

"You're not coming?" she asked.

I shook my head. "I'm going with Henrik to get the dust we need to finish the time freezer. Tyr's bringing it to the safe house, so play with it while we're gone and do whatever adjustments you think are necessary to have it functional when we bring the dust."

Mia squeezed me back. "I will. You two take care of each other." She stepped back and Elsa swooped in, wrapping her arms around me.

"I'm so sorry, Brynn. I know this brings up bad memories. Your aura's off. I'll do an emotional cleansing if you want one when you get back." Elsa kept her voice low.

"Thanks. I'm okay." I spoke through an oversized

smile. *Fake it 'til you make it.* History never repeated itself... did it?

"Heimdall." Tyr's voice boomed in the clearing. "Open the Bifrost. Two destinations. Northwest compound first. We're going to the safe house."

A brilliant light filled the clearing, so bright my hand flew to my face. I squinted as the colors illuminated the dirt, running the spectrum from red to indigo. Forse and Elsa stepped into the Bifrost, hands clasped and eyes closed. Like me, Elsa thought the transports sucked. She was toying with a remedy to quell the nausea. If I was better at the natural sciences, I'd have volunteered to help. But my strengths, like Henrik's, were more technologically oriented.

That didn't stop me from volunteering to test her Anti-Nausea Bifrost Blend when it was ready.

With a flash, Elsa and Forse disappeared, and Tyr pushed Mia's luggage into the circle. He held out a hand and she cautiously took it, shooting me a look that made it clear she was none too thrilled to be traveling by rainbow. Tyr wrapped her tightly in his arms and whispered something in her ear that seemed to calm her. She rested her head against his chest and closed her eyes. Tyr settled his chin on her forehead and looked at Henrik and me in turn. Before he flashed out of the clearing, he mouthed two words—*for ære.*

For honor. It was why we fought—what we strove to protect. It was the very purpose of our immortal existence, and it was the reason Henrik and I stepped willingly into the blinding light once our friends vacated it, knowing full well we might never return to the sleepy little hamlet of Arcata. Because even though we'd built a life there, that life would mean nothing if the very source of love Odin gifted to the realms was really and truly gone. Without Freya, love would turn to hatred. Mortals would surrender to their demons, immortals would forget their sense of purpose, and the realms, one by one, would fall into darkness. It had happened before.

But it wouldn't happen again.

"You ready?" I held out my hand, and Henrik took it. His familiar grip was reassuring. Wherever this journey took us, he'd be right there at my side. And so far, there hadn't been an obstacle we couldn't tase, implode, or outsmart into submission.

We really were the *perfekt* team.

"Let's do this. Heimdall, to Alfheim." Henrik gave a gentle squeeze, and I matched the pressure.

"To Alfheim," I echoed.

Maybe it was my anxiety over the transport, or maybe it was just a trick of the *extremely* intense light, but I could have sworn Henrik paled as he named our destination. Before I could study him further, Heimdall sent us rocketing through the realms and across the rainbow bridge that served as Asgard's private highway through the cosmos. The familiar sensation of bones being sucked tight against flesh made me queasy, and Henrik's clenched jaw made me wonder if he was really upset about Freya... or if there was something more going on.

Either way, he'd have to put a lock on whatever he felt. If the light wasn't playing tricks on me, it looked like Heimdall was about to drop us right smack dab into a field filled with meadow elves. And from the looks of things, they weren't expecting company.

CHAPTER 4

"**MY SISTERS, RAISE YOUR** hearts to the sun. Raise your consciousness to Mother Goddess, She who nourishes the spirit and encompasses the being." The white-clad woman opened her arms to the sky, her eyes closed in blissful rapture. A half-dozen identically dressed meadow elves formed a circle around her, mirroring her movements, like a sea of land-dwelling anemone shifting lyrically in the breeze. Asgardian schooling was heavy on the linguistics, so translating the elf's words was easy enough. Understanding why she was saying them, however, was another matter. *Raised consciousness?* "There She is. I can feel Her light glowing brighter. Can you feel the elements warming in gratitude? They welcome our worship. They thrive with our blessing. Only through giving your mind, body, and spirit to Mother Goddess can we truly *see* what is meant to be *seen*. Can you *feel*

how much brighter the sun shines on us as we give Her our praise?"

The Bifrost retracted above us while I focused on staying upright. As he always did, Henrik held out his forearm so I had something to hold on to while I gathered my bearings. He rested his other hand on the middle of my back, and I drew on his relaxed energy while I willed my stomach to settle. Henrik knew I hated having a weakness so we never discussed my travel sickness. He just kept us cloaked and let me hold his arm until I stopped heaving.

Gods, he was romantic. It was *so* unfair the valkyrie code prohibited me from dating until I reached the rank of captain. Right then all I wanted to do was jump into Henrik's spectacular arms, lace my fingers through his hair and—

"Now elevate your consciousness further, up, up, up until you touch the very beams Mother Goddess sends down. Beams of love that envelop the soul in a welcoming embrace."

My eyebrows shot up at the meadow elf's words. Mother Goddess? Soul envelop? These ladies were nuttier than the fruitcake Mia baked at Halloween. They made Midgard's hippies seem unfortunately uptight.

"Here, put this on." Henrik pulled a bracelet out of his backpack and shoved it at me. At the same time, he pushed one over his own wrist. "It's a charm blocker. Keeps them from getting to you."

"*Takk*," I whispered gratefully. It'd been a while since my last trip to Alfheim, but I remembered finding myself skipping through the meadow, picking daisies to offer Mother Goddess. Elves had exceptional powers of suggestion.

"Sorry, ladies. It's not Mother Sun. The light was just our ride." Henrik removed our cloak and slipped easily into the elves' language. He held out his hands and walked calmly toward the circle. I watched his cargo-clad posterior flex with each step, the tight muscles moving back and forth beneath the snugly fitted fabric in a hypnotic pattern. *Sigh.* "Heimdall must have thought this clearing was empty when he dropped us in. Didn't mean to disturb your, eh, worship."

The circle of meadow elves erupted into positively giddy giggles. The girls bounced up and down, their eyes fixated on Henrik like he was the second coming of their Mother Goddess in a deliciously exquisite, masculine form. *And they haven't even checked out his butt. Good luck, elves.*

"Did you say Heimdall sent you here? That would make you members of the Aesir. My apologies, Asgardians. You must have traveled very far to join us." The woman in the center bowed, and the rest of the elves stopped giggling and followed suit. Up close I could see why the woman acted as the leader—wisdom lined her wrinkled face, and an air of authority emanated from the top of her greying hair all the way down to her bare feet. She must have had a few centuries on the maidens

59

who gathered around her. They looked like the equivalent of Midgardian high-schoolers, with their glossy curls, sparkling eyes, and smooth skin that shone in the early morning light.

"No worries." Henrik gave an easy smile, and the giggles erupted again. I wanted to roll my eyes, but honestly, I couldn't blame them. When Henrik smiled, he tended to get what he wanted. Popping that dimple was simply unfair.

The sun was just rising on Alfheim, and the meadow we'd touched down in was dusted with dew. A circle of weeping willows stood like sentinels on the field's border, guarding a plethora of purple and yellow wildflowers, lavender hyacinths, and those tiny white flowery puffs that looked like snowballs—I could never remember their name. The sky reflected a dusty rose-pink as the sun slowly peeked over the grass-covered mountain. And immediately in front of me, seven meadow elves hiked up their flowing white dresses that didn't have so much as a hint of a grass stain, and skipped gleefully toward Henrik.

"You poor thing," one clucked in a tone so lilting, for a minute I thought she was singing. "You must be *exhausted* from traveling."

"Come with us." Another beckoned. "Let Mother Goddess *nourish* your energy. Your levels must be low after your journey from Asgard."

I pushed myself closer to Henrik. If his charm blocker failed, I wanted to be right there to pull him out. I had a good idea how the elfster wanted to "nourish" his energy. And if anyone was going to provide that particular service for him, it would be *me*. Someday. Gods, *please*, someday. "Why do they assume we came here from Asgard?"

"We told them Heimdall dropped us in here, so I guess they connected the dots about where we're from. It wouldn't occur to them that we were spending time in the mortals' realm. Most light elves avoid the place, unless they're low on… uh, reproductive options."

That made sense. Alfheim only hosted races of light elves, most of whom were female. This meant they occasionally sought out non-natives to re-populate their species. Beyond biological purposes, the elves tended to avoid outside contact with anyone who wasn't from Alfheim or Asgard. It was a tactical choice designed to preserve the realm's security. Not that they needed additional security—Alfheim was rarely under threat, thanks to its residents' alluring attributes.

When the light elves swore off violence centuries ago, Odin gifted each race with an entrancing power designed for defense. Their enchantments came from their physical attributes. Meadow elves neutralized an attacker by tossing their hair. The ripples of the movement caused their follicles to emit a hallucinogenic chemical that caused a recipient to feel dizzy. This would slow a pursuer enough that the elves could enchant them into a sleep before running away. Water elves could induce inebriation by flicking their tails at their victim—a particularly dangerous power since it was performed near a body of water and often led to accidental drowning. Solar elves refracted the sun's rays to distract an enemy, though they rarely needed to —as the second most beautiful residents of Alfheim, male pursuers were, as a rule, so enthralled with the vision of a solar elf, they very rarely attacked.

But the most dangerous residents of Alfheim were the fairies—the *älva*. Though non-violent like the rest of the realm, they were devastatingly beautiful, and terrifyingly cunning. They might not cut out the throat of a victim, but they wouldn't hesitate to lay claim to his heart. *Älva* considered all male visitors to the realm fair game. They only had to breathe on a victim to claim complete and total control of his devotion for a few years.

Or so I'd read in my textbooks. As a junior valkyrie, my visits here had been brief and void of any drama.

Until today.

"Come with us, sir." One of the younger meadow elves took Henrik by the elbow and pulled him toward her. I reached out and gripped his hand, anchoring him to me. The young elf pinched her lips into a thin line.

"No sir here." Henrik laughed. "I'm just a body-guard. And so is she." Henrik tilted his head in my direction.

"Hi." I raised my free hand in a small wave. "I'm Brynn. This is Henrik. We're looking for, uh... who exactly are we looking for?" Henrik never told me the name of his *älva* dust supplier. In fact, he'd only brought home one batch since I'd joined Tyr's team two years back.

Henrik looked at the gaggle of elves shooting him goo-goo eyes. "We're looking for Finnea," Henrik offered. "Do you guys know where we can find her?"

The cluster dispersed as the girls scampered behind their leader. The older woman lifted her chin and met Henrik's gaze. "Are you sure you wish to see Finnea? Perhaps your *soul* would be better served from engaging in worship with *us*." She stressed the last word.

"Yeah, my soul would be better off doing a *lot* of things besides tracking down Finnea. But orders are orders. Have you seen her?" The twinkle left Henrik's eyes. He met the leader's stare with steely focus.

"She usually convenes at the waterfall alone. She does not have many friends." The woman's mouth turned down in disapproval.

"Don't I know it." Henrik ran his free hand through his hair. "The waterfall's that way, *ja?*" He jutted his chin to the right.

"You are correct." The woman walked forward and placed her hand on Henrik's shoulder. "May the peace, and love, and strength of Mother Goddess be with you on your journey. And should you find yourself in need of *nourishment...* you are always welcome to return to us." She tossed her long grey hair, and I held my breath. A wave of what I could only describe as love blanketed the grove, enveloping Henrik and me in its warmth. I cringed as I waited for the inevitable pull toward the woman—the one that would bind me under her spell. But the only pull I felt was on my hand, as Henrik led me away from the meadow elves and in the direction of the waterfall.

"That's really generous of you, ladies. *Takk*—Brynn and I appreciate the hospitality." With a jaunty wave, Henrik dropped my hand and we broke into a light jog. We moved across the meadow, through the oak trees, and onto a clover-lined path I presumed led to the waterfall.

"You don't want to go back?" I asked in confusion. The enchantment hadn't worked on me, but maybe it was because I was a girl. Elves had little use for female visitors from a reproductive standpoint.

"Nope." Henrik held up his wrist and my eyes fell on the bracelet.

"Oh. Oh!" My mouth fell open. "It worked! The charm blocker worked!"

"Of course it worked." Henrik rolled his eyes without breaking his run. "When has a piece of my tech ever *not* worked?"

Now was probably *not* the time to remind him about our initial model for the nano-molecular particle accelerators. Odin's pear orchard stood as testimony to our failed attempt at advancing implosive technology.

"Henrik Andersson." I ran at his side. "You are, quite simply, the most brilliant scientific mind of our day.

Nobody is immune to elf charms. Nobody. I'm not even going to ask what you put into these things."

"Yeah, don't." Henrik slowed to a walk. I followed suit. He wrapped long fingers around my wrist, circling the bracelet. My eyelids fluttered. *Stop it, Brynn.* "Take this thing off the minute we Bifrost out of here. I didn't have time to study the long-term effects."

"Fair enough." Goosebumps still peppered my skin where he touched me. I let out an involuntary shiver, and Henrik ran his other hand over my arm.

"You cold, *sötnos?*" He pulled me closer and slipped his arms around my back. It was a comforting gesture, one intended to create warmth. And it did create warmth. Just not the kind my elf-magnet *friend* probably intended.

"I'm okay." I rested my cheek on the board that was his chest and let my mind wander as Henrik slowly moved his thumbs along the muscles of my back. The motion smoothed the knots that had tripled in size since Freya's disappearance.

Freya's disappearance...

My mind tried to push out the mental pictures of the last time this happened—the waiting, the searching, the gut-wrenching terror as we prepared for the inevitable, and finally, shortly after Freya was returned, the official visit from Odin's guard. His announcement of what we'd lost nearly ripped my soul in two, with a tear so deep there was no question of it ever fully healing—mitigation was the best I could hope for. I'd silenced all thoughts of those hellish weeks in the aftermath where I'd struggled to stay afloat; when I'd accepted there would be hole in my heart from then to eternity. I'd buried that agony deep in the emotional vault to be lost forever. But as I rested my head against Henrik's torso and allowed myself to relax in his embrace, a jolt of pain struck my gut. *Get it together, Aksel. Now.* I jumped out of Henrik's arms, slamming the door against the flood of memories that threatened to undo my *perfekt* control. It was the blessing and the curse of being immortal—I had all the time in the world to understand *why* things had to happen the way they did, but I'd drive myself to madness if I allowed the sheer weight of centuries of memories to pull too heavily on my consciousness. I was *really* good at letting things go. Really good. But every once in a while, a figment from my past came back to haunt me.

Even though I gave that figment a Viking funeral long ago.

"Brynn! Wait!" Henrik's voice sounded far away. I hadn't realized I was running, but now I found it almost impossible to stop. My legs moved without a conscious connection to my brain. My feet pounded against the soft clovers, the pace matching the pulse of blood against my ears. I ran and I ran until I sucked in air and my chest felt raw. The burn in my muscles was searing, punishing. It grounded me in the physical realm, tearing me away from the anguish in my mind. *Never go back.*

"Brynn!" Henrik's hand on my arm jolted me back to the present. He whirled me around, and I was so discombobulated I fell right into him. He wrapped a heavy arm around me, holding me firmly in place. I threw my arms around his waist and squeezed, anchoring myself to him. "Brynn?" Henrik leaned back, lifting my chin with one finger. Grey-blue eyes bore down, looking so intent I thought he might be able to see right through me. "What just happened?"

"Nothing." I hiccupped. I wanted to look away, tear my eyes from that too-intense gaze. But being this close to Henrik was mesmerizing. Enchanting. He was every bit as dazzling as the elves and fairies whose charms we were trying to avoid.

Too bad his magic bracelet didn't block out guys.

"Were you thinking about last time?" he asked in a soft voice. I wanted to lie, to tell him I was fine, over it, and that it was locked away in the black box in my chest where I stored all unwanted emotions so my *perfekt* control never wavered. Henrik's pupils dilated in concern, and the color of his eyes shifted to a slightly deeper blue. Gods, I couldn't lie to him. I'd tell Henrik anything he wanted to know. Ever.

"Oh, Brynnie." Henrik rubbed my jaw between his thumb and pointer finger. "I'm so sorry. I should have thought about what losing Freya again would do to you. If you want, I can take you home and—"

"No." I shook my head violently. "I'm in this with you. I may not have been old enough to do anything to help back then, but this time I am. You and I, we're going to take that perp down. Or her. Or them. Whatever. And then we're going to make whoever it is pay."

"Brynnie, Brynnie, Brynnie." Henrik rested his chin on the top of my head. "You are something else."

"Yeah," I murmured, trying to ignore the smell of sunshine coming off his chest. How was it possible for someone to smell like, well... like happy? Henrik smelled like happy.

"No, I mean it." Henrik pulled back. His thick hair was disheveled from our jog, but his eyes bore their telltale twinkle, as if he viewed the world as an adventure yet to be conquered. Immortality had always been so *easy* for Henrik. For me, some days, it felt inescapable.

"You mean what exactly?" I fumbled, forgetting our conversation.

"You're something else. You're strong. You're smart. You've been through Helheim, but you don't let the past drag you down." He moved his thumb to stroke my jaw and I felt a pull in my belly. "If I'd seen what you saw..."

"You've seen worse," I reminded him. "You were Elite Team before you were Tyr's guard. I know the kinds of assignments Odin sends that group on."

"Yeah, but there's a big difference. Those were just assignments—no personal ties. What you saw—"

Henrik broke off as I held a finger to his lips. Despite everything I'd done to put my emotions on lockdown, my eyes pooled with tears. I squeezed them shut to stop the inevitable embarrassment. "Can we talk about something else?" I begged. It was hard enough to keep the door locked without someone bringing it up. Especially someone I already felt vulnerable around. My gaze darted from left to right, looking for something—anything—to talk about. "Like, uh... that."

I exhaled slowly as I took in our surroundings. A crystal blue pond lay to my right, its surface barely disturbed by the cascade of water tumbling down a moss-lined mountain. Grey stones intercepted the liquid at regular intervals, creating a white mist that framed the waterfall from top to bottom. Clovers and wildflowers surrounded the pool, and pink and purple butterflies darted from bloom to bloom, wings flapping gently in the light breeze.

"I guess this is the waterfall?" I shook my head at my obvious words. "It's so... it's so..." Words failed me, and the nearness of my memories mingled with the thrill of Henrik's touch, causing my eyes to water anew. He was here. He was safe. He was... doing everything he could to make me feel better, and I was crying on him. *Weakling*. This was *so* unprofessional. I pounded my fist against his chest. "Dang it! Sorry, Henrik. Just give me a minute and I'll be normal again."

"Brynn," Henrik soothed. He laid his cheek on top of my head and rubbed my lower back. His hands traced a familiar pattern, and I started to calm, as if his touch drew the pain right from my heart. *Typical*. The god was totally out of my reach, but he was the only one who knew how to make me feel better. His hands moved lower, the tips of his fingers dancing just above the waistband of my cargos. Correction. Henrik

Andersson didn't know how to make me feel *better*. He knew how to make me feel *amazing*. My heart thudded so hard, he probably felt it through the thin fabric of my T-shirt. Hopefully he'd just think I was nervous about our mission or something lame. *Poker face, Brynn. Control. Control.*

"Talk to me," Henrik ordered, and any hope for resolve vanished at his commanding tone. "I want to be here for you, but I can only help if you let me."

My jaw twitched, and a traitorous tear trickled down my face. This time I didn't know what to blame —my heartache at my memories, or my frustration at having spent a lifetime loving someone who'd be married with kids long before Freya ever released me from her convent. Sometimes life was so unfair. Being of Asgard required a life of sacrifice—I got that. But did I have to sacrifice the thing I'd wanted with all my heart for *my whole entire existence?*

Oh, gods. What did the contract matter at this point? If the past was any indication, it wouldn't be long before all Hel broke loose. And if, Odin forbid, it was *Henrik* that I lost this time around, did I really want to spend the rest of my existence knowing I didn't tell him how I felt while he was still alive? *Still alive...* I drew a shaky breath at the thought of a world without Henrik. *Regroup, Aksel. Nobody's dying... not today, at least.* But I didn't know what tomorrow would bring. The fact was, with Freya gone, there was a very high likelihood the realms would go mad very, very soon. And if we didn't recover Freya before the realms began their descent into darkness... if I really did lose Henrik... *Breathe, Brynn. It's going to be okay. I think.* I drew my shoulders. The worst case scenario was a very real possibility. And if it came to fruition, I needed to know that I'd laid all my cards on the table with the god who meant more to me than anything in the cosmos.

Without giving it another thought I reached up and cupped Henrik's face. My small hands barely covered his broad cheeks, day-old whiskers scratching my palms. Henrik's eyes widened, and before I lost my nerve I pulled him down to me. I stood on tiptoe and pressed my lips against his. I'd imagined Henrik's lips would feel rough, but they were softer than the Egyptian cotton sheets Mia recently snuck into every room in the cabin, and touching them sent sparks of heat straight through me. I ran my tongue lightly along the spot where his top and bottom lip met and let out a sigh. He even *tasted* like happy. Sunshine, and salt water, and fresh air and calm. I pressed against him and kissed him harder, giving in to the explosion of joy bursting inside my brain like a New Year's fireworks display. I was kissing Henrik Andersson. *Kissing Henrik Andersson!* It was the culmination of every dream I'd ever had coming to fruition in one glorious, beautiful, picture-*perfekt* package—in front of a waterfall, no less. I couldn't have planned this better if I'd tried. Mortals would make movies about this moment. Composers would write symphonies. Wagner's successors would have to add a new movement to *Flight of the Valkyries* just to honor the beauty of this impossibly ideal experience.

In my euphoria, I completely failed to notice one very important detail.

Henrik wasn't kissing me back.

In fact, he pushed me away.

CHAPTER 5

STRONG HANDS WRAPPED AROUND my biceps and lifted me upward. Henrik pulled his head back and set me on the ground an arm's length away. He held me as I looked up in confusion.

"Henrik?" I asked, tilting my head to the side. His face was steady, the look in his eyes one of compassion. *Oh, gods.* He felt sorry for me.

Recognition fell like a wet blanket. Humiliation cascaded in waves, intensified by the realization that in one moment of stupidity I'd completely and totally mutilated any chance I ever had at preserving the single most important relationship in my world. *Oh gods, oh gods, oh gods.*

"I... I..." I turned to run, but Henrik's grip was too tight. He held me in place, refusing to let me escape the horror of my gross misjudgment. "I am so sorry," I whispered. Forget the time freezer; the next invention on my list was a time *reverser*. I'd have given anything to erase the last sixty seconds of my life.

"Don't be sorry." Henrik's sympathetic gaze was beyond humiliating. *Dear Mother Goddess of Alfheim, in whom I previously did not believe. Sorry about that. If you're listening, pretty please open up the ground and swallow me whole. 'Kay? Skål, Brynn.*

"I'm sorry," I repeated. Henrik kept looking at me. *Now would be a great time for that earth-swallowing bit, Mother Goddess.*

"Don't apologize for doing that. Ever." Henrik spoke very calmly, like he was afraid he'd spook the crazy girl who just mauled him. "But you know we can't, Brynn. You're a valkyrie. If Freya found out we kissed, she'd withhold your true love come promotion time."

Heat prickled my skin as blood rushed to my face. "I don't care. That's the stupidest rule I've ever heard."

"You may not care, but I do." Henrik kept his eyes locked on mine. "Listen very carefully, Brynn. You've got a lot riding on keeping that vow. If you maintain your purity until you reach rank—"

I threw my ponytail over my shoulder and glared. "Do you hear how archaic it is? *Maintain my purity?* What is this, Victorian England?"

"It's the valkyrie code. And it's important to you."

"Not as important as some things," I whispered. The tears pooled anew. This time I didn't try to stop them.

Henrik's expression softened and his eyes turned another shade darker. He shook his head and took a step back. His hands released my arms, and I felt the divide grow between us. *Oh gods. No, no, no.* "Listen to me, *sötnos*. I've known you your entire life. And I love you enough to remind you that as a valkyrie, that code is the single most important thing in your existence. I know it's hard. I followed the same code at the Academy. The difference is, Odin gave me a squadron of assassins to oversee for holding up my end of the bargain; I didn't get rewarded with my *perfekt* match like you will." Henrik's mouth turned down in a frown.

"I don't care," I muttered. I'd given up hope on the whole ground-swallowing thing. Now I just wanted this mortifying conversation to end, and for everything to go back to the way it was.

"You should care." He spoke fiercely, as if he were trying to convince us both, but I was too humiliated to do more than stare at my boots. That Mother Goddess was going to have a lot of explaining to do, if she existed anywhere in this realm. Or anywhere at all.

"It's not like anyone would know. Freya's not here," I muttered to my feet.

"Freya's not here?" a musical voice called from across the pond. The notes carried on a warm breeze, light and lilting... and devastatingly ill-timed. "Pity. I was *so* hoping we could catch up, one love goddess to another."

Henrik's spine straightened. "*Perfekt* timing as always, Finnea."

Curiosity body-checked mortification, and I followed Henrik's gaze. A shiny-haired, long-legged *fairy* made her way toward us. Lavender curls cascaded to her obnoxiously small waist, while two transparent wings framed her body like a pale indigo halo. She wore a strapless mini-dress that barely covered her irritatingly ample assets, hugged her nonexistent belly, and flared into a tulle tutu that stopped halfway down her thigh. Shiny leather boots in the brightest of purples covered calves that looked like she must have spent her developmental years *en pointe*. Their heels added another four inches to her already nearly six feet of height, which meant that by the time she finished sashaying around the clover-strewn path and made it to us, she stood at least a whole foot taller than me.

What I ask is for the ground to swallow me whole, and what I get is an honest-to-goodness fairy? Whoever governs this realm has a seriously cruel sense of humor.

"Henrik, darling. It's been far too long since you've paid me a little... visit." Finnea twirled a lavender curl with one finger as she walked. When she got to us, she reached out to put her free hand on Henrik's bicep. Since we were still only standing a foot apart, it could have been an accident that Finnea's long fingernail speared my arm as she reached for Henrik's. But judging by the way she sneered at me, it probably wasn't. *Wench. That hurt.*

"You brought a *girl*? To *our* spot?" Finnea looked down her aquiline nose in disgust. Her steely green eyes seethed distaste, and if the way she flared her delicate nostrils was any indication, I'd have said she wasn't my biggest fan.

Since my face was level with a pair of barely

contained boobs I'd have given my eyeteeth for, and the flesh on my arm was slightly tender from the jab she'd inflicted, the feeling was just the slightest bit mutual.

Our spot? Was Finnea Henrik's... back the Bifrost up. Did Henrik have a secret girlfriend? No wonder he hadn't kissed me back. *Oh, gods.* Could this day get any worse?

Henrik's shoulders tensed, and he shifted his weight. Everything about him screamed "uncomfortable," but he reached out to pull Finnea into a hug. A *welcoming* hug.

What the Helheim had become of my life?

"Finnea, this is Brynn. We work together." His fingers rested lightly on the fairy's forearm, and a lead balloon landed in my stomach. We *work together?* We shared a house, a charge, and an entire lifetime of memories, but all we did was *work together?*

I clenched my jaw so hard it popped in protest.

"You *only* work with her?" Finnea managed to inject so much disdain in the last word, it was all I could do not to stick my tongue out at her. As Finnea glared at Henrik, he glanced at me. There was none of the usual affection in his eyes, and not so much as a hint of the mortifying moment we'd just shared. His neutral face was the picture of practiced calm.

But his right eye twitched.

Whatever. I'd just decided to bolt back to the Bifrost when Finnea turned to examine her nails, her self-satisfied smirk reflecting off the pond. The minute her gaze left Henrik, his expression shifted and morphed into a mask of remorse. I blinked back tears that were *so* not invited to this party, and Henrik shook his head. He mouthed the word *please*, and glanced down at his bracelet. What did that even mean? Henrik usually made sense. He was predictable and steadfast and logical, and above all else, consistent. In battle and in life, his actions aligned with whichever strategy would yield the most favorable outcome.

So what the Helheim was he doing dissing me for this… this… *fairy*?

Before I could wrap my head around the nightmare that was my day, Finnea turned around and Henrik became the picture of apathy once again. Well, not apathy, exactly. More like ice king. The expression he gave me was firmly on the jotun side of frosty. He ran his hands up Finnea's bare arms and let his eyes linger on those unfairly oversized boobs. "Good to see you again, Nea-Nea," he murmured.

Nea-Nea? The black box of pent-up emotion wanted to explode in my chest. So they *did* have a past. Or maybe a present. Mia's birthday cake threatened to make a violent and unsightly return. *Don't be sick, don't be sick. Don't let the stupid fairy know she's winning.*

Finnea's existence wasn't a surprise; Henrik had been going to see an *älva* for years—long before I'd joined Tyr's team, and on one occasion right after I signed on as Tyr's second. I'd thought the fairy was his dust supplier—a benevolent drug dealer who sprinkled magic fairy dust on worthy Asgardians as part of

Odin's plan for the greater good. But seeing her here spilling out of her stupid mini-dress and into Henrik's ogling eyes...well, *skit*. Finnea didn't look like a drug dealer. And something told me *they* didn't just work together.

With Henrik's attention locked on her boobs, Finnea's smirk developed into a full-fledged grin. "It's good to see you too, darling. Why don't we go back to my tree and get reacquainted?" She flicked a hand in my direction. "Your little work friend here can enjoy the waterfall. Be a dear, won't you, Brie, and pick us some berries to go with breakfast?"

"It's Brynn," I corrected through gritted teeth. "And I'm not going anywhere. Not without my partner." I planted my hands firmly on my hips and stared Henrik down. I shot a pointed glance at his bracelet. If the charm blocker worked as well as he claimed it did, this little display with Finnea was all his idiot boy hormones.

"Actually, Brynn, I do need a few minutes alone with Finnea." Henrik spoke impassively. My jaw burned as I ground my teeth together. *Whatever, Henrik.*

"Mmm." Finnea ran her finger along Henrik's cheek. She was so tall, she barely had to reach up to touch his traitorous face. "I think I'll need more than a few minutes."

Henrik locked his hands firmly around Finnea's waist and picked her up. She gave a soft giggle that echoed across the pond like a chorus of tinkling bells. "Henrik!" she squealed. But her laughter slowed when he set her down an arm's length away. My stomach settled at her indignant expression. *Been there, sister.* And by the time he dropped his hands and folded them across his chest, her amusement was completely gone. "What the Hel?"

"Listen, I really enjoy our time together. I mean, believe me, I *really* enjoy it," Henrik began. My stomach resumed the fevered churn of an Olympic rower. Now he was just being a troll.

Finnea stamped her foot. "Are you saying we're over?"

The churning slowed. Was he?

"I do need to talk to you about our… arrangement, *ja*. But first, I need you to do something for me." Henrik stepped into her space and whispered in her ear. Finnea's face went hard, then softened just a bit, then finally broke into a satisfied expression.

"I see." She gave a small nod. "And in exchange you'll…" She leaned forward to whisper in Henrik's ear. Since her shiny wall of hair blocked my view, I couldn't read his expression, but his voice sounded clear as a bell when he pulled back and swore to do what she asked. Finnea broke into an ear-splitting grin, and pulled a small pink satchel out of the top of her boot. "You have yourself a deal, darling. Hold this." She passed him the satchel. I shot Henrik a look. What was going on?

Finnea tossed her lavender hair and looked over her shoulder, flexing her wings as she did so. They took on a pearlescent glow, and she flapped them nine times.

With each pulse she rose a foot off the ground, so that on the final movement she hovered well above us, one leg bent with her toe pointed at her knee. She twirled a tight spiral, creating a shower of glitter I assumed came from her wings. It rained down, peppering the ground —and my right arm—in a glimmering hue. With hands cupped together, Finnea captured a portion of the glitter in her palms, then slowly lowered herself to the ground. Henrik held out the pouch and she emptied her hands with care, dusting the granules into the pink sleeve.

So *that* was where *älva* dust came from.

"Brie, love, be a dear and take this back to your colleagues." Finnea took the pouch from Henrik's hands and held it out.

I swiped sparkles off my arm as my eyes found Henrik's. "Come on, Henrik. We got what we came for. Let's go."

"Not so fast." Finnea trailed her finger along Henrik's chest. "I believe we have a little matter of payment to work out."

Henrik grimaced. "I'm afraid she's right. Brynn, Heimdall can drop the Bifrost on the east side of the waterfall. It's secure enough. Take the dust to the safe house, and come back when Tyr has new orders."

"You want me to leave without you?" I balked. Raging fire giants, spear-throwing jotuns, and homicidal dwarves I could handle. But bailing on your partner in the middle of a recon mission? That was unprecedented. And *so* unacceptable.

Finnea thrust the pouch at me, and I snatched it up with a scowl.

"A deal's a deal." Henrik sounded resigned, but he gave me a firm nod. "If you're not back within three hours, I'll meet you at the compound."

Finnea looked absolutely giddy. I felt well beyond nauseated.

"Whatever, Henrik. It's your funeral." I turned around.

"Heimdall," Henrik called out. "Open the Bifrost."

A brilliant beam shot across the sky and over the waterfall, and landed just behind the pond. I didn't feel my legs move as I covered the ground. Without a backward glance, I stepped into the rainbow's light and gripped the straps of my shouldered backpack. "To the safe house," I said in a level tone, no longer caring that perfect Finnea was twirling her perfect hair and positioning her perfect body as close to Henrik as inhumanly possible. I'd bypassed anger as I sped through mortification, and I was officially over it. Hundreds of years of love and friendship stuffed themselves firmly into the black box in my chest, to be dealt with later. Or never. I didn't care.

When the Bifrost failed to transport me, I repeated myself, slightly louder this time. "To the safe house. Fast."

Black boxes were indestructible, *ja*. But just in case mine had a leak, a timely departure from this stupid realm would be nice.

The wind began with a deafening roar as I was

sucked into the sky. But it wasn't loud enough to drown out the tinkling giggles I heard beneath me. Or the low murmur of the voice I wanted reassurance from more than anything in all the realms, whispering sweet nothings to a girl who was my opposite in every conceivable way.

CHAPTER 6

"THAT WAS FAST." TYR looked up from his tinkering as I stormed across the porch and yanked open the door. He sat at the kitchen table of his house in the compound. The time freezer lay in front of him, casing open and wires spilling out.

"*Ja.*" I ripped the charm blocker off my wrist and reached behind me to shove it into my backpack, catching the door with my hip. *Stupid fairy charms.*

"Oh my god, Brynn. Are you okay?" Mia jumped up from her seat next to Tyr and raced to my side. She threw her arms around me in a characteristic display of warmth, and pulled me through the French doors that separated the thick grey boards of the porch from the honey wood floors of the beach house. I wiped my feet on the rug as I walked, not wanting to track sand into Tyr's pristine abode. He and Mia were sticklers for tidiness. And Hel hath no fury like two obsessive cleaners thwarted.

"*Hei*," I mumbled into Mia's shoulder. "I got the dust."

Mia released me, and I tossed the small pink bag toward the table. It sprouted the paper-thin wings of a butterfly and fluttered onto the surface with a delicate *plink*. Mia's eyes only widened a little.

"You're getting used to all the weird, aren't you?" I asked.

"Not in the slightest." She shook her head. "But I'm getting a better poker face."

Behind her, Tyr snorted.

"Hush your mouth, Fredriksen." Mia shot him a glare that was more adoring than she probably intended. "Sit down, Brynn. I'll get you something to eat. You must be starving. And exhausted. And... upset? Why are you crying? Where's Henrik? Is he okay? Oh my god, what happened?"

"Henrik's fine." *Better than fine.* "And I'm not crying." I touched my cheeks, checking for evidence. Nope. Dry.

"I can still see the tire marks where your mascara drove the getaway car down your face." Mia pulled a tissue from the box on the table and passed it over. I swiped it beneath my eyes and sure enough, it came up dirty. *Stupid mascara.*

"What happened?" she asked again.

"I don't want to talk about it." My fingers shredded the tissue into tiny pieces. I felt Mia's stare, but I refused to look up. It wasn't like I was all goopy about my feelings for Henrik. Mia knew I liked him, and nothing got past Tyr, but it wasn't exactly something I wanted to dissect right here at the kitchen table. I'd thrown myself at my best friend, and he'd shot me down like an enemy drone in friendly territory. And now he was alone with Finnea, paying her back in ways I didn't even want to think about for the stupid magic dust we needed to save our friend. Sometimes life sucked so hard, I wanted to scream.

Knowing my life could literally go on *forever* made the screaming slightly less palatable. Asgardian Proverb #39: Today's heartache would be tomorrow's repressed memory.

"Fair enough," Mia said, after a long pause. I snuck a glance at Tyr and saw him shake his head at his girl-friend. I appreciated him keeping the female inquisition at bay, but I doubted it would last. Humans had this unfathomable desire to talk everything out. Asgardians knew the value of locking negative feelings deep in a vault and never, ever thinking about them again.

Well, every Asgardian except for Asgardian mothers. Apparently parental concern transcended realms.

"I'll make you a sandwich," Mia offered. "Tyr, can you show Brynn what I did to Barney?"

Thank you, I mouthed to Tyr as Mia busied herself in the kitchen.

Tyr just shrugged, but his eyes softened as he took in my expression. No doubt I looked like I'd been to Helheim and back. "Wanna see Barney?" he offered.

"Sure." I let out a breath as I smoothed the hairs of my unruly blond ponytail. I pulled out a chair and

86

tugged my backpack over my shoulder. Setting it on the table, I rifled through the contents, checking to see what I should restock while I was here.

When my fingers wrapped around two tiny spheres, I stilled. I'd totally forgotten about the forgetters. Henrik and I had invented them after playing a particularly mortifying game of "I Never" with his brother and sister-in-law. Since Gunnar and Inga had been married for-bloody-ever, and were best friends long before that, they already knew each other's embarrassing stories. And they knew just enough about me and Henrik to ask the kinds of questions that left us wishing we'd never agreed to play with them. So, being the brilliant scientific minds that we were, we'd hit the lab the very next morning and didn't leave until we came up with the forgetters. They were tiny balls that, when thrown, exploded and emitted an odorless gas that wiped the events of the previous twenty-four hours from memory. It was the manufactured equivalent of what Tyr could do with his magic—a brain wipe. We'd only made a dozen, half of which were functional. Since we'd used four in the test phase, there were only two left.

My mind weighed the pros and cons of using defensive technology to delete mortifying personal memories of one overly busty *älva* with a really stupid nickname. *Probably not the most judicious use of limited tech, Aksel.* But maybe if I only used one of them...

"Are you sure you want see Barney?" Tyr repeated.

"*Ja,*" I murmured distractedly, releasing the forgetters and zipping the backpack shut. Apparently I'd be living with my humiliation for years to come. "Wait, who's Barney? Did you guys get a cat?"

"No. No cats." Mia's voice was muffled by the thick refrigerator door. She pulled bread, cheese, meat, mustard and pickles out and deposited them on the counter, and set to work making one of her famous triple decker sandwiches.

My mood lifted infinitesimally as my friend moved around the kitchen. Gods, I was *so* glad Tyr got over himself and started dating her.

"Thanks for this. So who's Barney, if he's not a cat?" I asked.

"Well, we have Fred." She gestured to Tyr's prosthetic arm, which now bore all the realism of his original arm, thanks to that stupid *älva* dust. "We had to call the time freezer something, didn't we? Fred needed his best friend."

I stared blankly.

"Barney," she said slowly, as if talking to a small child. "You know, Fred and Barney?"

"Huh. Oh! Ha!" It was a pity laugh, and she knew it. "Sorry, long day. I'm not exactly running on all cylinders."

"Please." Mia picked up the plate, now teeming with food, and carried it to the table. She studied me with concern, and I lifted the sandwich to my lips to ease her worry. Mia was raised to believe a good meal could heal any injury, and since I had a black box of a Band-Aid on mine at the moment, I wasn't about to turn down *anything* my friend cooked. Ever. "You on your worst day are still better than the rest of us at our intellectual peak."

"Speak for yourself." Tyr winked at Mia and reached for the pickle on my plate.

"Hey!" I swatted his hand. "So what did you guys do to Barney?"

"Not what we did," Tyr corrected. "This was all Mia. She reconfigured the wiring so the circuits would stop overheating. She just moved this here"—he pointed —"to here, and added a neutralizing thermo-layer."

"You came up with that? That's brilliant." I bit into my sandwich. *Yum.*

"You don't have to sound so surprised," Mia said drily.

"It's not that. It's just that Henrik's been playing with this design a lot lately, and he never thought of doing it that way." I shook my head. Saying Henrik's name made the black box rattle. *Bury it, Brynn.* I drew air through my nose, then exhaled on a slow breath. I repeated the action, visualizing myself being anchored to the earth, to the present, to *this* moment in *this* kitchen with *these* two people. Asgardian Proverb #67: The past and the future were beyond my reach. The only moment I could control was the present.

"Well sometimes all you need is a fresh perspective to make you realize what you need has been sitting right in front of you all along." Mia tilted her head and gave me a significant look.

I bit into my sandwich again, forcing myself to

focus on the texture of the bread. Grainy. "This is really good. Where do you get the spicy mustard?"

"I think it comes from England. I'm not sure. One of your people dropped in on one of those flying horses with a fresh shipment this morning." Mia played with her necklace.

"The flying horses are pegasuses," I reminded her. "Who'd you get for your domestic valkyrie?" I took another bite and concentrated on the taste of each ingredient. Spicy mustard and peppered turkey danced a fiery tango in my mouth, and the weight in my chest lifted. There. I'd done it. *Perfekt* control. I rocked at this.

"Mist." Tyr eyed my pickle with longing, so I picked it up and took a bite.

"Delicious. Get your own lunch, Captain Klepto." I bit again.

"You're mean when you're hungry." Tyr pushed his chair back and stood.

"You want a sandwich, baby? I'll make it for you." Mia put her hands on the table and started to rise.

"Sit. Relax. You and Brynn need to catch up." Tyr kissed the top of her head as she sat. "I'll be upstairs in the study if you need me." He picked up Barney and the *älva* dust and walked toward the stairs, and I fought the urge to throw my sandwich at him. If he left, how was I going to fend off Mia's Henrik-related questions? *Get back here, War. For the love of Odin,* please *don't leave me alone with the mortal inquisition.* On the second step, Tyr turned turned around, and my heart soared. *He's staying. Thank gods.*

Tyr opened his mouth and squashed my hopes flat. "*Takk* for securing the *älva* dust, Brynn. I'll talk to Forse and we'll get the coordinates for your next destination squared away with Heimdall."

"How long do I have?" I stifled my glare. "Henrik told me to retrieve him if he wasn't back in three hours."

"I'll send you back within two. I want to speak with Odin to make sure nobody else has seen anything, and try to move Barney into beta phase. Now that we've got the dust, I can use my magic to implant it. But I don't anticipate the device being fully operational any time today. We have a few kinks to work out. We'll get you and Henrik rerouted and bring you back to base when you pick up more intel."

My fingers touched my forehead in mock salute. "Aye, aye."

Tyr rolled his eyes at me and took another step. Then he paused, and looked at me with an unreadable expression on his face. "Henrik okay out there?"

"He's taking one for the team," I said with false brightness. I bit down on my molars, sending a searing pain through my jaw. The black box exploded in my chest, and before I could stop myself I blurted, "Why didn't you tell me he had a girlfriend?"

Mia sucked in a breath. "Butter my flapjacks... Henrik has a girlfriend? I thought he liked Brynn!"

I snorted.

"He *had* a girlfriend," Tyr corrected. "And I didn't tell you because it wasn't relevant. He hasn't seen Nea-Nea in almost two years."

"Nea-Nea?" Mia covered her mouth with her manicured hand. "Please tell me her parents didn't name her that."

"They named her Finnea, but Henrik called her Nea-Nea. Once," I spat out. "And she's pure *älva*. Gorgeous, generous with her, eh, *dust*, and as you'd say Mia, warm as snow pudding."

"I say that?" Mia tilted her head.

"I don't know. Something like that. Point is, she's a jerk."

"Brynn. Be nice." Tyr bit back a smile. "She's done a lot to help us over the years."

"Yeah, well, Henrik's leveling the playing field on whatever debt you think we owe her." I dropped my head in my hands. What happened to my control? Oh, right. The guy I'd loved *forever* was doing Odin-knew-what with some big-breasted fairy, and all I could do about it was bring her stupid dust back to Tyr so we could save the Goddess of Love from whoever kidnapped her—the same Goddess of Love who might *never* lift her embargo on my going on an actual date—and stop the realms from falling into complete and total chaos. Again.

Sometimes being a valkyrie was unfathomably awful.

I drew a breath and tried not to sound bitter. "Henrik's holding up his end of whatever bargain he has

92

with her right now. He sent me back here to get me out of the way. Oh, and to pass on the dust."

"I'm sure it's not as bad as you think. This bargain, I mean." Mia reached across the table and touched my hand.

I rolled my head to the side so my cheek was flush with my arm. "I get that she's hot. I get that she's got that magic stupid *älva* charm. What I don't get is how the smartest guy I know could choose to be with someone so…"

"Thick? Dim witted? Vapid?" Tyr offered from the stairs.

"You see it too?" I trilled.

"Tyr! You just told Brynn to be nice!" Mia scolded.

"I know." Tyr frowned. "But Finnea's always irritated me. She's hot, I'll give her that, but that's about the only good thing I can say about her. The thing about *älva* is that they've got this weird ability to draw men in. The way she used to get under Henrik's skin… ugh." He shuddered. "I was glad when he decided to stop going to Alfheim."

"How long has it been since he's seen her?" Mia asked.

As Tyr shifted his gaze to me, one corner of his mouth turned up in his signature smirk. "His last visit was exactly one week after Brynn was assigned to our team. We've been rationing our *älva* dust since then. If you hadn't used the last of it on Fred here, he sure as Helheim wouldn't be there right now. That's the honest-to-Odin truth."

I raised an eyebrow at Tyr's implication. In no universe would *any* guy, much less Henrik Andersson, stop seeing an actual *älva* who looked like *that* on account of five-foot, two-inch, crazy-haired me. We just hadn't needed any *älva* dust since a week after I joined the team, that was all.

"Really?" Mia wound her hands together and leaned forward on her elbows. "Interesting. Brynn, how do you feel about that?"

"It doesn't matter." I picked at my fingernails. "Even if Tyr wasn't hallucinating, I'm not allowed to date until I make captain. The way Freya promotes, that could be decades away. And Henrik seems pretty happy with the bird in hand, at the moment."

"Henrik knows the rules." Tyr started up the stairs again. Now he spoke over his shoulder. "But I'll tell you this. He hasn't been on a single date with anyone since you showed up on our team."

The sound of Tyr's office door clicking into place was punctuated by the popping of my jaw as it fell open. At this rate, I was going to need to see Elsa about healing my poor face joint. But still. *No. Freaking. Way.*

"So, you were saying?" Mia rested her cheeks on her fists. "You're worried about some girl stealing your man?"

"He's not my man." I picked up my sandwich and finished it in hurried bites. "And besides," I mumbled through a mouthful of meat and cheese, "Finnea's got her *älva* paws all over him right now."

"Are his paws all over *her*?" Mia asked pointedly.

"Doesn't matter." I gave myself a second to finish chewing as I ran through images of purring and cooing my immortal eyes could never unsee. "He was giving off really weird vibes. But he's definitely *not* into me."

"Hmm." Mia ran her hands along the white table-cloth, smoothing out the wrinkles. "Look, I don't know exactly what happened in Alfheim, but I do know Henrik likes you. It's obvious to everyone. He's probably just holding back because he's following that rule. It's stupid that you're not allowed to date. You're, like, a million years old," she teased.

"You're telling me." Bitterness threatened to over-take me. I frowned. This wasn't like me. I was the queen of compartmentalization. I'd literally gotten an award for it as a junior valkyrie. Why was I letting Henrik's rebuff affect me so much?

Oh. *Oh.*

"Mia, how long have you been here at the beach house?" I asked.

"We got in sometime in the middle of the night, same time you left for Alfheim. And it's almost noon, so... I don't know. Ten hours? Twelve?"

"That's it?" I adjusted my ponytail. I was used to spending a lot of time with Freya, but half a day without her shouldn't have been long enough for her absence to affect me. Unless her captors took her straight to a dark realm. If that were the case, and the clock was already ticking...

This was *so* not good.

As Goddess of Love, Freya naturally emitted a

signal that could be felt throughout the realms. It cast a soothing glow over the residents of the light realms—Asgard, Vanaheim, Midgard, Alfheim, and the friendly pockets of the dwarves' realm. But if Freya entered a dark realm, that realm's boundary would act like a cage, keeping Freya's love from penetrating the atmosphere and illuminating the light worlds. The lack of love would create a blackness in the souls who depended on Freya's warmth to guide them. It would create unease in gods, mortals, and elves, and its effects would grip the valkyries especially hard, because of our close relationship with Freya. It would inevitably bring about desolation and destruction, just like it had when...

I sighed. We needed to get Freya back. For a lot of reasons.

"Do me a favor, will you?" My fingertips brushed the tablecloth. "Keep in touch with Heather and Charlotte and your brother and your parents. Give me a read on the human world when I check in with you."

"Sure. But why?" Mia asked.

"Because there's going to come a tipping point where Freya's absence starts to affect the mortals. And we're going to need to run interference with the humans so they don't hurt themselves if it comes to that."

Mia raised one perfectly sculpted eyebrow. "Fair enough. Now I adore you, Brynn. You know I do. But you look like you've been to hell and back. Can I do your makeup before Tyr sends you back to Elfheim?"

"It's Alfheim." I smiled. "And why not?"

Because it doesn't matter what *you look like. Henrik's just not that into you.*

Shut up, brain.

Mia ran upstairs and returned to the table with her makeup bag faster than I could finish off a dark elf. She pulled out a cleansing cloth and wiped the grime off my face, then got to work.

"So why exactly aren't you allowed to date anyone? Have you *ever* been on a date?" She dabbed foundation on a sponge and dotted it along my jawline.

"Of course I've been on a date." My words sounded clipped as I tried not to move my face. "I've only been a valkyrie for about a hundred years. Before that I was in school, and I didn't have this stupid restriction looming over me."

"So you can't date because you're a valkyrie? Are valkyries like Asgardian nuns?" Mia smoothed concealer under my eyes.

"Kind of." I paused. "Difference is, nuns never get to date—they're celibate for life. Our restriction terms out once we reach a certain rank. After that, we can get married and have families if we choose to. But most valkyries decide it's easier to adhere to the code without external ties."

"Explain," Mia said.

I thought for a moment. "Okay, here's the deal. There's no gain without sacrifice in Asgard. Duty to the realm is above all else. It's the way Odin sets things up."

"Lousy plan, if you ask me." Mia picked up her blending brush and set to task.

"Ain't that the truth," I muttered. "Well, Freya takes it a step further. She's structured the valkyries so we have to hit certain career milestones to earn certain privileges. Our jobs are a pretty big deal, and since we're warriors, soul gatherers, and *also* working for the living representation of love, Freya doesn't like emotions tainting our professional decisions. She needs valkyries to be hard; strong; willing to do whatever it takes for the protection of Asgard. But at the same time, because of her title, she knows the outcomes of our relationship futures and wants to make sure we guard our hearts for our future mate, if that's the path we choose to take." I rolled my eyes.

"So she's like an overbearing parent?" Mia laughed. "I know a thing or two about those."

"More like a loving big sister," I corrected. "She says maintaining the purity of our love is for our own good —that once we give a piece of our heart away, we can never get that piece back. So essentially, for our fifty to one hundred initial years of service, we're like the Romans' vestal virgins—locked in the training compound, only allowed out to perform domestic duties for the titled gods."

"Like Mist?" Mia wrinkled her forehead.

"Like Mist," I confirmed. "Freya's made an example of her, poor thing. She hasn't kept to her vow—she keeps finding herself in, uh, compromising positions with some of the titled's bodyguards."

Mia giggled. "She got caught?"

"Yeah. So Freya refuses to promote her until she upholds her vow for a full two decades."

"That's longer than I've been alive!" Mia looked appalled.

"You're a baby," I teased. "And I know it sounds like forever, but it's the blink of an eye to an immortal. Freya's honestly not asking that much. Being a valkyrie requires a very particular mindset, and she needs to know that every candidate can attain it. If they can't handle the sacrifice, they can always quit."

"Does anyone ever quit?" Mia held up an eye shadow brush. "Close your eyes."

I did as instructed. "Never. It's the most demanding, but also the most rewarding job a goddess can have. Well, a non-titled goddess," I corrected. "We get to protect the gods who do Odin's work. We're responsible for making sure the titleds—the gods who influence the fate of all the worlds—are safe. We get to choose the human soldiers with valor and *ære* worthy to ascend to Asgard. And when we reach captain rank, if we've served well and kept our focus on protecting the realm, then the Goddess of Love will reward us with our *perfekt* match. If we haven't devoted ourselves to the work, well, then she leaves it up to us to figure out our path. And hunt down our partners."

Mia coughed, and I opened my eyes. "Shut the front door. If you work hard and don't screw around, she'll hand over your soul mate? Forget overprotective parent, she sounds like a fairy godmother! That's an amazing deal!"

I wrinkled my nose. "It's a good deal *in theory*. But remember I'm immortal. Which means it could be tens or *hundreds* of years before I get promoted to captain. And that is a freaking long time to not date. I haven't even kissed a boy in over a century." Until this morning's debacle. But I was *so* not counting that as a kiss. Not out loud. Not ever.

"Oh, Lord." Mia leaned back in her chair, deflated. "That's a long time." She sat up again and picked up a brush. She dipped it in blush and applied it to my cheeks. "What about Freya? Is she allowed to date?"

"She can date." I nodded. "But she can't give her heart away. If she gets too close to a guy, her obligation to the Norns requires she break things off. Otherwise, she's too emotional to oversee her duties. She took a vow to remain neutral in all things." My eyes narrowed as I recited Freya's mantra from memory. "You can't have *perfekt* control if you're crazy in love."

Mia handed me a mascara wand. She held up her compact so I could do my lashes. "And that's why she won't let you date until you make captain. She's afraid you'll lose control—put whoever you fall in love with ahead of the realm."

"Exactly." I finished the second coat and handed back the wand. "It's not a huge deal. I knew this when I signed on for the job. And all things considered, Freya's moved me through the ranks really fast. I was a domestic valkyrie seventy human years ago—I had to bring titled gods their groceries, just like Mist is doing for you guys. And after that I joined a junior squadron, a senior squadron, and served three tours—two in Muspelheim, one in Jotunheim. When I was assigned as Tyr's second bodyguard a few years back, it was a really big deal. Nobody's been made second without at least two hundred years of service, well, ever."

Mia zipped up her makeup bag and glanced up the stairs. "You think Tyr had anything to do with that?"

"Maybe." I shrugged. "We were like family growing up. It makes sense we'd work well together. Or..." I stared at my cuticles.

"Or?" Mia prompted.

"Or maybe Freya felt bad for me. My folks weren't exactly thrilled when I joined up. They've made no secret about wanting grandbabies."

Mia laughed. "Mine do that to me and Jason too, though they'd *die* if we dropped out of college to start a family. Well, either way, it looks like you're tracking to move up faster than most. So maybe your happily-evah-aftah is coming sooner rather than later."

"Maybe." I shrugged. I wasn't sure what scared me more—the prospect of living another hundred chaste years in the convent of Saint Freya, or the day she presented me with my *perfekt* match. I'd always imagined it would be Henrik. But after today, it seemed pretty clear that *wasn't* happening. Even if he had kissed me back, one look at his ex and I knew for sure I wasn't his type. Leggy fairy I was not.

But I was a scrappy little warrior. And it was time

to rebuild that black box and compartmentalize my emotions once again. Enough feeling—it was time to fight for Freya.

"Okay, ladies." Tyr's footsteps thundered on the stairs. "Brynn's got to go to Muspelheim."

"Did Odin declare war?" I knew our leader had been furious when the fire giants admitted to harboring Hymir, but when the giant was spotted in Jotunheim last week, Odin had dialed down his anger at the flaming realm. Or so I'd thought.

"Not just yet. But Odin's ravens saw a bound female being moved through Muspelheim, and Forse's scout claims a new portal was opened near the volcano earlier today."

I jumped up so quickly, my chair clattered behind me. "What about Barney?" I asked as I righted it.

Tyr held the wire-riddled contraption in one hand. "He's not ready, but Mia and I will keep working on him until you get back. Catch the Bifrost into Alfheim and relay Forse's findings to Henrik. Then get over to Muspelheim as fast as you can. Forse's scout is a fire giant named Hyro."

"Did Hyro say anything else about the portal, other than that it was opened?" I questioned.

"No. Apparently the communicator she uses to talk to Forse is on the fritz, and that's all the information Justice was able to discern. So you need to find Hyro, learn everything you can about the portal, the volcano, any of it, and then report back to me. I don't want you making contact with the perps until Barney's operational. If they grabbed Freya out from under three of us, Odin knows what they could do to just two of you. Remember, if you feel your danger level is outside the norm, call me and I'll Bifrost in immediately."

"But Odin said it's a trap, and they want you to—"

"I don't care what Odin said." Tyr glowered. "I'm your commanding officer, and I'm ordering you to call me if you can't handle things on the ground. Am I clear?"

"Yes, sir." I saluted.

"Good. Here." Tyr pulled a painting away from the wall and pressed his hand to the pad behind it. A door swung open when the fingerprint scan was complete, and Tyr retrieved a small black satchel from within our hidden arsenal. "If you get into trouble with the fire giants, give them some of these rubies. Half is the payout we promised the scout for her intel. The other half should buy you enough time to run."

"Fair enough." I caught the satchel as Tyr threw it to me, and tucked it into my backpack. I shoved the straps of my bag over my arms, took my plate to the sink, and stopped just long enough to give Mia a hug. "Thanks for the sandwich. And the makeover. And the pep talk."

She squeezed me gently and pulled back, her face lined with worry. "Be extra careful. And tell Henrik if he doesn't take better care of you, I'll personally shoot him in the kneecaps."

I groaned as I darted out the door. "Thanks for that, mortal." I jumped off the porch and ran across the lawn, down the stairs, and onto the sand. The midday sun beat down on my all-black ensemble, and I stood still to soak up the warmth. Odin only knew what I'd walk in on in Alfheim, and I wanted to be able to visualize this peaceful moment... in case I needed to bleach my eyeballs once I arrived and saw what that wench was doing to Henrik.

Don't go there, brain.

"Heimdall, open the Bifrost!" I shouted. A dizzying beam of light shot down. "To Alfheim." I stepped inside the brilliant circle and gave my friends a small wave before my bones were sucked upward, my skin barely holding on. After several nausea-inducing seconds, I was right back where I started, looking around the pond for nymphie "Nea-Nea" and my so-called *work associate.*

Please let them have their clothes on. Please, for the love of all that is good and holy, let them be wearing clothes.

"Henrik! Get out here. We've got new orders," I bellowed into the flower-strewn space. My voice was so loud, the chorus of birds came to a screeching halt.

"Hey!" Finnea's surprised squeal broke through the silence. Henrik came tearing out from behind the waterfall, a glossy look in his eyes. Finnea stamped along behind him, adjusting her hair. I thanked every deity I could recall that neither was naked. "Get that rainbow out of here! We were *having* a *moment.*"

"Moment's over." I grabbed Henrik's hand and pulled him into the Bifrost with me. He reached down to grab his backpack, still propped against the rock on the side of the pond where he'd left it. "We've gotta dash. Nea-Nea, it's been a real peach." I waggled my fingers at her as Henrik ripped off his charm blockers and tossed them into his bag. I tried not to look victorious as he gripped my hand. What was the point? I might have been taking Henrik with me, but I had no claim on him. After all, he and I didn't exactly have the...history he had with *her*.

"See you later, Finnea." Henrik gave a small nod and met my gaze with an apologetic look. "Where to?"

"Heimdall," I called upward, refusing to let emotions cloud my focus. "Take us to Muspelheim."

And without a backward glance, we flew through the realms, leaving one *älva*-laden Helheim for one dripping in lava, flames, and the all powerful fire giants.

I didn't know which was worse.

CHAPTER 7

THE MINUTE THE BIFROST dropped us into Muspelheim, Henrik held out his arm. I reached for it instinctively, then pulled back. Instead of letting Henrik comfort me, I put my elbows on my thighs and bent over, drawing deep breaths until the heaving stopped. *Stupid Bifrost sickness.*

I stood quickly, and ignored the hurt look on Henrik's face. I could barely handle my own energy right now—no way could I take on his.

"Listen, Brynn. About what happened—"

I pulled a dagger out of each boot and shared one with my partner. "It doesn't matter. Follow protocol. We're cloaked, right?"

Henrik frowned, but waved his hand in front of us. "What the Hel? My magic's not working. Why would... oh, *skit.*"

"What?"

Henrik pointed. "We dropped in too close to the

castle. Royal residences are enchanted with enough dark magic to block my spells."

Fabulous.

"We're in the open, assess for immediate threats and find cover." Henrik positioned his back against mine in the standard formation so we could turn a quick circle. I inched away from the contact, staying close enough to feel the vibration of his movement and counter-shift accordingly, but far enough that I didn't *actually* have to touch him. I couldn't. We kept our weapons drawn as we examined every inch of our surroundings for prospective threats.

"Watchtower, my eleven o'clock," I murmured as I pivoted. "It looks unoccupied but it could have a drone."

Henrik tensed against my back, but kept moving in rotation. "Gathering of younglings, my ten o'clock. One additional presence, semi-mature, possibly a sibling or babysitter."

We continued our tight circle. "Guard just rounded the castle wall. Jeez, how'd he miss the Bifrost dropping in?" I asked.

Henrik pointed to a flaming tree on the opposite side of the castle. "He was probably distracted. I sent a detonator ahead of us as we left Alfheim, and the unsanctioned explosion should have pulled his focus." He sounded smug.

"Pretty pleased with yourself, *ja*, ace?" Oh, good. Joking took the edge off the pain. I'd have to remember that.

Henrik ignored me. "Best cover at my six o'clock," he deduced. "Near enough to the younglings we can determine whether they're being watched, and hopefully pick up some information on what's going on inside the castle. Do you think Freya's being held there?"

"Hardly likely." I'd have to catch Henrik up to speed once we found cover. "I'll follow you."

"Move out." Henrik crouched as he ran to the foliage he'd determined to be the safest hiding spot. I followed, cringing with every twig snap and leaf crunch. There was no way we wanted to get captured here. I'd sooner go to Helheim.

Helheim... I shuddered, pushing the underworld from my mind as I tucked my dagger back in my boot and dove into the bushes. Henrik and I crouched side by side behind a blue-leafed plant. I made sure to keep as many inches as possible between us.

"You're not going to touch me anymore?" Henrik's mouth turned down as he tucked my second dagger into his belt. "Brynn, you have to understand, as much as I wa—"

"Careful." I untucked the bottom of my T-shirt and used it to cover my fingers so I could pluck a bloom from the branch by Henrik's waist. As I tossed it onto the dirt, it burst into flames and rolled toward the castle. "Braxton bushes burn when they're touched. And as luck would have it, they're currently in season."

Henrik swore. "Brynn! I need you to listen to me."

I ignored his outburst as I plucked five more

blooms from the bush. When we were safe from becoming Braxton fodder, I looked up. "Didn't you learn about the fauna when you were here?"

Henrik gave me a long stare. I clung to the protective bubble I'd placed around myself, and let his wounded look bounce right off. After a pause, he shook his head and seemed to let it go. *Thank Odin.* "No, I didn't learn about fauna here. I never served in Muspelheim. My tours were in the cold realms. It's where I learned to weaponize ice."

"That's not good. Okay, Muspelheim is the complete opposite of Niflheim and Jotunheim in every possible way. You're going to have to think counterintuitively if you want to survive." I mentally ran through the obvious dangers he'd need to watch out for, letting science do what it always had and override my emotions. "Okay, avoid contact with anything blooming. It will either burn you or bite you. Obviously steer clear of the fire giants—even the little ones." I tilted my head at the gathering of younglings, each with mottled purple skin and big bulbous noses. The only obvious difference between them was their hair— each giant had a cascade of stringy strands that mimicked a different color of the rainbow. "And I'd say watch out for the guards, but all you really have to do is stay out of range of their weapons. They're embarrassingly slow in every regard—slow movers, slow reactors, slow thinkers..." I trailed off. Henrik looked at me with an expression that bordered adoration and awe. "Why are you staring like that?"

"You're so calm about all of this. Most goddesses freak out about this realm, but you act like it's no big deal."

"Because it's not a big deal." I shrugged. "Muspelheim may be the fiery embodiment of Hell the humans are so afraid of, but I did my tours here. Once you know what to avoid, it's not too unpleasant. Well, the sulfur stinks. But other than that, it's just another realm."

Henrik still stared, so I turned my attention to the younglings gathered twenty meters from the bush.

"Get to work, Andersson," I ordered.

"I'm so sorry, Brynnie," he murmured, squeezing my shoulder. My entire body stiffened. He was *not* supposed to be touching me. If he was sorry for not kissing me back, I didn't want to talk about it. And if he was sorry about the alone time he'd just spent with the fairy, well, then I *really* didn't want to talk about it.

"I said, get to work."

"Listen, I'm sorry I never told you Finnea and I used to have a thing." His fingertip grazed my collarbone, and I leaned farther away.

"You don't owe me an explanation. Let's just pretend none of today ever happened. Skip all the awkward."

"But, I—"

I inched as far away from Henrik as I could, given we were ensconced in a bush. We were *not* having this conversation. Me and my stupid kissy lips had ruined everything between us. The sooner we jumped into our new normal, the better. Uncomfortable *hei*s on our way to the kitchen, duct tape down the middle of our lab space so there could be no accidental touching, awkward side-hugs at celebratory gatherings—bring it on. If I could gather dead souls and carry them thousands of miles on pegasus-back, I could *so* handle this. "We've got a job to do. Can we please table this for now?" Or maybe for *always*?

Henrik didn't look happy; in fact, the line of his jaw strained like he was biting down really hard on something sour. But he gave a curt nod.

"Good. Because I need to brief you." I exhaled. Chapter closed. Black box repaired and sealed. Moving on. "So before Tyr sent me to, um, get you, he told me Forse had a scout in Muspelheim named Hyro. According to Hyro, a portal opened up by the volcano not that long ago."

"A new portal or an existing one?" Henrik asked.

"I don't know. And I don't know if it's powered by dark matter, but given it's in Muspelheim, odds are good it wasn't an Aesir that set it up. We're tasked with finding Hyro and obtaining any information the giant has about the portal and Freya's potential whereabouts."

Henrik nodded. He reached out and lightly placed his hand over my heart. The heat from his palm was a sharp contrast to the icy barrier that I'd erected between us this morning, and I drew a ragged breath.

"Listen, *sötnos...*" Henrik's words dropped off as I inched away.

"Please don't touch me," I whispered. I didn't stop moving until his hand fell away from my heart.

Henrik looked like I'd just slapped him. Our friendship had always been so easy. Well, it had been easy for him. I'd spent the last few centuries in love with a guy I'd never even had a chance with.

Sometimes what *was* just well and truly *sucked*.

"Brynnie—" Henrik started.

But I cut him off by placing my finger against my lips. The younglings had scattered from their circle, and were moving through the clearing. Some headed toward the castle, while others walked in our direction. We held very still—odds were they were headed in the direction of the garden to our left, maybe to pick berries or sit in the shade. Both suns now blazed directly overhead, making the ground even hotter than usual. The soles of my feet began to warm inside my boots, and I sorely regretted my black outfit. The color soaked up the heat like a sponge. Henrik must have been feeling the effects of the climate too, because he shifted beside me. As he did, he lost his balance, and in a move of uncharacteristic clumsiness, he tumbled out of the bush. He dropped flat on the ground, his face pressed against the dirt. He wore the regulation black camos and T-shirt, so he should have blended with the sooty earth. But he rolled once as he fell, and the movement caught the eyes of two of the younglings. They scampered to his side.

The one in the pink party dress clapped her hands gleefully. Since Asgardian secondary education covered all three of the fire giants' dialects, I knew the little partygoer was from the southern region the minute she opened her mouth. "Ooh, a prince! I asked for one for my birthday, and I got him!"

Henrik remained prone on the ground. Apparently Asgard's former Elite Team Captain now subscribed to the youngling school of hiding—if he couldn't see them, then they couldn't see him either. *Snort.*

"I don't know, Tullah." The one in the blue tutu wrinkled her round nose. "He looks kind of funny to me."

"Of course he does. He's a *human* prince. See the way his ears aren't pointy? You're the only one who wants an elf prince, Sabby."

The little giants thought Henrik was a human. *Double snort.*

"Yeah." Sabby poked Henrik's head with the toe of her shoe. For the first time, he lifted his head from the dirt and opened his eyes. Since he didn't appear in imminent need of rescuing, I decided to let him run lead on this one.

"Ooh, he's *handsome!*" Tullah lay with her belly on the dirt and propped her chin in her hands. She blinked adoringly at Henrik, now inches from his face. "Hello, prince. You probably can't understand me because you only speak human, right?"

"Uh, hello." Henrik slipped into Tullah's dialect as he lifted one hand from the ground in an awkward wave. If he wasn't in immediate danger of blowing our cover, I'd have laughed out loud. As it was, I permitted myself one inward chuckle. A long one. This totally took the edge off my morning of mortification. *Thank you, karma.*

"Are you here for my birthday? We're having a tea party. Nanny just went in to get cake. Do you like cake? I bet you do. All princes like cake. And dancing. And balls." Tullah twirled her ankles in the air. "Do you want to have a ball? I do. I'm a beautiful dancer. Want to see?"

She jumped to her feet, and leapt into the air with all the grace of a dizzy rhino. Then she dipped into a low bow.

"Wow, Tullah. That was *really* good." Sabby looked genuinely impressed.

"I know." Tullah skipped back to where Henrik still lay prone, and squatted down. "Do *you* want to dance with me? Is that why Daddy sent you?"

"I... er... you see, uh, Tullah, is it?" Henrik stammered.

"Yep." The little girl nodded happily.

"Right. Well you see, Tullah, your, uh, daddy, wanted me to be a surprise for later in your party. After your cake. So be a good girl and go on back to the rest of your guests, okay?" Henrik pushed himself to his feet and patted the tiny giant on the head. She scrunched her face into a pout and stamped her foot.

"No! I want you to dance with me, and I want you to do it *now!*" The last word came on a howl, and Henrik rushed to cover her mouth with his hands.

"Shh!" He looked around wildly. "Somebody will

hear you! Oh!" He pulled his hand away from the girl's mouth and rubbed it. "You bit me!"

"I don't *caaaare!*" Tullah wailed. "It's my birthday and I want to dance with a *priiince!*"

"Okay, okay." Henrik ran his hand through his soot-covered hair. "Let's be quick about it, though. You wouldn't want to keep your party guests waiting."

"Oh, no." Sabby shook her head seriously. "You have to dance in front of everybody. Tullah said she was going to get a prince for her birthday and nobody believed her. If you don't do it over there"—she jutted her chin—"they'll think she made it all up."

"Yeah, but..." Henrik stalled. What could he say? If he danced with her in the open, he'd risk exposing himself to her Nanny and whatever guards watched this little girly gathering. But if he said no, the cater-wauling of a spoiled little giantess would give away our location for sure. "Okay. How about this? You want to call your friends over here, and they can watch us dance? See, I have to stay here, under the trees. Human princes are sensitive to heat, and those two suns of yours would make me burn."

The girls' eyes widened. "Burn? No!" Sabby cried.

"To a crisp," he embellished, sensing a loophole. "I'd fry right up and disappear if I stepped out there. And then I wouldn't get to dance with you on your birthday." Henrik molded his face into a mask of sorrow. Tullah's bottom lip quivered.

"I don't want you to die," she said sadly.

"Me neither," Sabby chimed in.

115

"Well that is *very* generous of you." Henrik winked at the girls, and they giggled. "So go get your friends. I'll wait right here."

Tullah tapped her foot. "How do I know you won't disappear?"

She was good. Henrik's body language practically screamed *the minute you walk away I'm out of here.* He was seriously off his game this afternoon.

Henrik crouched down so he was at her eye level. "Because a prince never breaks his word."

A small *V* formed between Tullah's eyebrows. "Nuh-uh. Sabby, you stay here and make sure he doesn't run away. I'll go get the girls."

"'Kay." Sabby scooted closer to Henrik. Her tiny purple hand reached up to hold his calloused peach one, and she appraised him through mud-brown eyes. "Don't move."

"Wouldn't dream of it." Henrik gave her a charming smile. When she turned to watch her friend's progress across the field, he chanced a glance at the bush where I was hidden. *Help,* he mouthed.

I raised my shoulders, palms to the sky. There really wasn't much I could do without exposing my position to the tiny giant. We could always make a run for it—if we were fast enough, only the two younglings would know we'd ever been there in the first place. All things considered, that seemed like the best option. I pulled back the branches, preparing to bolt, but stopped when I saw Henrik shake his head.

"Got 'em!" Tullah's tiny voice sounded much closer

than I'd expected. Had she really made it to the castle wall and back already? Maybe she wasn't full giant. She moved too quickly for her kind.

"Ooh!" A chorus of little girls squealed in delight as they gathered around Henrik. I slunk back into the bush, careful not to make a noise as the party guests circled their "prince."

"He's so handsome!"

"I'll bet he has a beautiful princess back home."

"How come you always get the best presents?"

The girls' enthusiasm bubbled to a fevered pitch, and Henrik held up his hands. "Ladies," he declared, his voice halting the percolating conversations. "I am Prince Henrik of, eh, Midgard, and I have been sent to honor the birthday girl with a dance, at the request of... of... what's your daddy's name, sweetheart?"

"Surtr," Tullah said proudly.

The blood drained from my face. Since the girls were hanging around the castle, I'd figured they belonged to someone important. But I'd hoped Tullah was a senator's daughter, or maybe a high-ranking military officer's kid. *Skit. This day seriously sucks.* Tullah's dad, Surtr, was the king of the fire giants. He loathed Asgardians more than any leader before him, and he'd launched more than one hundred direct attacks on our realm just during my lifetime. Surtr was the *last* creature we wanted alerted to our presence. We were supposed to drop in on Muspelheim undetected, and now Henrik had an audience with the realm's littlest princess.

Navigational fail.

"Right. Surtr sent me. Okay then, let's dance. And then, I'm afraid, I need to get straight back to Midgard. Very important princely business awaits me there." Henrik shot an anxious look at my hiding place, and I gave a tight nod. As he held out his hand and led the squealing birthday girl in a waltz, I rifled quietly though the contents of my backpack. My weapons inventory was sadly lacking—I only had the vacuum, a nano-molecular particle accelerator and my sheathed rapier, plus the two daggers hidden in my boots. Correction—one dagger. Henrik had tucked the second one into his belt when we'd taken cover. Shoot. None of those were going to do us a bit of good. I checked the front pocket of the pack and felt a small sphere. My fingers wrapped around it, and when I pulled it out I had to bite back a yelp of joy.

Thank Odin! The forgetters.

Henrik continued his dance as I mulled over the best way to use the memory-wiping orbs. If I threw them at the group now, I'd hit Henrik too. The effects would be immediate, and I needed him at full capacity when we tracked down Hyro. It wouldn't help anyone if I were the only one on this mission aware of its purpose. I'd have to catch Henrik's attention and alert him to the plan. Then I'd throw one of the forgetters at the little giants, and Henrik and I could run as if our lives depended on it.

In all likelihood, they probably did.

Henrik marched Tullah in increasingly larger

circles, and I realized he was guiding her near enough the bush that I'd be able to catch his eye. Parting the leaves as gently as I could, I settled the forgetter in my palm and held it up. Henrik's eyes twinkled. He led Tullah away from the bush, and twirled her in a dizzying circle before stepping back and bowing low to the ground.

"Thank you for the dance, sweetheart." He offered a wink that left several of the tiny giants giggling. "But I'm afraid I must return to—"

"There you are!" The giants' nanny came rushing out of the castle wall, the ground shaking under the weight of her footsteps. My heart came to a standstill. "I thought you were coming inside for cake. You girls scared me half to—" She broke off at the sight of Henrik. He rose slowly from his bow as the girls rushed to his side, grabbing at his hands.

"Look, Nanny! Tullah got a real prince for her birthday."

"Can you believe it?"

"Did you know he was coming?"

The girls clamored over each other in their enthusiasm to show off their prize. Henrik took cautious steps backward, assessing Nanny's reaction. As I watched, her face worked through surprise, embarrassment, and then finally, outrage. I knew what came next. As she opened her mouth to call for the guards, I leapt from the bush and barked one word to Henrik.

"Run!"

Henrik parted the sea of adoring girls and took off

at a full sprint. I followed suit, turning as I ran to aim the forgetter at the cluster just as Nanny bellowed for backup.

"Guards! Trespassers in Muspelheim! South of the castle wa—"

But Nanny never got to finish her warning. I launched the tiny ball at the group and glanced over my shoulder as it exploded thirty meters behind me, leaving a silvery film in its wake. In the seconds I permitted myself to watch them, the girls shook their heads and looked at each other in confusion. No doubt they wondered how they'd ended up in party dresses, playing in the forest.

CHAPTER 8

"NICE PLAN, BRYNN." HENRIK held up his palm and I slapped a high five as we ran. My stomach barely even fluttered at the contact. *Better.* "I can't believe you thought to bring a forgetter with us."

"I didn't." My feet pounded against the soot. "I guess it's been a while since I cleaned out that pocket of my backpack. Apparently I left two in there."

"Well, fast thinking, then. Those were good times, *ja*? We haven't invented chemical tech in a while. What do you say we get back to basics like that? We've been so focused on harnessing the dark elements and developing the weapons that can—" Henrik glanced over his shoulder and skidded to a stop. I followed suit.

"What is it?" I asked.

Henrik grimaced. "That was a short reprieve."

I squared my shoulders, fists at my side, and followed his gaze. Sure enough, a squadron of six fire giants barreled through the forest like a herd of angry cattle. The black scabs covering their purple skin gave off actual sparks, the physical manifestation of their fury. They swung their arms over their heads in a display of aggression, and one reared its head back and emitted a stream of fire. Honest-to-goodness fire.

"What the Helheim did he just do?" I gaped. I pulled my dagger out of my boot as Henrik studied the stream.

"Is that not normal?" he asked.

"No." I shook my head. "Not at *all*. They're supposed to *live* in a realm of fire, not create it *with their mouths*."

Henrik pulled a particle accelerator from his backpack and threw it at me. He drew his sword and crouched in a fighting stance. "In that case, *sötnos*, weapon up. We'll debilitate this crew before we find Hyro."

"With pleasure." And it would be. After the morning I'd had, I needed to work out some anger. Killing bad guys was just what the healer ordered.

"You take right, I'll take left?" Henrik offered.

"But the ones on the left are bigger. You sure you can handle them, Henrik?"

"I'll take my chances." He grinned.

"Well in that case, I'll let you be the gentleman today. Righties, here I come." I took a deep breath to ground myself as the giants descended upon us. With thunderous battle cries, Henrik and I sprang into action. He charged the giant coming from the left, while I pocketed the particle accelerator and lunged. I threw the full weight of my five-foot, two-inch frame behind my dagger and pierced the hardened thigh of the fire giant who had the misfortune of being first on scene. Wrapping both hands around the handle of my blade, I pulled it horizontally, slicing through cloth, skin, and after a forceful wrench, bone, before pulling my dagger free. The giant fell to the ground, his leg hanging at an unnatural angle, almost completely severed from his body. He let out a wail and threw his head back in agony, emitting a stream of fire that ignited the needles of the tree above him. Navy liquid gushed from his severed limb and he twitched before falling still.

One down, five to go.

Henrik swung his sword at the giant nearest him, so I turned my attention to Rightie Number Two. He launched his enormous body at me, leaping through the air in a disturbing display of grace. I flung myself onto the ground and rolled out of the way, fighting panic as I moved. This wasn't right. Fire giants weren't supposed to be this fast. Or this coordinated. And they sure as Helheim didn't shoot fire out of their mouths. Had they evolved since my last tour? It was a valid hypothesis, but this wasn't the time to mull it over. I needed to figure out how to debilitate this squadron before they brought our mission to an abrupt and unsightly end.

A flash of silver blurred by, and Henrik's sword flew through the air, landing neatly in the spine of the fire giant I'd just escaped. It pierced the flesh, and Henrik leapt off the chest of his recently departed conquest, following the trajectory of his blade. The giant convulsed as Henrik landed on its back and drove his sword deeper. He wrenched it from side to side, barely flinching as navy blood spewed from the wound and covered his face. As he drew his weapon from his victim, another giant launched itself at his unsuspecting frame. I pulled the particle accelerator from my pocket, unlocked the safety and fired at the giant, who imploded on impact, leaving nothing more than a spray of ash in his wake. The remaining giants scurried backward, hastily retreating from their newly departed —yet still smoking—comrade. They looked back and forth between me and the ashes, possibly wondering if they'd be next.

Oh, you will be.

"Four down," I called to Henrik.

"Two to go." He grinned. In spite of myself, I grinned back. Ending Asgard's enemies always gave me a rush. And doing this right now was kind of like a really bizarre therapy. Fighting alongside Henrik was natural, and easy, and strangely satisfying. Maybe we'd been through enough together that we'd get through this, too.

And maybe I shouldn't judge myself *too* harshly for checking out Henrik's butt as he stood up.

I wiped the smirk off my face as I angled my body toward the remaining two giants. They still stared at the ashes, but I doubted the reprieve would last long. We needed to strike before they could. "It's two to two." I recounted our kill tally as I pocketed my gun and drew my dagger. "Let's make this interesting. If I end both of the survivors, I win, and you'll have to bake me a pie. I'll take your grandmother's Dutch Apple Crumble, *takk*."

"Not a chance, Brynnie. This round's mine, and when I win you'll have to do my laundry for a week." Henrik crossed to my side.

"It's on, Andersson." I dropped into a low crouch and brought my dagger to eye level.

"You could take them right now with the particle accelerator," Henrik pointed out.

"Yeah, I could." I rocked back and forth on the balls of my feet. "But where's the fun in that?"

Henrik shot me a wink and leapt at our opponents. He swung his sword in a high circle, striking one giant's arm and cutting it clean off. The giant howled. I darted for the nearest tree, running up the base of the trunk and pivoting to launch myself into the air. I aimed for the giant's shoulders, wrapping my legs around its neck and squeezing hard. With both palms around my dagger, I slammed my fists into its skull so my blade pierced the bone and struck the soft matter beneath. The giant tumbled to the ground and I fell with him, rolling until I struck the base of a nearby tree. My right leg throbbed, pinned beneath the dead weight of Muspelheim's finest, and I swore out loud as pain shot through me.

Henrik turned his head at the sound of my curse, and his attacker seized the opportunity. The oversized ogre cocked his arm and struck Henrik on the side of the head with a forceful backhand. Henrik soared through the air. He landed in a heap beside me, still gripping his sword. A trickle of blood oozed from his temple, and he remained still as the giant thundered toward us.

"Henrik!" I pushed myself to a sitting position and reached over to shake my partner. He lifted his head groggily. "You have to get up! I can't move my leg and —oh, *skit.*"

I ripped the sword from Henrik's hand and held it over his body as the giant reared his head and let out a roar. My arms went on lockdown as I braced for the onslaught of fire. Thanks to the grace of Odin—and the extremely strong deflective spell Asgardian craftsmen placed on all of our weapons—the blaze made an about face the moment it made contact with Henrik's sword. My muscles vibrated with the impact of the stream, but I held tight as the fire bounced back at the monster, incinerating the giant on contact, so he was no more than a pile of ash atop the remains of his fallen comrade. I dropped the sword, now blistering my hands, and leaned back against the trunk of the tree with an exhausted sigh.

"Four to two. You owe me a pie." I ignored the fissures of pain in my leg and snuck a glance at Henrik. He'd rolled onto his back, and now stared at me with undeserved admiration. It hadn't been *that* grueling of a battle; we'd had way worse.

"Brynn." Henrik shook his head. His eyes moved to the giant pinning my leg and he jumped to his feet.

"Oh, man." He wrapped both arms around the remains of the beast, but the monster wouldn't budge. "They're *förbaskat* heavy." Henrik grunted.

"You're telling me," I muttered. It was my leg being crushed.

Henrik picked up his sword, tossed it back and forth between his hands until it cooled, and held it over his head. "Close your eyes and cover your nose and mouth," he ordered. "They seem to spray when they're cut, and internalizing the blood would make unnecessary work for Elsa."

I did as instructed, and wiped giant blood from my face as Henrik sawed through the oversized limb pinning my calf to the dirt. When he'd severed the offending body part, he rolled it to the side and lifted me gingerly in his arms. I held on to his neck and tried not to look overly affected. The guy had just sawed off a monster's limb for me. It was kind of a moment.

"You saved me." Henrik stared.

"Yeah, well." I shrugged. "You cut that giant leg off me. We're partners. It's what we do."

Henrik lifted me from the carnage while I tried not to think about the pain shooting through my crushed limb. The way our bodies healed, it would reset itself within a minute or two. But for now, it was undeniably agonizing. The pain prevented me from jumping out of Henrik's arms and putting a healthy distance between us. *Looks like I found my new mantra—distance makes the heart grow ambivalent-er. Or something like that.*

"*Takk, sötnos,*" Henrik said.

"No problem."

Henrik held my gaze. "Listen, Brynnie. We need to talk about what happened in Alfheim."

"We really don't," I pleaded. "I said we could drop it." If memory served correctly, I'd actually *begged* him to drop it. The universe was *not* giving me what I wanted today.

"Yeah, well, that doesn't work for me. I need you to know that nothing happened between Finnea and me after you left. I offered her a deal, and she took it."

I broke eye contact. "You paid her back for the dust. You don't have to tell me the details."

"No." Henrik spoke so fiercely I looked up. "I offered her a trade. *Älva* experience heightened powers when they're involved with an Aesir. It's what made our arrangement symbiotic, and it's why she's been reluctant to break off our, uh, our thing. I told her if she'd continue to supply my team with the *älva* dust we need to develop our defense systems, I'd let her take her pick of this year's graduating Academy class. There's a line of warriors a kilometer long who'd give up their immortality to enter into a relationship with an actual fairy. They've been under lock and key for the duration of their studies, you know?"

"Wait." My brows scrunched. "You're saying you *didn't* sleep with Finnea after you sent me back to Tyr?"

"I haven't slept with Finnea since you joined our team." Henrik stared at me intently.

I blinked. Then my face scrunched up as a wave of pain ripped through the lower half of my body.

"What's wrong?" Henrik's voice dripped with anxiety.

"Just an after pain. I should be good in another minute." If I willed it, it would come true. "Put me down so I can get the blood flowing again."

Henrik set me gently on my feet and I tested my weight. It felt uncomfortably tender, but I'd felt worse.

"You okay to move or do you need me to carry you?"

"I should be okay soon."

"We need to put as much space as possible between us and these guys before the next group catches up." Henrik held out his arms to lift me, but I shook my head.

"What do you mean the next group?"

A wave of thunder rolled over the forest. The ground shook, and Muspelheim's bizarre truck-sized birds evacuated their treetop perches with loud cries of protest. In the distance, at least three squadrons of fire giants raced through the forest. I couldn't make out their features, but I saw a minimum of ten distinct streams of fire shoot through the air, incinerating trees and clearing their path. At this rate, they'd be on top of us in under a minute.

Healing time was over.

"Where's the bribe?" I ripped my backpack off my back and dug through it.

"What bribe? What are you doing? We have to go, *now*." Henrik urged, as a fresh stream of fire lit up the sky.

I dumped the contents of the black satchel into my palm and shared half with Henrik. "Here. The rubies. Tyr gave them to me to pay off the scout, but he gave me extra to use as bait—he says they'll buy us time with the fire breathers. The giants might want our blood, but they'll want the rubies more. Scatter a few of them around, it should buy us enough time to..." To what, exactly? We still hadn't found Hyro, and Tyr wouldn't be happy if we called for the Bifrost to bring us back without the intel we came for.

'Course, Elsa wouldn't be happy if we came home with charred limbs. With the amount of dark energy emanating from the fire giants, burnt arms could take days for her to heal.

"Throw all of the rubies and run, Brynn. We'll figure out how to pay off the scout later." Henrik flung his gems in a wide arc, and I followed suit. Then we took off. I ignored the searing pain in my right leg as we raced through the forest without any idea of what we were running toward.

Gods, I hoped we weren't heading straight into a trap.

CHAPTER 9

"**T**YR SAID THEY COULD be bought off with rubies!" My words came in short gasps. Henrik and I had been running a good five minutes, and we still hadn't put enough distance between us and our pursuers to outmaneuver them. These were *not* the fire giants I'd seen on my tours of duty.

"Yeah, well, we also thought they were *slow of movement and thought.*" Henrik's voice parroted what Professor Mikstram had taught us in high school. "Apparently they've evolved." Even though he was running every bit as fast as I was, he barely sounded winded—which was totally unfair, given I worked out twice as hard as he did. *Stupid injury. Finish healing, already.*

"Apparently." I pumped my burning legs harder, springing off the tips of my toes to lengthen my strides as we sprinted through yet *another* elderwood grove. Great Odin, how many of these things were we going to run through? I made a sharp right turn and called to Henrik. "This way!" I bolted in the direction of Muspelheim's sole saltwater lake, knowing we could power-swim across and summon the Bifrost before the iodine-averse fire giants caught up. Forget finding Forse's contact; we needed to get out of here. And no way was I asking Heimdall to open up the bridge until we'd put some distance between those freakishly fast beasts and us. We couldn't chance porting one of them back to the safe house.

"Get in here. Quick," a scratchy voice beckoned from up ahead. It sounded as if it came from behind the arch of boulders twenty-five meters away. "Back here. Before they catch you."

Henrik raised an eyebrow and I blinked, not breaking my run. On the one hand, it was suicide to trust *anyone* in Muspelheim. The odds were good whoever was behind that rock wanted to maim us, grill us, or turn us over to Surtr in exchange for... well, whatever fire giants found valuable these days, since apparently the value of rubies had plummeted. The price for two Asgardian heads must have gone up.

On the other hand, the streams of flame shooting at us were only getting closer. And if my visual assessment was accurate, the fire-breathing mutants were no more than fifteen meters behind us, twenty tops. If we didn't lose them, and fast, we wouldn't be heading back to Midgard without some serious blisters... or worse. Chances were the monsters would be more than happy to serve up flambéed Asgardian for tea.

"What do you think?" I tipped my head toward the boulder arch. We were only ten meters away.

Henrik shook his head. "My gut says no. But if we don't take cover, they're going to roast us. Do you see any other options?"

I scanned the grove. There was nothing but trees in any direction. A glance over my shoulder proved Henrik was right—a thick billow of smoke crawled through the foliage like Freya's forest cats stalking a reindeer. The giants spouted fire with each exhale, incinerating trees on contact. There was no way we'd make it if they got even ten feet closer.

"That arch is the only break in the tree zone I can see. Climbing the elderwood is out, since the whole trunk seems go up in smoke the minute the base is charred." I squared my shoulders and darted to the right. "Do it."

Henrik followed me without question, flinging his body over mine as we dove through the small opening in the arch. He wrapped his arms around my chest and tucked his legs against me, rotating so his body bore the impact of our fall. His back made a dull thud as it struck the hard dirt. My landing was slightly less uncomfortable, thanks to the thick layer of muscle adorning Henrik's chest, which I *so* didn't think about because I was erecting *extremely major* boundaries today. Boundaries that *totally* didn't include committing the sensation of Henrik's body wrapped around mine to memory, because I *absolutely* was not going to relive this moment every night from here to forever.

That would have been pathetic, after all.

We skidded another meter, Henrik gripping me tightly and my hands locked around his thick forearms for the sole reason of not flying off and hitting my head and being an ineffective partner. *That* would have been irresponsible. Then we came to a stop and leapt to our feet, backs close together—but not actually touching because, boundaries—in a defensive stance.

The cave was too dark to see anything at first, but our pursuers' peculiar breathing habits were quick to remedy that. We heard the thundering of their footsteps right before our shelter was illuminated with the thick, hot light of fire breath. The light shot right past the opening of the arch and faded as the fire giants drove forward into the grove, decimating the fauna and sparing us.

When I finally permitted myself to breathe, the smell of burnt wood overwhelmed my nasal cavity. It stung at the back of my throat, and made my eyes feel like they'd been scrubbed with sandpaper and rinsed with alcohol. *What the Helheim?*

"You okay, Brynn?" Henrik punctuated each whispered word with a muffled cough. No doubt the black smoke affected him too. I didn't have to see through my burning eyeballs to know his sword was drawn.

"Yeah. I can't see so great though." I rubbed the back of one hand against each of my eyes in turn. The other pulled my dagger out of my boot and held it steady. This situation wasn't ideal, but it wouldn't be the first time I'd fought blind.

"You don't need your weapons in here." The scratchy voice came from my left, and I whirled around, blade at chest level.

"Identify yourself," Henrik barked.

"Chill out. I'm Hyro. Your friend Forse's... eh... acquaintance?" The scratchy voice rose on the last word, and for the first time I realized its owner was female.

"Prove it. Because we are having one *skit*-tastic day, and the only faces I want to see right now are friendly ones." Henrik guided me behind him with one hand. He was giving me time to clear my vision, and I rubbed frantically at my eyes, making the most of the lull in the action. Things could get heated fast around here. *Ha!*

Apparently, smoke inhalation made me think I was funny.

"Fine." The voice sighed, affecting a tone of long-suffering patience. "You're here because somebody stole your love goddess. You're afraid of the chaos that will envelop the realms. You're looking for a scout that knows something about a portal and a bound female." My vision *finally* returned and I squinted through the darkness to see a curvy girl who didn't look much older than seventeen in mortal years, twirling her cherry-red hair as if she was bored. "Did I pass?"

"I think we're good," I whispered to Henrik. "I can see now. And I can totally take her if it comes to it."

The girl's bulbous nose scrunched up. "That was rude,"

"Sorry. But like he said, we're having a lousy day." I stepped around Henrik and held out my hand. "I'm Brynn. This is Henrik. You're Hyro?"

"Yep."

Henrik stepped to my side and lowered his sword to shake her hand. "*Hei* Hyro. Huh. Your name rhymes with pyro. Your parents must have a wicked sense of humor."

Hyro blinked at him.

"You know," Henrik explained. "Because you're a fire giant. Pyro... Hyro..."

"Real original." Hyro rolled her eyes. She tilted her head back and exhaled violently, shooting a stream of flame out of her nose. Henrik and I both ducked, but the flame shot well over our heads, lighting a sconce hanging on the rocky wall. She repeated the movement three more times, until a flaming wall sconce lit each corner of the tiny room. Hyro leaned back against the grey wall of the cave, her arms wrapped around her waist, with one black boot crossed over her ankle in a pose that screamed *defiant teenager* way more than it screamed *formidable fire giant*. "I thought you might want to be able to see stuff," Hyro offered by way of explanation.

"Thanks." Henrik rubbed his free hand over the back of his neck. "Wait. If you're a fire giant, why are you so... well... short?"

I jabbed him in the ribs with my elbow, and he rubbed his side. "Ow, Brynn!"

"Sorry about him. He doesn't get out much."

"No, he's right." Hyro pushed herself off the wall so she stood at her full height. "I'm four feet, eight inches. I don't exactly fit the mold."

"Maybe not," I admitted. "But that doesn't give the foreigner an excuse to be rude." I shot Henrik the stink eye, and he had the decency to look embarrassed.

"Sorry, Hyro. Last rude thing out of my mouth. Scout's honor." Henrik held up his fingers in a webbed trio, and the laugh escaped my mouth before I could stop it.

"That's *Star Trek*, you nitwit. Boy scouts do *this*." I held up three fingers and Henrik mirrored the gesture, the serious expression never leaving his face.

"Right then. Scout's honor." He held the pose, then broke into a grin. "Love that about you, Brynnie. I learn something new every day." He reached out to cuff my shoulder, pushing my *perfekt* control toward its breaking point.

Hyro studied her fingernails. "So, what do you need from me? Forse's message said you needed info on the girl I saw this morning. What else?"

"Honestly, anything you can tell us about, well, anything would help." I tucked my dagger into my boot and motioned for Henrik to sheathe his sword. "We don't know who took Freya, where they took her, or what they're planning to do with her. If you've seen any unusual activity around here, anything at all, it could help point us to our next destination."

Hyro twirled a lock of her crimson hair. "Anything, huh?"

"Anything," Henrik confirmed.

"Okay. I might have a few things for you. But first, did you bring what Forse promised?" Hyro looked from Henrik to me.

"Uh, we brought the rubies, yeah." Henrik rubbed the back of his neck again.

Hyro wrapped a strand of hair around her pinky. "So? Where are they?"

"They're, um… they're back at the castle." The words tumbled out of my mouth. "We accidentally dropped in closer than we meant to, and the guards got real aggressive and charged at us, and before we knew what was happening we… we…"

"We threw the rubies at them and ran." Henrik shrugged. "In hindsight, it wasn't our brightest idea. We're usually a lot smarter."

Hyro's eyes narrowed to slits. "You threw Asgardian rubies at the palace *guards*? Seriously?"

My hands landed firmly on my hips. "Like I said, they were chasing us. *Chasing* us. Since when did they get so fast, anyway? I swear when I was here before, they moved at, like, a quarter of that speed."

"Freaky, right? Things are totally different here since the volcano erupted," Hyro said.

"The volcano?" Henrik wrinkled his brow. "That thing's been dormant for centuries."

"Exactly." Hyro's glare softened. Now she looked wistful, almost sad. "There were reports of a dark magic trace around the base, so a handful of the guards went to check it out. Rumor is, by the time they reached the mountain the magic was so thick they could barely see two feet in front of them. I guess they pushed forward, because their communication devices were working up until right before the explosion, and at least one of them described what he saw. Thick black smoke circled the bottom of the volcano, much denser than anything we'd seen in that area before. It looked a lot like this, actually." As if to demonstrate, Hyro made her lips into an *O* and let out a breath. A dense mist swirled from her mouth, heavy as the morning fog on a cold day, and blacker than the remains of the elderwoods just outside the cave.

"Have you been doing that long?" I shifted my weight as a fresh wave of pain coursed through my injured leg. *Why isn't it healing faster?*

"Since the explosion." Hyro looked uncomfortable. "It just started after the dust settled."

Henrik stepped so he stood slightly in front of me. I appreciated the chivalry, but I didn't need protecting.

"Stand down, Hotshot. I was just telling you how bad it was at the volcano." Hyro studied the scraggly ends of her hair.

I nodded at Henrik. "So then what happened?"

She shrugged. "Nobody knows. One second they were talking about black smoke, and the heavy dark magic readings they picked up on their readers; the next, the volcano exploded and they were gone."

"You mean you lost communication with them?" Henrik prompted.

"Nope. Gone. The explosion must have buried

them." Hyro leaned back against the cave wall. She rested her head on the stone and stared up at the ceiling. "A second team went out to the site once the lava had cooled, but by the time they got there, there wasn't a trace of team one. No footprints, no bones, not even any weapons. Maybe the lava melted them down, or maybe they were just too buried to track. And when the second team came back, they were like super soldiers. They ran at four times their top training speed. They saw a good ten meters farther than they tested on their last optical exams. Their fire breathing had twice the power mine has now, and at least three times the heat. It was insane. When Surtr caught wind of what had happened to team two, he sent every member of his guard out to the site, hoping they'd return all hopped up on the juice, too. Now every member of the royal guard can run, fire breathe, and fight with the strength of... well..." Hyro met my eyes, "an Asgardian."

"Did something happen to them at the volcano? Did they run into anyone? Did someone turn them into what they are now?" I asked.

"Not that we know of. Each team was in communication with the base officer the entire time. Nobody mentioned seeing any strangers."

"What about the dark magic? Did any of the teams ever identify the source?" Henrik pressed.

Hyro toed the ground with her boot. "Nope. The official report said it was coming from a residence in the town at the foot of the volcano—that the owners had opened a portal to Helheim, and the energy of the *ikkedød*—Hel's freaky dead guards—set off the volcano. And maybe there was a portal, and maybe the *ikkedød* did have something to do with the explosion. But I know the owners of the house didn't have anything to do with opening any portals."

"How do you know that, Hyro?" I asked gently.

When Hyro finally looked up, tears brimmed in her eyes. "Because my parents owned that house. And they'd never invite Hel—or her minions—into our home. They were good giants."

I ignored the irony of the words. With the possible exception of the crying teenager in front of me, there was no such thing as a good fire giant. None that I'd met, anyway.

"You said they *were* good." Henrik wore the uncomfortable look all guys wear around crying females. "Did something happen?"

"Yeah." Hyro wiped her nose on the back of her hand. "The entire village was buried under the lava. My parents are dead. I would be too, if I hadn't been out hiking that day."

"Oh, Hyro. I'm so sorry." I stepped forward and pulled her into my arms. For a minute, I ignored the fact that Hyro was a stranger, a fire giant, and in all likelihood, an enemy to Asgard. Right then she was just a girl who'd lost people she loved more than anything in all the realms.

I could certainly relate to that.

"It's okay." Hyro squirmed her way out of my

embrace and offered a small smile. "It was a few months ago. It hurts less every day."

"I'm so sorry for your loss," I murmured words I'd spoken a thousand times before. After a beat, I looked up at Henrik in alarm. "This happened a few months ago? Did you hear anything about it?"

He shook his head with a frown. "No. That's really strange. We should have picked up on an atmospheric shift like that. If Ull didn't see a change in the winter weather patterns, then Tyr should have noticed the increase in soldier strength. Or Freya should have felt the heartbreak of everyone who lost their loved ones. Or…"

"Great Odin." I tugged at my ponytail. "So many levels of our security should have picked up on this. How did we miss it?"

"Surtr went to a lot of trouble to cover it up," Hyro offered. "There were no messages sent; he censored all the outgoing communications to make sure nobody let it out. And I don't know how your weather and heartbreak trackers work, but the rumor was he had one of our wizards cloak the entire region. Don't feel too bad about not seeing it—he didn't want you to."

"Guess that explains it," Henrik murmured, at the same time as I hissed at him, "Fire giants have *wizards*?"

Förbaskat.

"Hyro, you look way too young to be living on your own. Who's taking care of you?" I asked.

"I am." Hyro gave a sad smile, and my heart tugged. She shook her head. "Don't worry about me—I miss my parents, yeah. But the censors thought I was home that day. They tallied me in the lost count. I'm off the grid now, so I get to do whatever I want."

"Including helping Asgardians?" Henrik raised one eyebrow. "Why would you do that? And don't say it's for the rubies. We both know you could have asked a lot more of Forse, and he'd have sent it. We really will pay you back, I swear."

"I know you will. I can tell you're good guys." Hyro stared at her toes. "Surtr blamed my family for what happened. Somebody caused that explosion—maybe even opened a portal to Helheim. But it sure wasn't my parents."

"Then who did?" I mused.

"No idea." Hyro shrugged. "Do you want to hear about your friend?"

Henrik and I exchanged a glance. We could come back to the volcano talk later, when we were alone. Right now, Freya was our top priority.

I took a deep breath and nodded at Hyro, knowing her next words could mean the difference between peace and chaos across the cosmos. "Tell us what you know."

CHAPTER 10

HYRO HELD HER HAND up to her face. Her chipped purple fingernails looked dirty in the light. In that moment, I resolved to send her two dozen rubies. Three dozen, maybe. It had to be a living nightmare to exist off the grid in a realm filled with fire breathing giants.

"'Kay." She glanced up. "This morning I saw dragons flying over the grove."

"Dragons in Muspelheim?" Henrik's back stiffened.

"Weird, right? I haven't seen them here since I was little, so I got curious. I lost the first ones, but another group came in behind them, then another. There were enough that I was able to follow their trail all the way to the volcano."

"Did they see you?" I asked. Fire giants and dragons were allies, I guessed because of the whole fire element thing. But I didn't know how far that friendship went. Or what it would cost Hyro if she ratted them out.

"Nope. My traveling cloak matches the soot in that area. Their eyes are bad enough they'd think I was just part of the dirt from that distance."

Fair enough.

"So what did they do once they got to the volcano?" I winced as my leg throbbed anew. *Heal, already.*

"They circled it for a good five minutes, and then I got this really creepy feeling up and down my back, and I started to feel sick." Hyro rubbed her abdomen, as if she was reliving it.

"Dark magic," Henrik muttered to me. I nodded. Whenever I was exposed, I felt the exact same way.

"What happened next?" I prodded.

"There was this flash of light, and this purple haze formed around the top of the volcano. I contacted Forse as soon as I could, and told him a portal had opened."

Henrik nodded. "What happened after the haze formed?"

"Well, it got thicker, and I saw four dark things herding one smaller thing toward the volcano's base. It was hard to see through all the smoke, but all five of them were definitely wearing all black, and the smallest one had a black bag drawn over her head. I figured it was a girl because she had long reddish-blond hair sticking out from under the bag, and she was walking way too gracefully to be a guy. No offense." Hyro glanced at Henrik.

"None taken," he replied through gritted teeth. I knew he wasn't upset about Hyro's comment; he was upset because he knew as well as I did that we'd been *this close* to Freya, and she'd gotten away from us. Again.

"They took her through the portal, didn't they?" I asked.

Hyro tilted her head. "It looked like it. The dragons circled, then five of them swooped down and picked up the girl and each of the four dark things, flew them to the top of the volcano and dropped in with them, going right through that purple mist. The rest of the dragons followed, and they all just disappeared. It was the craziest thing I've ever seen. Like, ever."

"You're *sure* that's what happened?" Henrik pressed.

Hyro nodded. "Does it make any sense to you?"

Henrik and I exchanged a glance. Dragons? What did they have to do with our friend's abduction? And who were the four dark things? Were they the shadows we'd seen take Freya from Midgard, or were they something totally different?

"Not at the moment it doesn't. But we don't have the whole picture. Forse and Tyr might have come up with more intel by the time we get back to base. Maybe they can make sense of all this," I answered.

Hyro shifted her weight and stared at her nails. She let her hair fall in front of her face, acting as a shield. In the flickering light she looked unbelievably vulnerable. And while I appreciated the information she shared with us, Surtr would have her incarcerated... or incinerated... if he ever found out she was helping Asgardians. Whatever instinct had possessed her to

146

agree to act as Forse's spy could very well get her killed.

"Hyro, are you okay here? By yourself, I mean? Do you have any friends, or other family looking out for you?"

Hyro shook her head. "It's just me. Like I said, they counted me in the death toll after the explosion. I was supposed to graduate in a few months—now I don't have to enroll in Surtr's army like the rest of my class." She gave a tight smile. "Trust me, it's better this way. The mortality rate for first-year female recruits is... well, let's just say there's a reason you don't see a lot of lady fire giants."

Henrik gave a nod, and I bit my bottom lip. "We can't bring you back with us, since we're going to a safe house. But when we finish this mission, will you let us relocate you? You could start over somewhere, maybe... um..."

I wracked my brain. Where could we hide a teenage fire giant with hair so red it practically glowed, breath that turned to fire, and flesh that completely betrayed what she was? It wasn't like the humans on Midgard could walk by a violet-skinned girl without doing a double take. Especially if she sneezed flames on them.

Hyro saw my confusion and touched my arm. "It's okay. I know I don't fit anywhere. The trolls are afraid of me, the dwarves would rather collect the bounty Surtr would put on my head if he found out I was a refugee, and the humans..." She shrugged. "I'm fine here. Honest. I have a semi-permanent camp in a forest nearby, and I've gotten pretty good at hunting. Plus, it's a lot less lonely now that Forse talks to me. Or it was, before today. This stopped working right after I told Forse about the portal." Hyro pulled a small communication device out of her pocket. "I'm not sure how I'm going to talk to him now."

"Hey, I made that!" Henrik blurted. "That klepto Forse stole it without even asking."

Hyro's eyes turned down as she offered it to Henrik. "Do you want it back?"

"No, keep it. But let me see what's wrong with it." Henrik picked up the device and turned it over. He opened the back panel and studied the communicator's guts. "Ah." He pulled a key out of his pocket and poked at the wiring until I heard a small pop. With a smile he replaced the panel, and handed the device back to Hyro. "All fixed."

"Thanks." Gratitude laced Hyro's tone.

"No worries. I'm glad it's getting good use. I didn't know it could reach this many realms away."

When Henrik puffed out his chest, I groaned. "Henrik."

"What?" He held out his arms. "Just taking a moment to appreciate the awesomeness that is me."

"I helped develop that, remember? In fact, wasn't I the one who reconfigured the chip so it could transmit beyond the home realm's gravitational sphere?"

Henrik waved a hand. "Po-tay-toe, po-tah-toe. Either way, it's a sweet little machine. Use it in good health."

"Um… thank you?" Hyro tucked the communicator back in her pocket.

"Come on, Brynn. We'd better get back to Forse and Tyr with all of this." Henrik stuck out his hand, and the girl shook it. "Thank you for everything you've done for us. We'd have been fire giant fodder if you hadn't shown us this cave."

Hyro grinned. "It was nice to have someone to talk to for a while."

My eyes prickled. I had so much—my parents, my brother, my friends, the entire Asgardian society. This girl was so young, and she had nobody. "Hyro, are you sure you don't want us to relocate you? We can find an encampment that will welcome you. You wouldn't be the first refugee we've relocated. And you shouldn't have to be all by yourself."

"If I ever change my mind, I know how to reach you." Hyro patted her pocket. "But really, I'm fine here. And now that I'm on your team, I actually have a purpose. Forse said the girl you're looking for is somebody real important to all of us."

My throat constricted. "She is."

"Well, then I'll keep an ear to the ground and pass along anything that might help you guys find her." Hyro nodded.

"Aren't you afraid Surtr is going to catch you?" Henrik wasn't being snarky; he genuinely didn't understand why someone so young would take such a huge risk for strangers.

"A little," Hyro admitted. "But after seeing the dark

magic and the portal open up in the volcano, I'm willing to bet whoever's behind your friend's disappearance is responsible for my parents' deaths, too. Surtr might not have cared about all the people that died in that explosion, but I did. They were my friends." Hyro's eyes brimmed with moisture. She quickly pressed the heels of her hands to her eyes, stopping the overflow. "Anyway. I'm happy to help."

"Thank you, Hyro," Henrik spoke sincerely.

"Yeah. Thank you." I gently touched her elbow, and tilted my head toward the entrance of the cave. It was probably safe to call for the Bifrost now. "Well, if you change your mind, let Forse know and we'll evaluate our camps and determine the best relocation for you. And I'll have a messenger deliver three bags of rubies to this cave. Asgard doesn't have any dragons, but if you see a pegasus fly by, you'll know it's ours."

"Thanks." Hyro shot me a grin so sincere, the fire in the sconces glinted off her sharp, yellow teeth. I returned the gesture, then followed Henrik out of the cave, ignoring the protests of my injured leg. *Why hasn't it healed itself?*

At the entrance, we paused to scan what was left of the grove. It was nothing but black soot, grey smoke, and the scent of freshly cremated trees.

I sighed. "I guess we can call for the Bifrost right here, *ja*? No need to get to the water anymore."

"Agreed." Henrik shifted his backpack with one hand, and looked at my awkward posture. "Is your leg still not better?"

"Not yet." I gritted my teeth. "Just get us home. Elsa can fix it."

"Heimdall!" Henrik shouted from my side. "Open the Bifrost."

In a flash of light and color, the Bifrost came shooting down from the tar-colored sky. It lit up the clearing, filling my body with energy as it prepared to suck us up, away from the fiery realm of Muspelheim and back to the safety of the beach house, where our friends were waiting. As my feet left the ground I caught a glimpse of a young girl standing at the entrance to the cave, hidden behind a wall of red hair. She gave a small wave before ducking back into the safety of her enclosure. It wasn't right. We would find a safe place to move Hyro. Running from cave to cave in Muspelheim was no kind of life.

But unless we found Freya in the next few days, *none* of us would have any kind of life. My brain grasped at every bit of information Hyro had shared, from the four black figures herding Freya, to the dragons circling the purple mist. Time was closing in, and we needed to piece everything together.

Fast.

CHAPTER 11

"WHAT THE HELL? YOU guys scared me to death!" Mia sat on the sand in front of the safe house, wrapped in a thick blanket. Her knuckles were white as she clutched her phone to her ear, and she breathed erratic breaths at the same time as she glared at me.

"Sorry." My leg throbbed and my nausea ebbed as I jumped from the landing area. A beam of light retracted above us, disappearing in the thick coastal clouds. "It's just the Bifrost."

"Shh," Mia hissed. Then she spoke into her phone. "What? No, you heard wrong. Brynn just got home and said there's a *light frost* outside. Winters are cold here, you know?"

Henrik let out a soft chuckle. "She's good."

"If she's going to hang with Tyr, she better be," I muttered. Our war god had more secrets than a phoenix had feathers.

"Right, Jason. I hear you. I'll talk to Mama about the holidays." Mia paused. Her mouth turned in a frown. "I said I'll talk to her! You don't have to be rude about it."

Henrik jogged to my side, and we exchanged a look. Mia's brother was never rude to her. Jason teased the daylights out of her, but he loved Mia with all his heart, and treated her with the kind of respect all men should have for women. This wasn't normal.

This was because of Freya's absence.

This was *so* not good.

"Goodbye," Mia harrumphed. She hung up the phone and wrapped her blanket tighter around her.

"*Hei*, Mia." Henrik lowered himself down next to her on the sand. He kept his movements slow and deliberate. I mirrored his action, so we framed our friend.

"Hi," she muttered.

"It's awfully cold out here. Do you want to head inside?" I offered.

"No. I just need some fresh air." Her words sounded clipped.

"Mia." I hesitated. "Is everything okay?"

"Yes." She answered too quickly.

Henrik nudged her with his shoulder, then pulled his beloved fake eyeglasses out of his backpack and slid them over his nose. "Amelia Ahlström, as your T.A. I want you to remember you can come to me with any problem. Any time. Even if it's got nothing to do with math."

Mia looked up at Henrik and burst out laughing.

"You don't have to wear those around me. I know they're just for show."

"Maybe." Henrik looked smug. "But I got you to laugh, didn't I?"

My lips curved up in a smile. Henrik was such a *nörd*. What Mia didn't realize was that he actually *liked* wearing the clear-lensed glasses. He claimed he wore them to blend with mortals, but I knew he thought they made him look smart.

What he didn't know was that the glasses added an extra hot edge to the sexy assassin vibe. *Like he needs an additional edge...*

"Alright." Mia hiccupped. "I'll tell you. But don't tell Tyr. He's got enough going on already."

I glanced back at the house. "Is he inside?"

"Nope. He's off fighting dragons. Again." Mia shook her head as Henrik and I exchanged a worried glance. Tyr knew not to leave the realm without a bodyguard. Something big must have been going down for him to take off without us. Either that, or he was making a point to Odin about calling his own shots while he was in Midgard. *Boys.* "Apparently there was another uprising in one of your heims. Dwarfheim, I think."

Henrik's back straightened. "Nidavellir? That's the third time in a month. Do you know why?"

"I didn't ask. He ran out of here in a hurry." She squeezed the blanket around her knees. "Why are all the dragons being so uppity lately?"

"I'm not sure," I admitted. "The scout we just met said they've been acting weird where she is, too."

"Oh, good. So you did find her." Mia exhaled in relief. "Any good news?"

"None to speak of." Henrik pushed his glasses up his nose. My stomach fluttered. *Seriously. Stop it.*

"Whatcha reading?" I toed the book laying open in the sand. "*Norse Mythology* by John Lindow. Huh."

"It's the really helpful one I've been using to help me understand what's going on in World Myths in Art. I thought I found a paragraph on you, Brynn—it said a girl named Brynhild was the fairest of all the valkyries. But Elsa told me she was someone else."

"Oh, she's someone else, all right." I snorted. "Brynhild's the fairest. And the fastest. And the most full of herself. She's Freya's second in command, so I guess now that Freya's missing, she's running the show. I probably should have checked in with her before I took off with Henrik, but Tyr's orders trump hers anyway, so it wouldn't have mattered."

Mia looked up. "I'll bet that *really* lit a fire in her britches. Elsa also told me she's not a fan of your relationship with Henrik on account of him shooting her down in high school."

"Elsa talks too much," Henrik muttered.

"And we don't have a relationship," I was quick to add. "We're just… work associates."

Henrik gave me a disappointed look, but he couldn't exactly argue. They'd been his words, after all.

"Back to business." Henrik drew his shoulders up. "What's going on with your brother, Mia?"

"Oh. That." Mia blew at an errant strand of hair. "He

wants my folks to come to California for Christmas instead of doing the traditional thing at home. Says he's sick of east coast weather, and the 'stupid girls' after him at school, and his 'asinine professors' and, well, everything. He's in a seriously awful mood. I've never seen him like this."

"He was rude to you?" I pressed.

"Yeah." Mia shrugged. "Maybe exams are getting to him. They're coming up soon. Speaking of, any chance we'll be out of here by end of next week? Or do I need Dr. Fredriksen to come up with a medical excuse for missing my tests? For the record, I *really* do not want to miss exams. It is *extremely* difficult to retain this much information, and I do not want to have to study over Christmas vacation." Mia stared each of us down.

"I'd love to say yes, but we can't make any promises. It all depends on when we recover Freya." Henrik studied Mia. "Have you noticed any other mortals acting differently?"

"Um…" Mia bit her bottom lip. "Well, Heather and Charlotte seem kind of off. Charlotte texted me about Heather not holding up her end of the chore chart. And Heather e-mailed to tell me her boyfriend's being a jerk and she's swearing off all men." Mia's lips formed a small *O*. "That's not good, is it? Is Freya's disappearance causing their bad moods?"

"Let's just hope they're having a rough week." Henrik shot me a look behind Mia's back. *Rough week* my right hook. The mortals could feel the effects of Freya's absence. I already felt off, which meant the rest of the immortals wouldn't be far behind. And then it was a short journey until the aura of the cosmos turned dark and everything descended into absolute chaos.

So, so not good.

Assuming Odin was taking this seriously, we should have every available squadron on a god-hunt by now. We needed to get our newest intel to Forse, so he could disseminate it through the ranks.

"Mia, is Forse in his house?" I asked.

Before she could answer, a blinding light broke through the sky. It shot down on the sand, depositing a blood-caked, mud splattered, thoroughly exhausted God of War in its wake. We'd *definitely* be having a talk about his unchaperoned excursion later. As I gritted my teeth, the Bifrost retracted and Tyr moved slowly across the sand.

He was limping.

"Oh my god, what happened?" Mia threw her blanket on the ground and ran to her boyfriend. "Your face is… and your clothes are… oh Tyr, what did they do to you?"

"It's okay. I'm okay." Tyr held out his arms and Mia tucked herself into them. When she was enveloped in his massive embrace, her shoulders shook. The sounds of her whimpers weren't far behind.

"I hate seeing you hurt," she sobbed. I caught Henrik's eye. Mia was usually stronger than this. Yes, she hated that Tyr's job put him in danger. But I hadn't seen her cry over his injuries since… well, since we nearly lost him to Fenrir.

The mortals were *definitely* getting hit early this time.

Tyr rested his chin on Mia's head. "I know, baby. Sorry to run out on you like that. But I'm just fine, and everything's sorted." He shot Henrik a look. "For now."

Mia pulled her head back. "What do you mean for now? Did you kill the dragons? Or tame them? Or whatever you guys do to dragons?"

Tyr wrapped his arm around her waist and turned her toward the house. "Why don't we all go inside? Brynn, grab Forse and Elsa. I think we'd better have a meeting."

"And a healing." I nodded at his wounds. "My leg's not exactly in mint condition at the moment—maybe she'll do a two-fer."

"I don't need a healing," Tyr grumbled.

"Big baby." I rolled my eyes.

Henrik picked up Mia's blanket and book and walked to Tyr's house while I ran to Forse's. There were only a handful of homes in the tiny cove, each boasting Cape Cod-style façades and connected by an emerald green lawn. Elsa's lights were off, so I rapped on Forse's door. Sure enough, they answered it together, and after a brief explanation I brought them back to Tyr's, Elsa's healing box in tow. In no time, five gods and one mortal were gathered on the couches framing the big stone fireplace. Someone had lit a fire, and Mia sat beneath a thick quilt with her knees tucked to her chin.

"Good. We're all here." Tyr rubbed his girlfriend's

shoulder with one hand and ran the other through his hair. He'd changed into a clean shirt in the time it took me to fetch our friends, and though the wounds on his face looked like they were trying to knit themselves shut, blood was still caked on his cheeks. I wondered if it was his or a dragon's.

"We're all here, *kille*. Start talking." Henrik leaned forward, elbows on his knees.

"Something's going down with the dragons," Tyr began. "I don't know what, and I don't know why. But that initial skirmish we saw a few weeks ago in Nidavellir was just the beginning. Back then they were fighting amongst themselves, posturing for dominance. The dwarves were only getting hurt when they tried to intervene. Now the dwarves are being outright attacked. The dragons turned on them, and they're getting more aggressive. And the dragons' numbers are down—either they're killing each other off, or they're transferring to another realm."

"They're transferring," I confirmed. "Forse's scout in Muspelheim reported a group of dragons entering a portal in the volcano. If they're transferring realms in Muspelheim, they could definitely be doing it in Nidavellir."

Henrik rubbed his neck. "Do you suppose they took Freya through the Muspelheim portal to Nidavellir? Then what's happened to the missing dragons?"

"Maybe there's another portal from Nidavellir to a second realm," I mused. "Or maybe the portals can go to more than one location. Tyr, is it safe to go back there to investigate? Or are the dragons still attacking?"

"It's safe at the moment. Odin sent the Elite Team to cover me, and we were able to subdue a good number of them. The ones we could find, anyway." Tyr rubbed the stubble on his chin. "You think there are two portals in Nidavellir?"

"Well, the dragons in Muspelheim had to come from somewhere," I pointed out. I quickly recapped what Hyro had told us about the unusual dragon presence, the existence of fire giant wizards, the weird energy around the portal, and the bizarre mutation of Muspelheim's normally sluggish fire giants into full-blown super soldiers. "It's insane there right now—the giants are even *breathing* fire, shooting the hot stuff out of their mouths a ridiculous distance."

Henrik leaned back to stare at me. "It's almost like they've taken on the qualities of the dragons."

My eyes widened as I stared back. "That's never happened before. There can't be an inter-species transmutation of powers. Can there?"

"Just because it's never been done before doesn't mean it's impossible," Henrik pointed out. "Think about it. Idunn spliced apple specimens until she came up with the immortality blend. Odin spliced raven genes until he created Huginn and Muninn, the ultimate eyes in the sky. Who's to say it couldn't be done inter-speciously?"

"Maybe," I conceded. "But inter-realm species? That's just playing with fire."

Elsa giggled from the end of the couch. "Isn't that what they've created? Fire-breathing fire giants?"

Henrik and I inhaled simultaneously.

"Oh my gods. Do you realize what this means?" I asked him.

"They've found a way to create hybrid dark species. How? Their energy levels should be disparate enough to kill off the invading genes." The thought tumbled out of Henrik's mouth.

I matched his pace. "Unless the dominant gene's been enchanted to accept the recessive one. Could a spell like that even exist? And how long would it hold?"

"And what happens when it wears off? If the specimen contains warring genes and one side wins out, what happens to the host body?" Henrik continued. "Does it return to its original state or does it die?"

"Could a corporeal being even withstand that kind of internal dissention?" I asked.

"Uh, Einstein? Tesla?" Mia held up her hands in a cross. "Time out. The rest of us can't keep up."

Henrik took a breath. "Brynn and I are wondering... if it's possible that the fire giants actually got some kind of genetic transplant from the dragons. Magically. If that happened, they could have taken on some of the dragons' physical capabilities, like the fire breathing."

"But because a magical transfer is finite, unlike a physical transfer, the magic would eventually wear off and the transferred genes would be at odds with the pre-existing genetics of the host body. So what's going to happen to the fire giants then?" I asked.

"And how is the transfer taking place? Is that how the volcanic explosion plays into this? Is everything that goes near that volcano in Muspelheim infected with some airborne dragon pathogen? Or does the spell target specific individuals with a certain predisposition?" Henrik asked.

"And how do the biomechanics break down?" I wondered. "Are the host bodies the only susceptible organisms, or is this something endemic? Could it spread?"

"And if it spreads, what's the transfer mechanism? Are we talking cellular level, airborne pathogens, Odin forbid, a mushroom cloud..." Henrik trailed off.

"And most importantly"—I shot him a look—"what does this mean for us? Does it have anything to do with Freya? Is whoever's taken her controlling the dragons too? What's their ultimate goal?"

"I'm glad we've got *Brynnrik* working on this." Elsa rested her head on the back of the couch. "But why do I feel like we're even further from figuring this out than we were yesterday?"

"We know there's a portal between Nidavellir and Muspelheim, though whether it goes on to a second destination, we can't say. We know Freya was taken through it. And we know the dragons are involved in some way." Tyr nodded at Henrik and me. "Your next stop's going to be Nidavellir. Search the area for Freya, and pay our dragon guy a visit. He may have some insight."

"You have a dragon guy?" Mia sounded incredulous.

"We've got a guy for everything, *prinsessa*." Tyr kissed the top of her head.

"Oh, there's one more thing you should know." I leaned forward and spoke directly to Tyr. "The mortals are feeling Freya's absence. The effects are taking hold sooner than we'd expected."

Tyr glanced at Mia, then set his mouth in a firm line. When he spoke, it wasn't conversational. It was a command. "Henrik, Brynn, go catch some sleep. When you wake up, head straight to Nidavellir and track down Berling. Then report back here and we'll regroup." A deep *V* formed between his brows. "We need to fix this fast."

Henrik reached over to squeeze my knee and I bit down on the inside of my cheek. This was not the time for another black box explosion. Or even a fissure.

My world view narrowed to a singular focus. The dragons were inconsequential. We just had to get our love goddess back.

Everything depended on it.

"Um, guys?" Elsa raised her hand. "Healings first. Then sleep."

"I'm good. Just take care of Brynn," Tyr ordered.

"No can do, brother. Those wounds should have closed themselves up by now. You've obviously got dark remnants in there, coupled with whatever you had left after the Arcata attack." Elsa tapped her foot.

"You didn't let her heal you when you got here?" I turned on the god of stubbornness. "Tyr, you're our leader. If something happens to you, we're all screwed."

"And also, we like you," Mia pointed out.

"Thanks for the concern, Brynn," Tyr said wryly.

"You know what I mean. Stop being a stubborn pig and take your healing like a man." I stormed up the stairs to Tyr's office, pausing at the landing to look at the sea of shocked faces. "Oh, like you weren't all thinking it."

Mia's tranquil voice cut through the tension. "Actually, I'm kind of curious about how all of this works. That one after Fenrir happened so fast. Would it be okay if I watched?"

Elsa looked thoughtful. "Emotional healings are private, but Tyr's not getting one of those. I don't see any reason you can't observe a physical healing. It might give you a better understanding of how our systems operate."

"I'll whip up a batch of my *amazing* Swedish pancakes while you lot are getting patched up. Healings, snacks, and sleep should make everything right— at least for tonight. *Ja, sötnos?*" Henrik shot me a wink.

"There's very little your pancakes can't fix," I admitted begrudgingly. "But let's do this fast. We need to get back in the field as soon as possible."

A lot of lives depended on it.

CHAPTER 12

I TURNED ON ONE heel and walked through the French doors that marked the barrier between the upstairs landing and Tyr's office. A massive window took up almost the entire beach-facing wall of the large room, flooding the space with natural light. A leather sectional was cozied against the glass, with a separate foot stool positioned a few feet away. The desk and chair butted against the smaller window, the one facing Freya's house. A dresser stood on the wall beside the door, boasting hurricane glasses filled with smooth stones and candles, and the door to the en suite bathroom occupied the fourth wall, a jetted tub just visible beyond the frame. A long soak suddenly sounded heavenly.

Maybe tomorrow. First we had to track down our love goddess.

"Mia, take the desk chair and sit in the corner. Tyr, Brynn, the couch is yours. Sit down, feet flat on the floor, and hands on your knees, facing up so I can scan you." Elsa issued her orders as she strode into the room, a pitcher of water in one hand and her healing box in the other. She set both on the desk and used her magic to open the box, removing two small cups before shifting through ingredients with delicate fingers.

Mia took her seat. Tyr closed the French doors behind him before walking across the room. "You doing all right, Brynn? You're moodier than usual."

"Shut *up*, Tyr!" I dropped into my appointed seat on the couch.

"I think Brynn might benefit from an emotional healing, as well as a physical one," Elsa said calmly. "This is a lot to process, and although she's doing really well managing everything..." She turned to me. "You really are doing brilliantly, love."

"Uh, thanks?" I crossed my arms.

"All things considered, an overall purification might do a world of good," Elsa finished.

Having the realm's High Healer as your in-house nursemaid had its benefits, as we'd seen when she saved Tyr's life. But it also had major drawbacks. Sometimes I just wanted one of those regular medicinal healings the normal healers gave, not one of Elsa's full-service hippie-dippy deals.

"I appreciate it, Elsa, I really do. But time's of the essence, and I really want to get back into the field as soon as possible. Can we table the emotional cleansing until *after* we get Freya back?" I asked.

"Brynn." The corners of Elsa's mouth turned down. "Your energy's totally closed off."

"Sorry, Elsa." I was. She was one of the sweetest goddesses in Asgard, and none of this was her fault. "Long day."

"Long life," she pointed out.

"You can say that again," Tyr muttered.

"And an emotional cleansing won't be effective if you're not open to it, so maybe waiting a few more days might not be a bad thing. But when you're ready, I want you to let me know so I can effectuate the closure you need on this."

"Thanks." With everything else going on, I wasn't ready to go *there*.

"So, how exactly does all of this work?" Mia craned her neck from her spot at the desk. She'd dug a pencil and paper out of the drawer and was poised to take notes.

Typical Mia.

Elsa turned from her healing kit and walked to Tyr. "We do things a little differently in Asgard. You mortals like to compartmentalize your systems. You see a medical doctor for a physical injury, a religious leader for a spiritual ailment, and you more or less neglect your energetic systems entirely. But where we're from, we recognize the entire being—physical, spiritual, and energetic—as one entity. And a weakness in one area can lead to an injury to the whole. Does that make sense?"

"Kind of." Mia looked up from her note taking. "Y'all take a holistic approach to medicine."

"More of an integrative approach," Elsa corrected. "Because we learn to command our energy from an early age, we're able to create somewhat of a bubble around ourselves. The bubble keeps us from co-mingling our energetic spheres, and maintains the purity and invincibility of our corporeal form. You call it immortality; we call it energy medicine."

"Fascinating." Mia's pencil scribbled furiously.

"But sometimes we drop our guard," Elsa continued. "We let our bubbles slip; we release our energy and forget to call it back; we allow someone's energy to enter into our space. That's when we get injured. That's when real damage can occur."

"Hold on. I thought Tyr was bleeding because a dragon bit him." Mia looked confused.

"That's part of it." Elsa knelt at Tyr's side, and took his palm between her hands. She closed her eyes, took a breath, and exhaled slowly. Then she waited.

In the meantime, Mia looked like she might jump out of her chair. Her eyes darted to me, and I held up one finger, signaling for her to wait. Elsa needed to focus while she assessed Tyr's wounds.

"Good. These injuries are purely physical. Tyr, you're suffering from a basic dark magic malady. What happened with the dragon?" Elsa asked.

"Its head nicked me with a fang on descent after I decapitated it." Tyr shrugged.

"Oh my god!" Mia paled.

"It happens." I shrugged. "Tyr can take a dragon fang."

"He can," Elsa assured Mia. "Tyr's wound is an example of an unavoidable injury—if an Asgardian is struck by an object laced with dark magic—a jotun spear, or a dragon's tooth—"

"Or a homicidal wolf?" Mia interjected.

"Exactly. Dark magic compromises our self-healing ability. Thankfully, I've got a prescription for that."

"Like a medicine?" Mia asked.

"Kind of," Elsa agreed. "Watch, Mia. Tyr, close your eyes."

Tyr did as instructed, leaning against the back of the couch and stretching out his legs. "Give me your worst, sis."

Elsa held out her hands and ran them over Tyr's body without touching him. She paused over his leg and his stomach, where his clothing was stained with blood. Elsa furrowed her brow, then placed one palm a few inches above his thigh, and the other over his belly button. She drew a deep breath and exhaled forcefully, then moved her hands in a slow figure-eight pattern. She continued the motion, drawing her palms up slowly with each cycle until her hands were level with her shoulders. I knew from experience she'd just taken all the dark energy out of Tyr's body. I also knew from experience it hurt like Mother Frigga. But Tyr didn't flinch. In fact, it was entirely possible he'd fallen asleep.

Show-off.

When Elsa's arms were at ninety degrees to her

torso, she flicked her fingers, as if she was whisking away a pesky fly, not banishing dark energy to the tenth realm.

Double show-off.

With the darkness removed, Elsa took a clear crystal from her box and rubbed it between her palms, set it down, and brought her hands back to Tyr's injuries. She took a breath and pushed healing energy into the wounds. The trickle of blood stopped immediately, as Tyr's stomach and thigh began to heal themselves.

I snuck a glance at Mia. She looked like she'd just walked in on a herd of baby pegasuses learning to fly. She was equal parts shock and awe as her orderly mind struggled to process what she saw. I got it; if I hadn't been born into it, it would be hard to believe this kind of healing was possible. It certainly defied the mortal science Mia grew up on.

Life with us definitely involved a steep learning curve.

Elsa cleared her throat and pulled two vials out of her healing kit. With the physical portion of her task complete, she could attend to Tyr's energetic needs.

"These are botanical extracts." Elsa held up the vials so Mia could see. "Both human and Asgardian bodies are comprised mostly of water, and plant cells can manipulate the water's energy. I have my junior healers locate plants containing specific frequencies—one plant's cells might minimize anxiety, another can improve focus—you get the idea. My juniors bring the plants to me and I distill their essences. Right now, I'm going to administer some pine and red chestnut to your boyfriend."

"Again with the pine?" Tyr groaned.

"When you learn to let go of your guilt, I'll take you off the pine. The red chestnut, I think, you'd better just get used to. I don't see you not worrying any time soon. Now open your mouth," Elsa ordered. Tyr did, and she placed two drops from each of the vials underneath his tongue.

"Are we finished?" Tyr murmured after he'd swallowed.

"You are. Now, lie there and regenerate. *Calmly,*" Elsa instructed. Tyr became the picture of relaxation.

While Mia scribbled furiously on her paper, Elsa stepped to my side. "May I?" she asked, and I nodded. She took my hand between hers and closed her eyes. I did the same, opening myself up to her energy. Things would go a lot faster if I dropped my walls.

Defenses down.

"Ouch," Elsa clucked, as I let her see my worst.

"Tell me about it," I muttered.

"What's happening?" Mia asked.

"Brynn's physical ailment was caused by an energetic deficiency. Would you please tell Mia what happened in Muspelheim?" Elsa asked.

"Henrik and I were fighting giants, and one landed on my leg after I killed him. Crushed it." I shrugged.

Mia cringed.

"Now the body of a fire giant, in and of itself, is not

laced with dark magic. Its weapons might be, or what-ever fire they're breathing these days might be enchanted. But a corpse shouldn't have kept Brynn's leg from healing itself."

"So why didn't it?" Mia asked.

I snuck a glance at Tyr. He lay on the couch, eyes closed as he allowed his body to regenerate. But I knew what he was thinking. He'd know whose energy was all up in my space.

Odin bless him for keeping his mouth shut.

"Brynn's at an energetic imbalance. I need to recall her energy from all of the places she's left it behind— Brynn has a *lot* of energy and she tends to forget to keep it with her." Elsa tutted. "And I'll need to eject the foreign energy from her space. That will restore her energetic order so her body can heal itself."

Mia's eyes widened. "Where'd you learn that kind of magic?"

Elsa shook her head. "It's not magic, Mia. It's energy. Mortals can do it, too."

"Get. Out." Mia's jaw fell open.

I tilted my head. "I've never understood that about your race, Mia. You're so intent on placing everything into identifiable boxes. Even your religions are at war with each other, literally at war, to prove that their god is the true god. It never occurs to humans that one supreme being could reveal Himself in countless ways to countless cultures in the manner each would best understand Him, or that all physical and energetic systems could be interconnected."

"Their race is young," Tyr spoke without opening his eyes. "The light elves only reached that level of consciousness a few millennia ago."

"True," Elsa agreed. "And a small number of the mortals already understand all of this. It's just a matter of their being able to open the minds of the others to accept what is."

As Mia mulled that over, Henrik called from downstairs. "Swedish pancakes are ready! I've got lemon-sugar ones, lingonberry ones, *and* Nutella ones. You're welcome, folks."

Tyr sat up. "Check me again, Elsa. I think I've regenerated."

Elsa scooted over so she could take Tyr's hand in hers. After a moment, she nodded. "You're all clear. Mia, I'm afraid this is where you'll need to leave. Take my brother and get out of here. Grab some pancakes, maybe take a walk before bed, talk through everything you've just seen and let Tyr help you make sense of it. I need a few minutes alone with Miss Brynn."

Mia nodded. "Thanks for letting me watch. I have, like, a million more questions, but I guess we've got time, right?"

Tyr walked to her side and put a hand on her lower back. He leaned down to kiss the top of her head. "We have forever. Come on, we can talk over pancakes." He guided her out of the office, leaving me with the person who could see through all my wounds, physical and otherwise.

Elsa closed the door behind Tyr and moved to stand

in front of me. The two of us stared at each other for what felt like *forever* without blinking. Finally, Elsa gave a small smile, lowered herself onto a chair, and pulled it so she sat right across from me. There was enough space between our knees so we didn't touch, but we were close enough that I knew our energetic spheres bumped up against each other.

Just like she wanted them to.

"It's up to you, Brynn. How do you want to play this?" Elsa asked.

"You're the intuitive one. Shouldn't you tell me my best path and set me on it?" I asked.

Elsa looked disappointed again. "That's not how this works, and you know it."

"I know," I muttered. "And I realize it's in everybody's best interest if I let you fix me and go to Nidavellir with all my ducks in a row, but *förbaskat*, Elsa, it's still too raw. I know I'll have to access those memories in order for you to heal me, and I'm just not ready to relive that all over again. It's too painful."

"I can certainly respect that." Elsa reached out to clasp my hand. "But putting *that* particular elephant from your past aside, Brynn, there's a lot going on with you right now. Your energy is all over the place. I can see you're thinking about the past, and worrying about what Freya's absence means for your future. You're living in fear of what was and what might be, and you're completely ungrounded from the present. *That's* the reason you got hurt. *That's* the reason Tyr's afraid to send you back into the field tonight. He can't see everything I can, but he's bound to pick up on the fear in your aura."

"He can see it?"

"It's really thick," Elsa confirmed. "Is it more than just... is there more to it than thinking about what happened last time?"

I squeezed my eyes shut. This was *so* not something I wanted to talk about.

Thankfully with Elsa, not talking was always an option.

Instead, I pushed the image of me kissing Henrik followed by Henrik's rebuff, toward my friend.

"Mmm," she murmured, her face impassive. "That's rough."

"You think?"

Elsa breathed deeply and released my hand. I opened my eyes and watched as she held her hands out in front of her. She lowered them gently into her lap, then nodded. "You're concerned about how this is going to affect the friendship," she surmised.

"*Ja.*"

"Fair enough. Let's get you back in control of your own energy. You know you can't control his choices. But you can control how presently you walk your path. And when you are truly present, there can be no fear." Elsa smiled.

Clearly, the clairvoyant had never been truly present with a horde of angry fire giants.

"You misunderstand," Elsa corrected. It was creepy how she could do that. "Fear is the absence of presence.

It exists in the past, or the future. But in this moment, this reality, there is only presence. There is only being. There can be no fear."

"You say that all the time." I shook my head. "It's not so easy for me.

"Because you're good at many things, Brynn Aksel, but owning your energy is not one of them. Ground yourself for me—anchor your body to the earth, and recall all of the energy you've scattered around this week."

I closed my eyes again and forced myself into the moment, opened my palms and pictured each spot I'd spent time, sucking the energy pricks from each of the coordinates.

"Good," Elsa praised. "Now fully inhabit *your* space. And draw on the golden energy that is uniquely yours —pull it from above and let it flow through your body until your cells buzz with your unique imprint."

"You're healing me," I complained.

"I'm grounding you," Elsa corrected. "If I was healing you, you'd know."

Fine.

"I heard that." Elsa sighed.

I drew a breath and refocused.

"Good. Now *this* is your most productive space. This is where you are fully *you*. And in this now, there is no fear, is there?"

"No," I admitted. I felt alive. Focused.

I felt powerful.

"Now, I want you to try to inhabit this space all the

time. Especially when you leave for Nidavellir. I know it's hard for you, so until we get to that proper healing, I'm going to give you something to retain this state. But remember, this is like a bandage—a quick fix. The deeper healing requires more work."

I opened my eyes. Elsa lifted the pitcher from the desk and filled one of the cups with water. She grabbed a small vial out of her healing kit and unscrewed the lid before adding a few drops to the water and handing the cup to me.

"What was that?" I asked after I drank.

"Mimulus essence. This, combined with the grounding, should help keep your fear of losing Henrik's friendship at bay for a few days. Hopefully that's all we'll need to bring our girl home." Elsa picked up the clear crystal again, and rubbed it between her palms. Then she stood, and packed up her kit. "And after that, when you're ready to tackle the deeper thing, I'm here. You know where to find me."

I stood and bent into a stretch. Healings, even minor ones, took it out of me. "Thanks Elsa. It's a crazy life we lead, *ja*?"

"*Ja*," she agreed. "The Norns only hand out what we can take, but I'll be honest—there are times when the sheer weight of it all feels unbearable. Sometimes I worry Mia won't be able to handle it. What's everyday for us is overwhelming to her. I can see that."

I picked up an errant vial from the desk and placed it in Elsa's kit. "I understand what you're saying, but Mia's a fighter. Every time we give her a new piece of the puzzle, she retreats to internalize it, then comes back more resolved than ever. She's going to be a force to be reckoned with by the time she fully commits to this. And then whoever's not on our side better watch out."

Elsa smiled, and closed her kit. "I hope you're right, Brynn. We sure could use her energy on our team."

"Oh, come on." I cuffed Elsa on the shoulder. "With guardians like us to keep her on the straight and narrow, she'll be signing on to full-time Asgardian duty in no time."

"But how?" Elsa walked to the door. She paused with her hand on the knob. "Odin's never turned a human before. And even if we use anti-aging enchantments, she's limited by her mortal form."

"I honestly don't know, but I wouldn't count her out." I shook my head. "I think we're both going to be surprised by what Mia's able to do with her gifts—mortal, or otherwise."

Elsa met my eyes with a wide smile and threw her arms around me. "Be careful out there, Brynn. You've got beautiful things to accomplish with that existence of yours."

I hugged her back, testing my weight on my right leg and exhaling at the absence of pain. *Well done, Elsa.*

"Keep everyone in check here while I'm gone," I said. "Once this whole Freya debacle is over, let's make getting Mia up to speed our top priority. We're going to need every hand on deck to make sure nothing gets through our defenses again."

Elsa nodded. "Agreed. Now get out of here. I believe a certain hot god has a fresh plate of hotcakes with your name on them."

I snorted as I opened the door. "Henrik's Hotcakes? Is that what we're calling the Swedish pancakes now?"

Elsa giggled. "I thinking Hottie's Hotcakes, or possibly *Perfekt* Pancakes, but yours is good too."

I wrapped my arm around Elsa's shoulders and steered her toward the stairs. "You're trouble, Fredriksen."

She looked at me with a laugh. "I am Tyr's sister. What else would you expect?"

CHAPTER 13

" **A**CCORDING TO FORSE, THE dragon guy's house should be three hundred meters east of the drop site. He's extremely cautious—he refused to give up any intel unless it was face-to-face. And whatever you do, don't call him Berling. He prefers Berry." Henrik held out his forearm as the Bifrost retracted. I shook my head, placing my elbows on my thighs and bending over until the heaving passed.

"You're going to have to touch me eventually," Henrik pointed out. "Things can't be weird with us forever."

I wiped my forehead with the back of my hand as I stood up. As much as I hoped he was right, I doubted things could ever be normal between us. Henrik grossly underestimated the deeply scarred girl psyche.

"I touched you in Muspelheim," I said, for the sake of argument.

"If you mean you let me carry you out of the fire

giant graveyard because you couldn't walk, that doesn't count."

"Whatever. Which way to Berry?"

Henrik pushed the thin silver frames up the bridge of his nose and jutted his chin. "Should be just over that hill."

"You know you don't have to wear your fake glasses. It's just us."

"Maybe," Henrik said. "But I've never met the dragon guy, and I want him to think I'm smart."

I rolled my eyes. "Just open your mouth and start talking. He'll figure it out pretty quick."

"Luck favors the prepared, *sötnos*. Now are you steady enough to walk or do you still feel unwell?"

I glared at Henrik as I stomped across the snow-dusted field. "I'm fine, *thank you very much*."

The low chuckle from behind let me know that Henrik followed.

We reached the hill without talking, and paused just below the top to assess the environment. Pink clouds, pastel songbirds, and a light layer of white covered the tapestry of trees.

I snuck a glance at Henrik. He stood at the crest of the hill, one leg in front of the other in a strong stance. One hand rested on the hilt of his sheathed broadsword, while the other shielded his eyes from the twin suns overhead. The light bounced off the waves of his hair, creating a halo effect. He looked every bit the conquering, avenging deity he was.

And he made my black box jump up and down in a

dance that showed *zero* respect to my flimsily erected boundaries.

"I assume Berry's place is somewhere in the trees?" I bounced on my toes to distract myself. A dense, deciduous forest rested at the base of the slope, its thick-trunked trees barren beneath the frost. A heavy fog settled on this side of the valley, filtering the early morning light. It was beautiful, the way the fog bathed the tree branches in a dim glow. It was the kind of place I'd always imagined Henrik grabbing me by the arms and pushing me up against the—

THWACK!

My wholly inappropriate train of thought came to a screeching halt as a large rock pelted me in the side.

"Look out!" I yelled.

Henrik and I dove for the ground, unsheathing our weapons as we moved. We leapt to our feet, blades out, and came face-to-face with an image so off-putting, I had to force myself not to scream like a Midgardian schoolgirl. A mottled face with beady eyes and pointed teeth sat atop a hunched body so gnarled with age or injury, just looking at it made my bones actually hurt. The creature drew back his fist to launch another rock, and Henrik jumped to action. He ran to the dwarf's side and wrenched the rock out of his hand.

"Stand down," Henrik commanded. The dwarf clawed at Henrik's arm, its yellowing nails leaving thick rake marks across Henrik's perfect skin. My partner picked the dwarf up by the scruff of the neck.

"Trespassers," the dwarf called in a shrill voice. The sound made me cringe.

"We're here by invitation of your king." Henrik lifted the dwarf higher, and the creature swung his legs in protest. "Should we tell him you're detaining an ally? I hear a century in the mines is the going rate for treason nowadays."

The dwarf fell still. His shoulders slumped in defeat, and he released his hold on Henrik's arm. "Proceed," he said. "But one misstep and..." The dwarf drew a slicing motion across his throat.

"Mmm-hmm." Henrik set the dwarf on the ground and it scampered off.

"What was that about?" I asked.

"Apparently King Hreidmar didn't alert the welcome wagon of our arrival." Henrik put his hand on the hilt of his sword and led the way into the woods. "It's probably better that way. Even with a hall pass, we're not exactly anyone's favorites around here. Asgardians have a reputation for using the dwarves to get what we want."

"I can't imagine why," I muttered as we walked through the trees. Our feet left light prints on the freshly fallen snow. "They've made practically every treasure we have—Mjölnir, Megingjörd, Járngreipr... hold up. Do they make things for anyone *other* than Thor?"

"Plenty," Henrik confirmed. "And they'll continue to —we pay them pretty well for their work. But helping us right now, well, they're just doing it because they like Freya. They always have."

The wicked dwarves had a soft spot for love. Who knew?

"Is this it?" I pointed at the tiny cottage hidden behind a thick grove of tree trunks. Its grey stone façade fit the cool atmosphere of the forest, and a trail of smoke emitted from its chimney.

"Should be." Henrik pulled a folded piece of paper from his pocket and read his tidy scrawl. "Forse says knock nine times and ask for Berry." He stuffed the paper back in his pocket and walked up to the door. He turned to me and waggled his eyebrows. "Secret code."

I giggled in spite of myself.

"Care to do the honors?" Henrik offered.

I squared my shoulders and knocked on the thick wooden planks. "Berry? Are you there?" I kept my voice quiet. By all accounts, Berry's was the only residence nearby, but apparently dwarves could sneak up on you.

"Who is it?" A hard voice came from the other side of the door.

"We're friends of Tyr and Forse. They sent us to ask you about the dragons?" We waited for what felt like an hour, but eventually the door cracked open. A tiny creature peeked around the handle, its face every bit as mottled as the one that had attacked Henrik. We appraised each other for a long beat before the door opened all the way and Berry stepped aside.

"Come in," he growled.

I nodded in gratitude as I stepped inside the little cottage, Henrik close behind. It was impeccably tidy, with a small kitchen off the entrance, a sitting area of sorts straight ahead, and what I assumed was a bedroom behind the door to my left.

Berry hurried to close the door behind us. "Tea?" He grunted.

"Um, yes please." I offered an unreturned smile. "Thank you."

Berry shuffled into the sitting area and put a kettle over the fire. He added leaves to a stone mortar, and ground them to a fine dust with a pestle. He portioned the mixture into three cups and waited until the kettle steamed before pouring the water. He held out the cups with a grunt. "Elderflower tea."

"Thank you." Henrik took two cups and handed one to me. He set his down on the low table and dug around in his backpack. He pulled out a small satchel and offered it to the dwarf. "Tyr sends these for you—he appreciates your help with this."

Berry took the satchel from Henrik and peeked inside. His face broke into a terrifying smile as he looked at the contents. Thank Odin he was on our side.

"Tell Tyr it is my honor to help. We will all fall if they keep Love from Asgard." Berry set the satchel on the mantel over the fire, and climbed into a leather armchair. He raised his mug to his lips. "To Freya," he saluted.

"To Freya." We mimicked his motion and sipped the tea. It burned my tongue, but it would have been poor form to refuse Berry's tribute. The last thing I wanted to do was get on his bad side. Dwarves lived by a very strict code. An eye for an eye. No favor without payment. Honor above all.

Though their definition of honor was slightly different than ours.

"We need your help." Henrik leaned forward, hands clasped and elbows on his knees. "Tyr says you might know why the dragons are acting weird. If they've got anything to do with Freya's disappearance, we need to figure it out." Henrik quickly recapped what we'd learned about the recent Nidavellir dragon uprisings, their sudden presence in Muspelheim and the transmutation of the fire giants, and the unusually fast reaction the mortals were having to Freya's absence.

Berry steepled his fingers. "The dragons are moving with more cohesion than usual. Normally the four main clans battle amongst themselves, but in the past month they have turned on us."

My eyes widened. "They're supposed to protect dwarves—or at least your minerals and treasures."

"They used to." Berry stared at his hands. "But now they are hunting my people."

Oh, Odin's ravens. This is so not good.

"The dragons gather at the base of Einak Mountain at sunrise and disappear for the day. After dark, they raid the villages, abducting any dwarf they can capture. Most of us took to the caves for protection." Now Berry's gnarled fingers cupped his tea.

"Why aren't you underground?" I asked.

"The dragons granted me immunity."

"Why would they do that?" Henrik wondered.

Berry lifted his shoulders. "Because I am their healer."

Back the Bifrost up. This little old man was... a veterinarian?

Henrik nodded. "And so long as you're useful as their healer, they let you live."

"Oh, you misunderstand." Berry shook his head. "They are not killing the dwarves they abduct. They take them to Nidhogg alive."

"Nidhogg?" I tried to keep the incredulity out of my voice. There was no way the dragon king from my childhood bedtime stories was real.

Berry raised one spiky eyebrow. "Have you heard of him?"

"Who hasn't?" I stared at Henrik. "He's not some fairytale villain?"

Henrik drained his cup and set it on the table. "It's news to me. There's actually a dragon king?"

Berry nodded. "I healed him once. He lives in Náströnd, protected by his guardians—dense, black shadows that shape-shift to take on whatever form serves their purpose. They are like the *ikkedød*, but crueler."

"We've seen them." I elbowed Henrik with enough enthusiasm that he rubbed his ribs. "Sorry. But now we know what they are. Those are the things from the attack footage, the ones that tried to kill Tyr, and abducted Freya."

"They sure are." Henrik narrowed his eyes.

"So the shadows are the guardians of Náströnd?" I continued. "Like, they guard the dragon king's lair? What do you call them?"

"Around here we call them the specters." Berry shivered.

The specters. Yeesh. Those things were seriously terrifying. And seriously powerful. They'd incapacitated the God of War and kidnapped the leader of the valkyries, all without suffering a single casualty.

I sipped my tea as my brain whirred. "I know Náströnd is in one of the dark realms, but just *where* is it exactly?"

The dwarf's face scrunched in distaste. "Helheim."

Double great. The dragon king lived in Helheim. And he commanded the dragons to bring live dwarves to... somewhere, in order to do... something.

Henrik leaned forward. "Do you have any idea what Nidhogg wants with the dwarves?"

"No." Berry's mouth turned down. "But if I had to guess, based on what you say about Muspelheim, I believe they have established a portal between Einak Mountain and the volcano in the fiery realm. And if Nidhogg plays a role, it is not out of the question to believe the portal goes beyond Muspelheim, straight to—"

"To Helheim," I groaned. "Ugh. They've got an army of captive dwarves guarding the Goddess of Love in Helheim."

"Not necessarily," Henrik mused. "Think about it.

We wonder how the inter-species mutation is happening, right? Dwarves and dragons share a realm; they breathe the same elements and consume the same minerals. They have a far more similar genetic makeup to dragons than fire giants do. No offense," he hastened.

"None taken," Berry assured him.

"So?" I asked.

"So, what if the dwarves aren't guarding Freya? What if, instead, whoever's orchestrating everything is using the dwarves as lab rats? Testing the transmutation on the more compatible species before integrating the more... lethal species?" Henrik rubbed the back of his neck.

"You think Nidhogg's testing the mutation out on the dwarves first? Maybe. But if it's already been successful with the fire giants, why hasn't he returned the dwarves to their realm?" I set down my mug.

"Maybe he can't." Henrik sighed. "Maybe the foreign genes killed them."

Berry stiffened in his chair. "A dragon would never kill a dwarf. Such an act would be dishonorable."

"Yeah, well, the dragons aren't injecting the genes themselves; they've got questionable fine motor skills, remember? Whoever's controlling them is doing that part," Henrik offered.

"Hold on," I interrupted. "You said something earlier about dwarves harvesting treasures and minerals from the mines, right?"

"Correct." Berry waited while I worked it out.

"Well, could there have been any minerals down there with transmutable properties? Something that might be able to effectuate the transfer of abilities from one species to another?" I asked.

Henrik sat up straighter.

I kept going. "Think about it, Berry. If you guys had some kind of an element that acted as a conductor, whether magically or naturally, couldn't the bad guys use that to create these super soldiers?"

"Like the ultimate power conductor. And if we find that and destroy it, it's game over for the new breed of Muspelheim monsters." Henrik leaned back and shot me a grin. "Nice logic."

"Don't give me the blue ribbon just yet," I cautioned. "The theory only works if a mineral like that exists."

We both turned to Berry and waited.

He sat very still. After a long moment he let out a slow breath and unclenched his fists. "We found a red crystal in one of the mines a while back. We had never seen one, so we took it to the lab to run some tests. It turned out the crystal was an anomaly. It refracted light, contained healing properties, and could act as an energy source like most of our crystals. But this one offered an additional capability."

"It could transfer abilities between beings?" I guessed.

Berry nodded. "We have some magic here. Not as much as you do in Asgard, but enough to generate light down in the mines and craft the treasures your people seem so fond of."

"You make pretty fabulous treasures," I praised.

"We do. We called on one of our light fairies and one of the muses who inspire our craftsmen, and they both agreed to test the red crystal." Berry leaned forward.

"Let me guess. You're now the proud owner of a glowing muse?" Henrik surmised.

"Exactly."

"Do you think the perps might have the crystal?" I asked. "Could they be using it to create these super soldiers?"

"It is the most plausible explanation." Berry rubbed his hands along the arms of the leather armchair. "I cannot think of another mineral capable of generating this result. And you say your science has not been able to foster it."

"Fan-bloody-tastic." Henrik dropped his head in his hands.

"No, this is good." I grinned. "We know what we're dealing with. Berry, if we destroy the crystal, its powers will be released, right? Meaning the super soldiers would lose their transmuted abilities, and go back to being, well, just plain fire giants?"

"In theory, yes. When a subterranean-based Nidavellir crystal is shattered, its power returns to the earth and it becomes just another rock."

"Okay. So to neutralize the giant threat, and put us back on an even playing field with at least one of the groups standing between us and Freya, we have to find the crystal and shatter it. We know the dragons are working under Nidhogg's control, and they're transferring their speed and flaming breath to the fire giants, possibly through an airborne substance via the Muspelheim volcano. That means Nidhogg's probably got the crystal—or whoever he's working for does. The real question is, who's controlling Nidhogg?" I thought out loud. "I can't see a dragon king wanting to genetically engineer super soldiers. Or kidnap our love goddess and send the realms into darkness. Besides total domination, what's in it for him?"

Henrik sucked in a breath. "Total domination. That's it."

"What's it?" I blinked.

"Brynn, think about it. Total domination. Tyr's best friend is abducted, and the realms are on the verge of crashing into darkness. Who do *you* think stands to gain the most from this?"

I blinked again.

"Okay." Henrik tried another tactic. "Who's been trying to bring Tyr to the dark side for, oh, forever? Who just sicced Tyr's childhood pet on everyone he knows and loves?"

I mulled it over. "Hymir?"

"Exactly."

I shook my head. "Hymir's not smart enough to get all these pieces moving together."

"Maybe he is not working alone." Berry tapped his fingers together. "Has the balance of power recently shifted in your realm? Do you have a new ally or a captive you did not have before?"

Henrik's head snapped up and he met my stare with wide eyes. "Fenrir," we whispered in unison.

Berry tilted his head. "You captured the wolf?"

"We did," I confirmed. "And we killed Garm in the process."

Berry leaned back in his chair. "Well then. You just made a legion of enemies. Garm was Nidhogg's daughter. Nidhogg gave her to Hel when she took command of the realm."

"Holy Mother Frigga." My hand flew to my forehead. "You killed a dragon princess, Henrik? That cannot be good for us."

"In my defense, she tried to kill me first. But if I killed Hel's guard dragon, and Freya and Tyr captured Hel's brother..." Henrik swore. "We've got the perfect storm of ticked off demons."

"Yeah, well, bad things come in threes, right? We've got Nidhogg and Hel mad at us. Who's the third? Is it Loki?" I wondered. He might have been on his uppers this month, but he was never a force to underestimate.

"Gods, who *isn't* mad at us these days?" Henrik rolled his eyes. "We've got two targets for now. Odds are good they've got enough to do with Freya's disappearance—we can catch our next link in Helheim."

"Stay away from Helheim," Berry warned. "There are rumors of dark factions moving together in its heart."

"Yeah, well, when *aren't* dark factions hanging out in Helheim?" Henrik shrugged. "Besides, if Freya's there, it doesn't matter. We have to go."

"Yeah, it looks like we're going to Hel." I sighed. "All we need is a hand basket."

"What's a hand basket going to do?" Henrik looked confused.

"Going to Hel? In a hand basket? It's one of Mia's funny sayings." I stared at Henrik's blank face. "I don't understand it either, but she says it a lot. Come on. We'd better move."

Henrik stood and shook Berry's hand. "Thank you. We truly appreciate your help."

Berry gave a tight smile. "Be careful. And bring Freya home safely."

"You have our word," Henrik vowed.

I shook Berry's hand and carried our mugs to the sink. Without needing to speak, Henrik and I raced for the clearing. Heimdall must have been watching—he lowered the Bifrost before we even called for it.

"To the safe house," Henrik ordered. "Let's finish this."

"Let's finish this," I repeated. I squeezed my eyes shut as we once again flew through the realms.

CHAPTER 14

MY NAUSEA EBBED AS I climbed the stairs from the beach to the safe house. Henrik walked behind me, his hands on my waist to steady residual wobbles.

"I hate the Bifrost," I muttered as we walked across the grass. Henrik fell into step beside me but kept his hand on my lower back. I *so very much* wished I could wrangle my little black box into submission.

Perfekt control was something of an enigma these days.

"There they are!" Mia's voice rang across the lawn. Through the open door I saw her leap from the couch and race toward the porch. She met us at the door. "Henrik," she hissed. "Drop your hand. Stop touching Brynn."

"I've been saying that all day," I grumbled.

"I can hear you, mortal." A cool voice came from inside. "You seriously think I couldn't see them walking here? Your eyesight might be pitifully poor, but Asgardian eyes see everything."

"Not everything," Forse muttered from the couch. "Or you'd know you didn't have a chance in—"

"Step aside, human. I need to talk with your *friend*." The voice dripped aural ice. My insides clenched as I un-shouldered my backpack and clutched it in my hands. *What did I do to tick off Freya's number two?*

Mia bit her bottom lip and did as instructed. She reached out to squeeze my arm as I stepped inside the house, Henrik at my side. His hand still rested on my lower back. Only now, the butterflies were gone.

"Brynhild." I lowered my head as protocol dictated after meeting her stare. "What brings you to Midgard?"

"You do, you insipid little child." Brynhild crossed her arms.

My backpack fell to the ground with a *clunk*.

"Hey." Henrik's voice was low and menacing. He stepped in front of me, shoulders pulled back and hands balled in fists. "Don't talk to her like that."

"Forgetting your place, *soldier*? Because with Freya gone, I command the valkyries, which ranks me well above you." Brynhild moved forward so she and Henrik stood eye to eye. Seriously, she matched his six-feet four-inches. In combat boots. Some goddesses got all the height.

"That's enough." Tyr's angry command boomed from the balcony over the living room. He thundered down the stairs and stood in front of the fireplace. His jaw was clenched, and the vein in his neck bulged as he glared at Brynhild. Mia, Elsa, Forse, Henrik and I watched him carefully. "I will *not* have you come into my house and talk to my team like that. Remember, Brynhild, this safe house is under *my* command. And I will eject any threat immediately. Including you."

"Well, Brynn is under *my* command. As Freya's second, oversight of the valkyries falls to me in her absence. And when one of our officers engages in an infraction this egregious, it's up to *me* to relieve her of her duties." Brynhild stared Tyr down.

"Relieve her of her duties?" Elsa gasped. "Brynn didn't do anything wrong! She and Henrik have been working day and night to find Freya."

"That's not all they've been doing day and night." Brynhild put her hands on her hips and turned to me. "Do you want to tell them about Alfheim, Brynn? Or should I?"

My throat closed up. She knew. Oh gods, how did she know? My one stupid mistake was going to cost me everything.

"Nothing happened, Brynhild. If anyone told you otherwise, it was a lie." Henrik's voice was steady, and I reached up to touch his arm in thanks. Whatever muscle my fingertips brushed was tense.

"Oh, really?" Brynhild smirked. "Because my source told me that you two were making out by the waterfall."

Humiliation washed over me in waves. Now all our friends knew about my mortification. Well, Elsa already knew, but she knew everything. The rest of them…

"You finally kissed?" Mia whispered out of the side of her mouth.

I shook my head. Technically, *we* hadn't done anything. I'd kissed. Henrik had rebuffed.

Then I'd asked the universe to swallow me whole.

"Your source was dead wrong." Henrik held up his hand. "On my honor as a warrior, I did not kiss Brynn."

Brynhild arched one pointed eyebrow and stepped closer to Henrik. "You're telling me my source is a liar?"

"I'm telling you your source misunderstood." Henrik stood his ground. "Valkyrie code states until a goddess reaches the rank of captain, she is not to engage in a physical relationship. Correct?"

"Correct." Brynhild crossed her arms. "And kissing constitutes a physical relationship. Brynn Aksel, you are hereby stripped of your duties as the war god's second bodyguard, and commanded to return to Asgard immediately for reassignment."

I clutched at my stomach as a fresh wave of nausea overtook me. This one had nothing to do with the Bifrost. "No." I gasped.

"No," Henrik growled. "Brynn didn't break her vow. The contract specifically defines a physical relationship as one involving the mutual engagement of both parties, *ja?*"

"So?" Brynhild's words seethed ice.

"So, that particular kiss was not mutual. Brynn was

really upset about losing Freya. She was emotional and confused and she kissed me, yes. But I did not engage. Without mutual engagement, she hasn't broken your code." Henrik crossed his arms, mirroring Brynhild's posture.

Brynhild glared. "Finnea said—"

"Finnea embellished," Henrik said firmly. "She has reasons of her own for wanting Brynn reassigned, as, I'm sure, do you." He took another step toward Brynhild. "Let it go. I didn't want you in Asgard, and I don't want you here. I don't do ice queens."

"Ooh!" Mia gasped. Brynhild whirled around and raised her palm, but Mia was nestled firmly beneath Tyr's arm. Brynhild caught his menacing stare and pulled back.

"Now that we've established nobody on my team has committed any infractions, I suggest you see yourself out." Tyr nodded at the back door. "You can leave Brynn's horse here. She won't be needing her to return to Asgard. Nice of you to bring her, though."

"Fang's here?" Mia asked. My mood skyrocketed. Having Fang around would be a tremendous asset, not to mention the fact that I'd missed her. I kept her back in Asgard for logistical reasons. Boarding a pegasus in Midgard was just not practical.

Brynhild stood her ground. "You're on thin ice, young lady. By all accounts, you should be on probation. You're lucky Henrik isn't into you."

"I never said I wasn't into her," Henrik corrected.

My heart leapt into my throat and began a frantic break dance. *What?*

"What did you say?" Brynhild's cry echoed my thought.

"I never said I wasn't into her," Henrik repeated. "I never said I *was* into her. I never addressed that subject, nor would I with anyone other than Brynn. What I did say was that I didn't kiss her back. You think I didn't know what would happen if I did?"

Brynhild and I probably looked like mirror images, both of our mouths falling open at breakneck speed.

As much as I'd screwed up our easy friendship, was there any chance I still had, well... a chance with Henrik Andersson?

"You'd best be on your way," Tyr ordered. He walked to the back door and pointed outside. "Don't let the Bifrost hit you on the way up."

Brynhild snapped her mouth shut and stormed out the door. She shouted over her shoulder as she marched, "You got off on a technicality, Aksel. Freya is *not* going to be impressed when she comes back."

"Don't forget your pony!" Mia called helpfully. "Elsa and I moved her and Fang to the driveway so they wouldn't chew up the back lawn."

Brynhild disappeared from view, then came back leading a black pegasus with a silver rope. She mounted the creature and flew away, no doubt wanting to put as much space as possible between us. She'd probably call for the Bifrost somewhere over the dunes.

"Well…" Tyr shrugged. "That was interesting."

Henrik turned around. When I dragged my gaze away from my boots, I saw concern in his eyes. "You okay?" he asked.

"Yep," I squeaked. Humiliation prickled my neck, and if the heat coming off my cheeks was any indication, I was probably ten different shades of red. *No point pretending anymore.* "I'm just embarrassed," I admitted. "I didn't want anybody to know about that. And, well, now you guys, and apparently the valkyrie administration, know what a loser I am."

"Hey," Mia protested.

Elsa shook her head. "Stop it, Brynn."

Henrik took my chin between his thumb and his forefinger. I tried to pull away, but he held tight. "You are *not* a loser. But you and I both know this isn't the time to talk about what happened in Alfheim." He tilted his head toward the couch, and I nodded. I forced my questions into a tight little file and stuffed it deep in the "Deal with Later" drawer. Asgard came first.

It always had.

"Henrik's right." I inhaled, willing the heat to ebb from my cheeks. "We learned something in Nidavellir that might lead us to Freya."

As everyone gathered on the couches, Henrik and I quickly recounted our conversation with Berry. When we'd finished, I leaned back on the couch and took a read of the room. Elsa frowned, her knees tucked to her chin, and her head nestled on Forse's shoulder. Forse's brow was furrowed, and he rubbed his forehead in concentration. Mia looked thoughtful, twirling one lock of brown hair. Tyr sat hunched on the couch with his elbows on his knees and a look of fury in his eyes.

"Sounds like it's time for us to go investigate the situation in Helheim," Tyr surmised.

"Us? I thought Odin ordered you to stay out of the field?" I blinked.

"Yeah, well, I'm voiding that order. Sending you two to Muspelheim on your own was bad enough. There's no way I'm letting you head into Helheim without me there to fight along side you." Tyr's eyes were steady.

Henrik nodded. "What's our departure time?"

"How's Barney coming along?" I asked Mia.

"He's nearly done." She smiled. "I was waiting for you and Henrik to make the final solder. We built it together; it didn't seem right to do it without you."

"Well then, what are we waiting for?" I stood quickly, ready to take action. And also, ready to leave the scene of today's humiliation. "Is everything set up in the office?"

Mia nodded.

"Excellent. And when we get back, you and I have something to discuss." Henrik looked at me levelly. I gulped.

A good something or a bad something? After the way he'd shut down Brynhild, maybe he didn't think I was a total troll.

I clung to that hope like a dwarf to a gem. I'd keep right on clinging for long as inhumanly possible.

"I know," I whispered.

Tyr cleared his throat, and I jumped. "Forse, stay back and protect the girls. Don't let anyone inside the sphere, not even Odin, without my signing off on it first. We're going to make a lot of enemies where we're going, and I'm not taking any chances with Elsa and Mia's safety."

"Consider it done." Forse nodded.

"Henrik, Brynn, go upstairs and finish the time freezer with Mia. Then grab every weapon you can fit on your person and meet me on the sand. I'll call for Heimdall when we're together." Tyr crossed to the painting by the staircase, removed it, and pressed his palm to the wall. When the fingerprint scan was complete, the door to the arsenal swung open. Tyr looked over his shoulder. "What are you waiting for? Get moving."

"Yes, sir." I saluted and followed Mia and Henrik to the office. Barney sat on the desk, a soldering iron nearby.

"Do you want to do the honors?" Mia asked, pointing to the iron.

I shot her a grin. "Nope. This one was your concept. We worked out the *älva* element and reconfigured the specs together, but the bulk of the design work was yours. You get to drive the golden stake."

Mia's smile stretched from ear to ear. "Well then, here goes." She picked up the safety goggles as Henrik and I stepped back. He leaned over to whisper in my ear, and I quelled the ensuing shivers. *Control, control, control.*

"Good call," he murmured. "Tyr may not let her walk into combat, but she's doing everything he *will* let her do to fight for Asgard. This device means a lot to her."

I didn't think Mia couldn't hear us over the crackling of the iron, but I looked at her just in case. She bit her bottom lip, her focus concentrated on the task in front of her. *Whew.*

When Mia finished, she held up the device triumphantly. "It's finished!"

"Extraordinary work, Mia. You must have one Hel of a math tutor." Henrik winked at Mia, and she stuck out her tongue.

"Something like that," she laughed.

"Let's test it out. Mia, may I do the honors?" Henrik reached for Barney.

Mia passed the time freezer. "Now remember, time will freeze for everyone except the person holding the device, and anyone *they're* touching at the moment of activation. We programmed it to work like a circuit, with the user being the stop gate. Anything you're not directly holding on to the instant you activate Barney is fair game for the energy to freeze. Are you comfortable doing it alone?"

"Absolutely." Henrik winked, and my heart thudded. Gods, my boundaries had *no* respect for me today. "Are you ladies ready?"

"You know we—" The words stopped in my throat

as a weird sensation rippled through my torso. It felt like a wave nudging at my skin, and making its way toward my heart before retreating. "Are," I finished. "Are you going to do it? Henrik?"

I looked around, but Henrik was gone. He'd been standing to my right just a second ago, but I hadn't seen him move to my left. He must have blurred.

Henrik chuckled, and Mia and I stared at him in confusion. "What's so funny?" she asked.

"Barney works." Henrik laughed. "And you should see your faces right now."

I touched my cheek, a warm sensation filling my fingertips. I felt inexplicably happy. "Wait. You just froze time?"

"I did," Henrik confirmed. "This baby is pure gold." He held up his hand and Mia slapped it in a high five. "Fang's out front, *ja*, Mia?"

"The pony? Yes. He's tied up to the front fence," Mia said.

Henrik grinned. "Great. Brynnie, grab Fang. I'll get the weapons and meet you out back."

"I dropped my backpack on the way in," I remembered. "The particle accelerator probably needs ammo."

"On it." Henrik strode out of the room, and I moved to follow.

Mia grabbed my arm as I walked past. "Brynn," she murmured. "Please be careful. I want you and Henrik to get your happily-evah-aftah, and you can't do that if you're dead."

"I have no intention of dying today," I reassured her.

"And I'd like that happily-ever-after as much as the next girl, but it's probably not happening with Henrik. The Brynhilds of the world aren't exactly doing me any favors."

"I thought she was supposed to be the 'fairest of all the valkyries.'" Mia quoted her book. "She's not that pretty, if you ask me. Henrik doesn't think so either. Did you see how he shot her down?"

"Yeah, well." I shifted from one foot to the other. "The line of gorgeous goddesses angling for Henrik's heart stretches a mile long. She wasn't the first, and she won't be the last."

"But the question is, which gorgeous goddess does *he* want?" Mia stared at me pointedly.

"Not me, if that's what you're thinking." I walked toward the door with a sigh.

Mia huffed behind me. "I swear, Asgardians are so dense."

I kept walking, but I couldn't help appreciating Mia's optimism. She was a good egg—I was glad Tyr had brought her into the fold.

I hoped we didn't run her off with all the weird.

"Take care of Forse and Elsa," I called over my shoulder. I ran outside, and untied Fang with a joyful squeal. "I missed you," I cried, as I patted her smooth white neck. She nuzzled my head, then followed as I led her to the backyard. When I reached the sand, Tyr and Henrik stood in an open area.

"Hold on, Brynn. I want Fang to stay here and protect the compound," Tyr spoke authoritatively.

"But I just got her back! And we could use her where we're going. Odin only knows what we're going to find, but my money's on a *lot* of dragons. A set of wings could come in handy," I countered.

"I can fly us wherever we need to go. Besides, once we reach Helheim, word of our presence will spread. And I'm sure there are plenty of enemies who'd love to take a crack at Mia and Elsa in our absence." Tyr made a good point.

"But nobody knows where we are. The compound's shielded and…" I faded off. "I get it. You can't be too safe. Fang, stay here. Protect the girls. If need be, herd them up and take them straight to Asgard. Heimdall will see you coming and make sure they're admitted."

Fang whinnied anxiously, and I patted her neck. "I'll be fine, I promise. We'll eat marshmallows when I get home. Now go."

I released her reins and she flew back to the house, positioned herself on the grass, and stood. *Good girl.*

"You ready?" Henrik held out my backpack and I shouldered it.

"As I'll ever be." I nodded, ignoring the way my skin tingled when he bumped against me. *Keep your energy to yourself, Aksel.*

"Heimdall," Tyr called. "Open the Bifrost."

I held my breath as the brilliant light beamed down from the sky.

"To Helheim!" Tyr cried. I closed my eyes as the light sucked us up through the sky, then deposited us in a realm so cold and dreary, my spirits sank on touchdown.

We weren't in Midgard anymore. This was Helheim.

And we had the fight of our lives ahead of us.

CHAPTER 15

"**FÖRBASKAT, HEIMDALL! I MEANT** Hel's gate. Not the outlands!" Tyr's voice thundered across the tundra. He sounded ticked, and rightfully so. Being on the outlands of Helheim was an absolute Asgardian nightmare.

Humans had it all wrong. Helheim wasn't the fiery, blazing pit of despair they imagined their Hell to be. It was actually really beautiful. And really cold. Helheim was a realm of primordial ice, its snowy landscape broken up by breathtaking mountains and icicle-laden trees that resembled the sequoias on Midgard, only with purple needles instead of green ones. It was located in the center of a realm called Niflheim, gifted by Odin to Loki and the giantess Angrboða's daughter, Hel. Hel ran the realm like the raging head case she was —I'd never met her in person, but I heard she was a terrifying half-god, half-skeleton hybrid. And that wasn't a dig at her weight; I'd read in my textbooks that the left side of her body was *only her bones.*

I'd seen weird in my day, but coming face-to-face with that might just land me in one of the healers' padded rooms for a little vacation.

"Dang it!" I hissed. My boots skidded across bulletproof ice as I struggled to find my footing. I placed one heel carefully on the slippery surface, and immediately found myself on my backside. *Ouch.* There would be a fat bruise on my butt in the morning. I looked to Henrik for help, but he was flailing around like a cartoon character. Tyr fared no better, lying flat on his back and swearing at the guardian of the Bifrost after taking his own tumble. This was bizarre.

Being Asgardians, cold weather elements weren't usually a problem for us. Our people did snow and ice like nobody's business. But things here were different. Everything in this realm felt completely foreign, from the abysmal aura and discolored flora, to the oppressive feeling of despair settling on my heart like a lead blanket, to the discombobulating ice.

I tucked my feet beneath me and pressed both palms to the frozen surface to push myself up. In seconds, I was right back on my bottom. I couldn't stand up to save my life.

"Tyr!" I shouted as a dense black shadow leapt from the branch of an eggplant-colored pine tree. "Encase us!"

"*Skit,*" Henrik muttered. From his prone position, he

had the perfect vantage point of the specter's descent. "Not those things again."

Tyr acted fast, wrangling himself to an unsteady crouch and aiming his palm at the sky. A silvery haze flew from his fingertips, but the motion threw him off balance, and he fell back on his butt before the magic could form a full protective dome. Instead the haze flickered, and struck the shadow, grazing its wing-shaped shoulder. The impact altered the specter's trajectory. Now it spiraled to the left, heading toward the pine tree with ever-increasing speed. On impact, the shadow shattered into shards of ash, slicing the top third of the tree clean off.

"Henrik!" I bellowed. The treetop was falling, and if it stayed its course, it would land on top of my partner. Henrik looked up from dragging his body across the ice by his fingertips—we'd all figured out there was no point in trying to walk. As he raised his arms to absorb the tree's impact, Tyr narrowed his eyes and held up his palm.

"On it," Tyr muttered, throwing up a protection. This time, the silvery dome formed just before the tree could pin the legs of the god I'd loved for centuries.

"Well, thanks for that," Henrik said, as he clawed his way to my side. Tyr bum-scooted over, so the three of us were huddled close together under the dome's safety. "I'd hate to design Fred 2.0: The Leg Version."

"Ha ha ha." Tyr waggled the fingers of his prosthetic arm. "Now put your strangely advanced brains to work and tell me why we can't walk on this ice."

I swiped the ground and held my hand up to my face. Tiny granules of ice stuck to my fingers, but they didn't feel cold. In fact... I wiggled experimentally on my bottom. *No freaking way.* "Henrik, look at this." I held my hand out, and he took it in both of his. I half-expected the slow heat radiating from his touch to melt the crystals.

"What exactly am I looking at?" he questioned.

"Irid crystals." I waited for his reaction.

"No. They don't exist." Henrik shook his head. Then he inched closer, staring at my fingertips in awe. "They don't exist?" This time it was a question.

"Then you tell me what I'm looking at. Because unless you can think of another molecule that's shatter-proof, temperature-proof, and by all accounts, Asgardian-proof, I'm all ears." I waited.

Henrik delivered.

"Holy Mother Frigga, they do exist." He dropped my hand and ran his fingers through his hair. It got wilder with every leg of our Find Freya tour. "Why didn't either of us ever think to check Helheim?"

"Um, because neither of us are stupid enough to go to Helheim *on purpose?*" I pointed out. "Henrik, do you realize what this means?"

"Hel, *ja*. If we collect sufficient samples we can complete production on the freezing beam, melting bow, and the climate suit. We can finally initiate research on the volcanoes of Muspelheim because we'll be insulated against the heat, and we can determine the elemental properties that make irid crystals impervious to Asgardian magic. Gods, Brynnie. There are so many possibilities."

"I know! We can isolate the source of the frost giants' power. We've never been able to pass through the gate to Jotunheim's treasure vault, because any warrior that enters goes into hypothermic shock on entry. Seriously ingenious system." I shivered.

"Don't remind me," Henrik muttered. I knew he'd been that frozen soldier on at least one mission, maybe more.

"Hey, *Brynnrik*. Would you two geniuses care to fill the halfling in on what's going on?" Tyr tapped his finger on his temple. We must have been quite the trio —Asgard's largest protector glaring in frustration while Henrik and I babbled excitedly, heads together, about the scientific advancements discovery of the irid crystals would bring to Asgard.

"Oh! Sorry! This is jus—"

"Huge." Henrik finished my sentence. "This is just huge. Possibly the hugest discovery in Asgardian science this century."

"Century?" I balked. "Millennia! This opens us up to endless possibilities for inter-realm exploration. Think of all the planets circling Muspelheim, Jotunheim, even Svartalfheim that have been off-limits before now due to climatic issues. We can send in teams to neutralize the outposts the giants think we don't know about."

Tyr held up a hand. "Never mind. I trust you will brief me on whatever has you so enthused later, *ja*? Because right now we've got another problem."

Tyr pointed one finger at a purple pine. My gaze shifted away from Henrik's shining eyes to the legion of dark shapes circling the top of the tree. The shadows were back.

And they seemed to have doubled in number.

"I don't suppose we're invisible under this dome?" I asked hopefully.

"*Skit.* I only threw up a shield. I should have thought about cloaking us." Tyr eyed the whirling circle. The shadows circled faster, moving closer to us with each turn.

"Want me to take care of it?" Henrik asked. His magic wasn't as strong as Tyr's, but it was good enough to get the job done. At least, it was strong enough in Asgard and Midgard. Hopefully the irid crystals wouldn't affect Henrik's abilities the way they seemed to affect our walking.

"I'm on it." Tyr held out his palm half a second too late. As if sensing his intention, the circle whirled with dizzying speed, creating a funnel. It bore down on us like an incensed tornado. My ears thrummed; the swirl gave off a deafening roar. And whether because of its force or the incapacitating effects of the irid crystals, the dome started to quiver.

"What is happening?" I watched in horror. "Tyr, things can't break your defenses. Even dark things."

"Yeah, well." Tyr held up both hands and Henrik followed suit. Their magic came together, holding a steady stream of silver at the dome. The tornado pulled back and jabbed, poking golf ball-sized holes in the surface of the sphere. Tyr and Henrik separated their streams, redirecting their magic so it patched each new hole as it appeared.

"Maybe we need to move to offensive." I nodded at the tornado, which peppered the dome like a jackhammer. It was punching holes into a large shape. "It's going to bust right through the hole like a perforated paper once it completes that circle."

"*Skit*," Henrik swore. "She's right. But letting it in might be the only way to defeat it."

Tyr nodded. He aimed a stream at me, trapping me in a thick silvery bubble. "We can't let this thing take all three of us out. Brynn, you're shielded and cloaked. We'll hold the specters off while you make a run for it. Crawl due south until you reach the cliffs behind the navy forest. Jump off the cliff, and aim straight for the blackest hole. The thickest part of the darkness is Hel's gate. We'll meet you there as soon as we neutralize the threat, but if we fail I need you to go after Freya on your own. Think you can handle that?"

He had to be kidding me. "I'm not going to Hel unless you're coming with me. Wait. That sounds bad. I mean—"

"I know what you mean." Tyr eyed me steadily. "And it's not a request. It's an order, Aksel. Our mission is to reclaim Freya. The realms are halfway to darkness, and if they descend fully, Hel claims them anyway. I won't have that for Mia. Now, on three, Henrik, pull your stream back and add it to mine. I'll release the dome, and hopefully our combined power will be enough to detonate those specters."

"What if—"

"Stop stalling, Brynn." Tyr shook his head. "Henrik, on my count."

"*Ja.*" Henrik squared his shoulders from his still-seated position. He shifted his stream to meet Tyr's.

"One. Two." Tyr counted.

"Be careful," I pleaded. My fingertips grazed Henrik's shoulder and he nodded.

"Always am, *sötnos.*"

"Three." Tyr dropped the dome, and he and Henrik aimed their stream at the tornado of specters. It quaked violently, then dove for the ground. It struck the ice like a cannonball, sending a quake across the impenetrable surface. I found myself splayed on my back, and scrambled quickly to my stomach so I could crawl my way toward the forest. The navy pines were a few hundred meters behind the purple pines, though from what I'd heard, a literal minefield separated the two species. No Asgardian had ever survived the crossing.

Not that it'd matter if I didn't get out of this clearing.

I snuck a glance over my shoulder as I shimmied across the crystallized ground. My stomach lurched as the tornado barreled down on Henrik and Tyr. They redirected their stream, silver light blasting the bottom of the funnel before it could strike. The blast flung the tornado due east, and it sucked up five of the pines in its path. It collected itself, and bore down again. This time it came so close to my friends that my eyes squeezed shut. When I managed to pry them open, the tornado quaked, and Tyr looked madder than a hot jotun. Henrik appeared calm as always, though I could sense his tension bubbling. Gods, I hoped we made it out of here. Even if I had to spend eternity in the friend zone, I couldn't imagine my life without Henrik in it.

The tornado dove again, and Tyr's voice rumbled across the tundra. "You sure as Helheim better be doing what I told you, Aksel!"

With a shaky breath, I turned my head and focused on the purple pines. I inched my way across the tundra without looking back. When I reached the dirt-strewn ground of the forest, I made my way to my feet with caution. When I was certain the dirt was void of irid crystals, I put one foot in front of the other and broke into a run. I didn't stop until I reached the border of the forests—the one that separated purple from navy. A field carpeted in thick, black grass served as the delineation between the two spaces. I knew it sheathed horrors beyond anything my mind could conceive.

I plopped myself onto the dirt and waited. What in Helheim was I supposed to do now?

CHAPTER 16

"**B**RYNN!"

OH THANK ODIN. I'd know that panicked voice anywhere.

"Henrik!" I shouted. "I'm in here! At the southern edge of the, uh, purple forest."

We seriously should have worked out the proper names for these places before we took this little pleasure cruise.

"We can't find you!" Henrik's panic increased.

"Maybe Tyr needs to drop the invisibility shield," I offered helpfully.

There was a pause before Henrik yelled again. "Okay, it's dropped. We still don't see you!"

"Follow the pinecone trail through the darker part of the purple trees," I called out. "I figured I might need to find my way back to you guys at some point, so I Hansel and Gretel-ed my way through the—"

My words were cut off with the crush of thick arms

around my shoulders. Henrik scooped me into a desperate hug, burying his face in my unruly curls.

"We thought you were dead." Henrik inhaled deeply.

"Nope. Not dead." My lips brushed against Henrik's neck as I spoke. It wasn't intentional or anything; he was holding me so close my lips didn't have anywhere else to go.

It was *so* not my fault I now knew what he tasted like. If sunshine counted as a taste.

"Gods, Brynn. When we couldn't find you, I thought, well." Henrik released his hold and let his arms slide around my waist. I reluctantly pulled my lips away from his neck, and studied his face. He looked harrowed, like he'd just seen a ghost... or a specter. But I got the feeling it wasn't the dark masses that caused the circles under his eyes, or the beads of sweat lining his forehead.

"Hey." I reached up to place my palm on his cheek. He leaned into my hand. "Are *you* okay?"

Henrik exhaled slowly, his cool breath brushing my face and sending an irritatingly familiar shiver down my spine. "Let's just stick together from now on, *ja*?"

"That's what I wanted in the first place, *thank you very much*."

"Great. Now that that's settled, do you two think we could carry on?" Tyr stood behind Henrik with his arms crossed.

"What happened to the specters?" I asked.

"We took care of the problem. Let's just say the

dragon king is going to need a new regime to protect him from now on." Tyr tilted his head toward the field. "By my calculations, Freya should be that way."

"Yeah." I hastened out of Henrik's arms and walked to the edge of the black grass. "And by *my* calculations, we'll be dead before we get halfway across."

"Why do you say that?" Tyr asked.

"I sent out a scout net."

"A scout net?" Tyr looked confused.

"Mia and I developed it last week," I explained. "Fortuitous, right? It's got two tiers; the first activates any airborne traps, the second tackles the ground. I fired a net off and the first tier got sucked out of the sky by something that was either really fast or really invisible—I never saw it. The second set off a series of mines hidden in the grass. Or maybe the blades themselves are the mines—I've never seen grass that color before; it could be weaponized, or infused with dark magic, or just plain possessed." I dropped to the ground and stared at the mystical field from a seated position.

"So I'm taking it I can't just fly us across. Whatever captured the net will capture us. *Förbaskat.*" Tyr rolled his head in a slow circle. His neck cracked in protest.

"I fired a second scout net and the same thing happened. I thought I might have detonated all the bombs with the first net, but maybe they regenerate or something." I fished the net gun out of my backpack and offered it to Tyr. "If you want to have another go, be my guest. But I've only got two more nets in there.

And we might want to hold on to them—I'm not sure what else is up ahead."

Henrik sat beside me and folded his hands together. I chewed on a nail while I stared at the black blades.

"What about the nano-molecular particle accelerator?" Henrik asked.

"I thought about that. Imploding the mines would activate the detonation, but if the bombs are regenerating we wouldn't have time to get across. If we tried to cross during the implosion, we'd get sucked in with it." I sighed. "I am flat out of ideas."

"Well, I'm not." Henrik gave me a devilish wink. "We can use the transporter to beam across the field."

I gasped. "You brought the transporter? Brilliant!"

"Won't we get blown up going over the field?" Tyr asked.

Henrik tapped his head. "We thought of that during beta phase. We figured we might need to use it to get from A to C without actually crossing the plane of B. The wormhole takes us outside the realm and spits us back out at our destination. So long as there isn't a trap in Helheim's atmosphere, we should be good."

Tyr narrowed his eyes. "And if there *is* a trap in the atmosphere?"

"Well, in that case we'll be dead, *kille*." Henrik grinned. "But we'll die warriors, so it's Valhalla, here we come."

My fist connected with Henrik's shoulder. "Don't worry about it, Tyr. If there was a trap in the atmosphere, it would have already been triggered by the Bifrost."

"Oh. Right." Tyr nodded. "Then let's do it."

Henrik stood and I followed suit. He unzipped his backpack and removed a small sphere with a red button. He offered it to me. "Care to do the honors?"

"Gladly." I pressed the red button, and a small black oval appeared at the edge of the grass. "Seriously? It couldn't show up, I don't know, *not* right over the danger zone?"

Henrik shook his head. We watched as the oval grew to the size of a doublewide door, purple energy swirling erratically in concentric circles along its border. "It only stays open for sixty seconds so we'd better move. Should we go separately or together?"

"Together," I answered. "Just in case we configured it wrong and it sends us to different places," I drew a breath before muttering, "or sends our body parts to different places."

"It could do that?" Tyr sounded alarmed.

"It could do anything," I admitted. "We didn't actually have time to test it out."

"You said beta phase," Tyr reminded me.

"It was a really rough beta," Henrik admitted.

"*Skit,*" Tyr swore. But he took my free hand and stepped to the edge of the grass, so he and Henrik had me bookended. "All right. Let's give this a go."

Henrik nodded. "For *ære,*" he said, as he gripped my hand. Then he leaned down and whispered, "I told you you'd have to touch me eventually."

I stuck out my tongue.

"For Asgard," Tyr chimed in from my left.

"For Freya," I whispered. I closed my eyes and counted down. "One. Two."

"Three," Henrik finished.

We jumped together, launching ourselves at the portal. It took Henrik first, then me, and finally Tyr. As I sent up a prayer, I felt a familiar suction. The portal used forces much stronger than the Bifrost, making this journey every bit as nauseating as the rainbow bridge I'd learned to loathe. We shot through the wormhole in a jerky pattern, and each turn sent a new surge of force from head to toe. We traveled too fast for sight to be effective—I couldn't even open my eyes. I tried to call out for Henrik, but the rush of wind was too loud to allow verbal communication. My fear diminished slightly at the steadying pressure of Henrik's hand on mine, and I clung tight to Tyr as I pulled him along behind me.

I'd thought the journey would last a few seconds, maybe half a minute, but as the forces pushed down and the wind whipped us in a violent trajectory, I realized we'd grossly underestimated the duration of this kind of travel. My muscles began to fatigue from the constant battering, and my hand slipped from Henrik's. He clamped down tighter, locking his fingers around my palm, but the forces were too strong for even his warrior grip. As I clung to his grasp, our hands slipped again, then again. With each twist of the sightless tunnel, our connection was loosened, until finally I lost him completely.

"Henrik!" I shrieked as I felt his fingertips slip from mine. But the word was hollow. It was like yelling into a void. "Henrik!" I shrieked again, clawing at the darkness in the vain hope that he'd reappear. But my hand closed on nothing, and as the wormhole whipped me back and forth along the trajectory back to Helheim, I lost Tyr too.

"No!" I stretched my hands out to both sides, desperately reaching for the gods who were my security; my world; my family. But there was nothing but air on either side of me. I was alone, completely alone in a black vacuum that we'd programmed to lead us straight to Hel.

And for the first time in a long time, I was afraid.

"Henrik! Tyr!" My volume alone would have earned me a lead role among the Berserkers. The transporter had dropped me in one piece right at the edge of the forest, but it closed without ejecting either of my friends.

This was Helheim. Both literally and figuratively.

I blurred through the trees, shrieking with a tenacity that would have awed any lurking Helbeast. I hit every corner of the forest, climbing to the navy-colored treetops when my ground search proved fruitless. It wasn't until I came to the edge of the ravine and stared into the black abyss of Hel's gate that I gave in to my tears.

"No." I cried softly at first, the drops falling from my eyes into the void below. As the seconds ticked by, my tears fell harder, coursing down my cheeks and disappearing into the darkness. "No!"

I threw my head back and wailed. Henrik and Tyr had been my world for, well, forever. They were the stinky boys who'd dug for worms and made mud pies with me when all the girls thought it was too gross. The only guys who fought me as hard as they could in combat class, because they knew what it meant to me to be treated like one of them. The boys next door who snuck me out of my house on summer nights to watch the aurora borealis. My childhood crush, who saved me from humiliation by stepping in as my Fall Ball date when I got stood up. The young warriors who'd refused to join the rest of the Elite Team on a recon mission the last time we lost Freya, choosing instead to stay by my side... and hold my hands through the entire ugly aftermath. The titled god who let me on his team even though I didn't have near enough seniority, simply to honor our friendship. The adorable guy who was trying *so very hard* to ignore the awkwardness between us so we wouldn't lose a near-millennia-long friendship.

Tyr and Henrik were everything to me. And now they were gone. The wormhole ate them.

And I had no idea where it had spit them out.

"I hate you, you stupid, friend-eating wormhole!" I

shrieked. Then I sobbed. I didn't care how ridiculous I sounded. Nobody was around to hear me anyway.

"Now, now, Brynnie. Why would you hate the wormhole? It got us over the grass safely. And it didn't even separate any of our parts." The voice was so jovial, so welcome, I was sure I'd imagined it.

"Henrik?" I turned around, not caring that snot dripped off my upper lip. "And Tyr? How are you... how did..." I took in the sight of my friends emerging from the trees with all of their limbs intact. "But I saw the portal close. You were trapped inside... weren't you?"

"No idea." Tyr shrugged. "We got separated, then the portal spit me out on the east edge of the forest. I hunted around for a good five minutes before I found this guy."

"And I was dropped on the west edge. I heard you shouting, but the portal broke my leg on exit. I called out but you were screaming too loud to hear me. By the time my leg healed itself, Tyr showed up, and we followed the sound of you cursing the wormhole."

My ponytail whipped back and forth as I took in the overly welcome sight of the family I'd thought I'd lost forever. Then I launched myself at my boys, catching them both in a tackle hug.

"Do not *ever* leave me in a wormhole *again*. *Ever*," I admonished. "You guys freaked me out!"

"Clearly," Tyr said drily. But he wrapped an arm around me and pressed his face to mine. Thick stubble prickled my cheek. "You're stuck with us, Brynn. You know that."

"I better be," I growled. I pulled back and appraised them both. "Are you okay to travel, Henrik? Or does your leg need more time to mend?"

"I'm healthy as a pegasus," he vowed. "And I just want to recover Freya and Bifrost out of here. I've had enough of this realm."

"Agreed." I took their hands and walked them to the edge of the ravine. "So this is Hel's gate. It looks to be about a hundred-meter drop, though it's so dark it could easily be twice that. And I'll be totally honest—I have no idea what's on the other side."

"Nobody does." Tyr studied the darkness below us. "I'd assume there's a guard down there. Garm used to protect the entrance, but Hel might not have replaced the dragon since we killed her."

I repressed a shudder at the thought of coming face-to-face with Hel. In school we'd learned that Hel herself was an abomination—half flesh, half bone, wholly evil. But for reasons only he'd ever know, Odin gave Hel dominion over Helheim and its constituents, from the *ikkedød* to the specters to the mortals who suffered an ignoble death—including the ignobility of dying of natural causes.

"There's something that's never sat right with me about Helheim." I turned to Tyr. "Why is it ignoble to die of natural causes? If a mortal lives a good life to old age, why banish him to Helheim?"

"A noble mortal dies a warrior," Henrik parroted Odin's code.

"Well, *ja*, but there aren't that many wars in Midgard at the moment. At least, not in first-world Midgard," I reminded him.

Tyr smiled. "Odin never meant it literally. Not every noble soul can die in battle. A warrior is someone who fights for *ære* in *any* capacity. Mortals whose choices shine light on the glory of the Asgardian virtues—honor, valor, truth, righteousness, and most importantly, kindness—are afforded seats at Valhalla. Those whose choices contribute to the dimming of Asgard's light are considered ignoble, and cast to Hel."

Well, *skit*. If Professor Meadows had covered that in her lecture, maybe I'd have gotten a better grade on my valkyrie entrance exam. Guess the assassins got a more thorough dose of history of the realms at the Academy.

Henrik glanced down at the darkness below, his hand still wrapped around mine. "Odin's inclusion of warriors of all kinds is at the very heart of *ære*. Every event, every choice, every action creates a ripple. And every one of us has the power to make those ripples beautiful... or choose to infect the realms with darkness." He met my gaze and traced a soft circle inside my palm with one finger. The action sent a warm shiver up my arm, and his words gave my heart a jolt. "I will always fight for beauty. For glory. For love, *sötnos*. What will you fight for?"

My breath caught at the endearment, and for the millionth time I wished I didn't have to live by Freya's stupid code. Because when Henrik talked about… well, all of *that*, it reminded me that he was one in a billion— that his heart was so kind, his mind so brilliant, his sense of honor so strong, I was lucky to be able to call him my friend. And if Freya didn't have her stupid rules, I'd have clubbed him over the head and demanded he release me from the friend zone right that very minute.

But Freya had her rules. And she needed our help. And right now, my hot-as-Helheim friend stared at me in earnest, awaiting some coherent reply. So I opened my mouth and blurted the first thing that came to mind.

"I fight for us." I squeezed Henrik's hand, then Tyr's, and looked at each of them in turn. "For all of us. For everything we've built, and everything we hope to accomplish." I drew a breath. "And I fight for the love I know the realms will lose if we don't bring back Freya. So let's go get our girl."

"Let's get our girl." Tyr smiled.

Henrik raised an eyebrow. "We jump on three?"

"On three," I confirmed. "One. Two." I squeezed my eyes shut.

"Three," Tyr finished.

We jumped as one, hands clasped as we once again plummeted through blackness.

CHAPTER 17

DESPITE MY FIRMLY CLOSED eyelids, I knew the exact moment we passed through Hel's gate. The air cooled to near freezing, my bones felt brittle as a dried out chicken carcass, and my joints ached with an intensity that was supposed to elude even aging Asgardians. I clung tightly to Tyr with one hand and Henrik with the other, hoping Tyr's flying ability would kick in and pull us up before we crashed. But we careened feet first toward the earth, landing with a painful crash that jarred my already throbbing joints and snapped my femur clean in two.

I swore. "That really, really hurts!"

Henrik reached over and placed his hands around my upper thigh. He guided it gently into place, speeding the healing process and distracting me from the pain at the same time. Now shards of agony alternated with warm pulses of an entirely more pleasant sensation. Henrik might not have had Tyr's powers, but darned if his hands didn't possess a magic all of their own.

Not the time, Brynn.

"Is that better?" Henrik asked after an unidentifiable length of time. I could have been staring at his strong hands for seconds or hours; I had no idea. But I shifted my weight so I rolled onto my injured leg, and winced.

"It's tender. But better, *ja*." I shifted again, and this time the pain was less intense. "I think the break mended, at least."

"Sorry about that. The drop was shorter than I expected." Tyr jumped to his feet and unsheathed his sword. "Let's find Freya and get out of this Hel-hole."

I tore my eyes away from Henrik, and followed Tyr's sightline. We'd landed in a darkened cavern, littered with heavy stones and blazing pits of fire. Our surroundings were nearly all black, from the soot beneath us to the rocky walls that rose indefinitely into the darkness above us. A group of bearded dragons rested in crevices along the walls, their yellow eyes reflecting the orange of the fires. In the distance stood a bridge, a narrow footpath spanning what appeared to be a bottomless ravine. And on the far end of the bridge stood a heavy iron door that I presumed to be our destination.

Just another day at work.

Henrik helped me stand before drawing his dagger. I opened my backpack and holstered an implosive gun, then checked my sheathed rapier. The fall hadn't broken it. *Good*. The lightweight sword would allow maximum mobility in the event we encountered something that moved especially fast, and the gun would take care of anything I couldn't debilitate in hand to hand combat.

"Oh!" I kept one eye on the dragons and reached in my backpack again, pulling out the time freezer and handing it to Henrik. "Here. You take Barney. I got to activate the wormhole of doom, so it's your turn."

"You sure?" Henrik tucked Barney into his back pocket. "I know you were excited to test him out."

I shrugged. "Fair's fair. I'll get the next one. Also, you still owe me a pie for winning the kill count in Muspelheim. I believe I requested your grandmother's Dutch Apple Crumble."

"You two are such *nörds*." Tyr cracked his neck. "Now can we *please* get moving? The love life, not to mention the good humor, of the entire cosmos is depending on us."

"Let's roll." Henrik marched forward, with Tyr on his heels.

Apparently they forgot rule number one of combat —when dropping in on a foreign zone, always assess the region for threats.

"Duck!" I yelled, as an enormous winged lizard dove from its perch.

Henrik and Tyr dropped and rolled with half a second to spare. The dragon swooped down on the spot they'd been standing, its black claws digging into the ground on its pass. It flapped its wings, soaring five stories with each pulse, then boomeranged back. This time, it opened its mouth and shot a stream of fire on its descent.

"Look out!" I yelled.

"On it." Henrik drew his sword and held it high. The fire struck the broad blade and ricocheted back at the dragon, singeing its talons. The animal let out a shriek and circled around, shaking its smoking toes as it flew. The whole thing would have been funny if we weren't in danger of becoming Asgardian flambé.

I ran to Henrik's side and drew the particle accelerator. "Want me to make it go away?"

"I do." He shifted, sword at eye level, mirroring the dragon's trajectory. "But unless we're planning on taking out an entire colony, I'd hold off on shooting the messenger."

"Point, Andersson." The rest of the bearded dragons shifted restlessly in their perches. I held my rapier at eye level and wedged myself between the boys. We watched as the dragon circled high above, then let out another stream of fire. Henrik easily deflected it with his sword, and the dragon flew to an empty crevice, narrowly avoiding another burn.

I took a count. Nine dragons sat as sentinels, standing between us and that big iron door.

Why couldn't Henrik have just broken Garm's leg? One single princessy guard-dragon would have been a *lot* easier to handle.

"Okay, what's the plan?" I turned my head to Tyr,

but kept my blade high. Dragons were fast, and I wasn't taking any chances.

"I'm assuming we have to get through the door." Tyr paused. "And I'm assuming they're going to try to stop us. If what the dwarf said is true, the dragon king Nidhogg is controlling them. We need to get him on our side so he tells *all* the dragons to back off, and so he helps us deactivate the Muspelheim super soldiers. We don't want to do anything more to anger Nidhogg, meaning do not kill another of his offspring, *Henrik*."

"Hey, that offspring was trying to kill you, so you're welcome," Henrik countered.

Tyr shrugged. "Either way, I'm guessing he's got another legion of monsters on the other side of that door, and we don't want to provoke him any more than absolutely necessary. What do we have by way of weapons?"

Henrik recounted our inventory. "We've got two broadswords, some daggers, a rapier, a vacuum, the particle accelerator, Barney, the transporter—not too keen on using that one again, not gonna lie—and the breakdown powder."

"What's the breakdown powder?" Tyr asked.

"It's epic." I grinned. "We're technically still testing it, but it's designed to deactivate dark magic-induced physical protections. So, if I applied it directly to Hel, her body would be as susceptible to light magic-laced weapons as our bodies are to dark magic-laced ones. She might still be able to control external objects with dark magic, but she couldn't protect herself with it like she can now. And we'd be able to take her out with our swords. Does that make sense?"

"Not really. But I trust you two." Tyr didn't take his eyes off the dragons. "Anything else in that bag?"

"The stunner," Henrik concluded, passing me a small wooden box.

"What's the stunner?" Tyr asked.

"You press a button and it sends out a sound wave that's at such an intense frequency, it literally paralyzes anyone in the room," I explained.

Henrik nodded. "We based the technology loosely on a dog whistle. Only the frequency needed to be low enough any corporeal being could hear it and—"

"As much as I love these little science lessons, we're in a bit of a hurry." Tyr jutted his chin at the wall of dragons. Several tails twitched.

"Right. Oh, *skit*." One of the dragons leapt from its perch. Henrik threw down his weapons and dropped to a fighting stance. He bent his knees and sprung from the ground, meeting the dragon in the air. He flung his body away from us, throwing the dragon off course. Instead of striking Tyr and me, it rammed into one of the bigger boulders near the edge of the ravine. The dragon roared, whipping its head from side to side as it tried to eject Henrik. But as good as he was with weapons, Henrik was even deadlier with his hands. He clung to the scaly skin, his fingers digging into the slippery surface as he climbed up the monster's neck. I heard the rip as Henrik tore the dragon's flesh. A thick, black liquid oozed from the wound, coating Henrik's arms and chest. His hands slipped; whether from the lubricating liquid or the violent wrenching of the dragon's neck I couldn't tell. But as I extracted the stunner from my backpack, the dragon pushed off the rock, soaring high into the black sky with my friend dangling one-handed from its open wound.

Förbaskat. Why did we leave Fang back at the compound? A flying warrior horse would have come in major handy.

I watched in horror as Henrik wrestled the dragon back to the ground, kicking as the dragon spiraled downward. He swung his legs up, straddling the dragon's neck and bending it into an unnatural angle while its brothers and sisters leapt from their rocky perches and descended on us with a cacophonous battle cry.

"Now would be a really good time to activate that stunner, *sötnos*," Henrik hollered.

"Oh. Right! Tyr, muffle our hearing. Right now!" I yelled.

Tyr held out his hand and muttered something under his breath. The shrieks of the dragons faded to silence as Tyr's enchantment took hold. He gave me a nod, and I pulled the string on the tiny wooden box in my hand. Heavy vibrations pulsed through me, alerting me to the stunner's activation. And even though I couldn't hear its wail, I knew the device worked; the eight dragons descending on us halted mid-air, while the one trying to skewer Henrik froze in a terrifying pose, its mouth open and its teeth just inches from Henrik's leg. Henrik shot me a glare that could have burned a hole in the sun. I was filled with too much tension to feel anything but relief at his safety.

"Oh my gods that was close!" I set the stunner on the ground and raced to the dragon. I held up my arms to help Henrik slide down, but he was too high. "Tyr, get over here and help me!" I turned around but Tyr was already at my side. He held the discarded swords in one hand, and reached up to help Henrik off the dragon with the other. When my partner's feet were safely on the ground, I flung my arms around his neck.

"Gods, Henrik, that was horrifying. I'm so sorry I didn't pull the trigger sooner. I guess I just—you're filthy." I pulled back, using one finger to touch the sticky black tar that covered his chest. And mine. "Oh, gross. Dragon blood."

Henrik tapped his ear and mouthed the words, *I can't hear you.*

Oh. Right. Tyr's spell.

Henrik motioned for us to follow him across the bridge. When we reached the other side, Tyr stepped around us and put his hand on the door.

Weapon up, he mouthed. Or spoke. We couldn't hear him either way.

Tyr handed us our swords before drawing his. He pushed the iron door open and waved us through. We stepped across the threshold, then ducked to the side, pressing our backs to the wall while Tyr closed the door and moved to stand beside us. He waved one finger in the air, and our hearing was restored.

"We safe from the sound waves?" he asked.

"Yes." I nodded. "I left the stunner in the cavern room, which means so long as the door stays closed, the waves can't reach us. We programmed them not to be able to travel through walls; only living, organic matter."

"Like dragon skulls." Henrik grinned.

"Excellent. With the dragons debilitated but not dead, I'm hoping we'll be able to reach a truce with Nidhogg. Assuming he's on the warpath because we killed his daughter, I'm banking on him being willing to trade our safe passage for the lives of the dragons back there." Tyr glanced at the door.

"Nice bargaining chip," I admired.

"Dragons are innately loyal. They feel every loss of their species." Tyr shrugged. "It'll just depend on how mad he is about Henrik here killing Garm."

"Again, you're welcome for me saving your life." Henrik rolled his eyes.

Tyr chuckled. "Onward and downward."

"You mean onward and upward, don't you?" I asked.

"Nope. Onward and downward." Tyr pointed at the spiral staircase descending underground. Well, more underground than we already were. "If the stories are true, we've got a few more levels until we reach our destination."

Nine levels of Helheim. Two down, seven to go.

"What are we waiting for?" I drew a breath and gripped Henrik and Tyr's hands. "Let's go to Hel."

The staircase to Hel's lair was a spiral of black rock on one side and endless abyss on the other, with the occasional fire-filled wall sconce to light the path. My toes caught on the uneven steps of the descent more than once, and if Henrik's enormous frame hadn't been right in front of me I would have tumbled headfirst into Odin knew what. The steps leveled off at several places, each time presenting an outlet that led to a thick indigo door. We didn't stop to linger on any of the landings; if the overwhelming feelings of negativity seeping through their cracks were any indication, each door marked the entry of another level of Helheim. At one door, my soul dropped with a heavy sense of fear; at the next I felt unaccountably hopeless, as if nothing would ever be right in the worlds again. Each feeling lifted as we continued our descent, so by the time we reached the sixth door I knew my emotions were being controlled by whatever corresponding level of Helheim we trudged by. Even so, the inexplicable rage building inside overwhelmed me to the point that I began to shake.

"Whoa there, sassy," Tyr said from behind. He placed his hand on my shoulder. "You doing okay?"

My hand removed his trespassing fingers faster than Thor could strike down an infidel with Mjölnir.

"Get your hands off me, you obsessive, controlling Neanderthal." I whirled on him.

Tyr glared at me. "What's your problem?"

"My problem is that I'm sick of you, of both of you"—I turned to yell at Henrik, since there were no favorites here—"thinking you know what's best for me. You're supposed to be my friends. Not my fathers. I don't need you to protect me from myself. Henrik, if you didn't want to kiss me you should have just said so, not pretended you were all noble and trying to protect my valkyrie virtue." I poked Henrik's chest. "That's an enormous lie and we both know it. And you, Tyr." I whipped around to glare at the war god. "I don't need you to act like you know *so much* about how I'm feeling *all the time*. Your title's just a job—it doesn't make you better than the rest of us. So stop acting all high and mighty and just be a normal guy for once in your existence. Both of you need to let me live my life and stop acting like you own me!"

I knew my fury was uncalled for, but I didn't feel like apologizing. Anger had painted my world crimson, and I couldn't see anything but rage. My soul felt the inexplicable need to get away—from this place, from my friends, from myself. I tried to storm past Henrik, but he placed large hands on my shoulders and held me in place. Though he stood two steps below me, he was still taller than me. Stupid gods and their stupid tallness. Height. Whatever.

"Let me go, Henrik," I snapped. "I told you before, I don't want you touching me anymore."

Henrik eyed me levelly. On the surface he was the picture of calm, but I knew him well enough to see the angry spark beneath his cool grey-blue eyes.

"Tyr, go ahead," he directed. "Your jaw's clenched, the vein in your forearm is throbbing; it's obvious the giant half of you feels the effects of what appears to be the *anger* level of Helheim. And I don't want you and Brynn feeding off each other."

Tyr shot Henrik a look that could have frozen a jotun, but he drew a breath and walked down the stairs. It didn't escape my notice that he bumped my shoulder harder than he needed to as he passed.

"I felt that, you jerk!" I lunged for his back. Henrik's tight hold on my shoulders was the only thing that kept me from falling off the ledge and into nothingness.

"Listen very closely, Brynn." Henrik stepped to the wall and pulled me with him. Our shoulders pressed against the cold rock. I shivered. "I know you're only saying these things because of the energy seeping out of that door."

"Nope." I shook my head angrily. "I mean it. You think you're so above everyone. Especially me. You humiliated me in Alfheim—*humiliated* me. And then you did it again in Midgard. You told *everyone* in front of Brynhild you didn't want to kiss me. I get it. You're not into me. You don't have to rub my face in it!"

Henrik moved one step up, raising his height another five inches. Now he nearly towered over me, like he always did. Ugh. Was posturing right now *really* necessary?

"Brynn Aksel, I never said I didn't want to kiss you."

"Well, you never said you did want to kiss me, did you? It's the same thing. You suck." I glared.

Henrik let out a frustrated huff. "Let's move away from the *anger* door, *ja?*" He pulled me down the stairs, until one hundred meters separated us from the indigo planks above. The rage began to seep out of me, replaced by a feeling of total humiliation. Again. *Oh, gods.*

"Henrik, I—" I stammered. "I'm sorry."

"Don't be." He turned again, standing two steps below me. Tyr was nowhere to be seen; he must have stormed all the way to the next landing. "Listen, the truth is, it doesn't matter how I feel about you. You're bound to Freya, and I won't have you lose your eligibility on my account."

So we were back to that party line.

"Don't look so disappointed. I need you to trust that I'm doing what's in *both* our best interests here. Can you do that for me? Please, *sötnos?*"

When I didn't answer, Henrik lifted my chin with one finger.

"Hey," he said softly. "It's not forever. You and I both know that. It's only until you hit that rank, right? And it's not for nothing; your job requires complete control over your emotions. Being together would complicate that and put you at unnecessary risk. Besides, our relationship has existed in *perfekt* balance for this long, what's another hundred or so years going to kill?"

"Me!" I blurted. "It's going to kill me!"

Henrik chuckled. "I highly doubt that. You're the toughest *flicka* I know."

Leave it to Henrik to call me a chick on the steps of Helheim.

I drew a breath. "I was a jerk. I'm sorry."

"Water under the Bifrost, Brynnie."

The ceiling became infinitely fascinating. "I have to apologize to Tyr, don't I?"

"Yep." Henrik nodded. "But you and I are good. Let's just get through the next century or two and trust Freya to have your best interests at heart when she doles out the *perfekt* matches, eh?"

I closed my eyes. If Freya didn't pick Henrik for me, so help me Odin I was quitting the valkyries and running screaming for the hills. Maybe the Berserkers would be hiring by then. They took females. And Henrik would make an epic trance-inducing warrior god...

"Where'd you go?" Henrik's voice brought me back to reality.

"Just hoping this ends well," I muttered.

"Things usually do." Henrik grinned. "We just need to trust in the innate goodness of the cosmos and know the elements, like us, are working together to rule the realms in *perfekt* balance."

I narrowed my eyes. "You sound like one of those new age meadow elves. Or Elsa."

Henrik laughed, the sound bouncing off the rocky walls. "They're not all crazy, you know."

"If you lot are done chatting, I've got a situation

down here." Tyr's voice came from somewhere in the darkness. Valkyrie fail. I'd left our charge on his own longer than absolutely necessary.

"On it." I nodded at Henrik, and we bolted down the stairs. When we got to the final landing, we skidded to a stop. Tyr stood just past the threshold of an open indigo door. And on the other side swarmed a horde that promised a fate worse than death.

CHAPTER 18

"**C**LOSE IN," TYR COMMANDED. Henrik and I drew our blades and formed a tight triangle with our commander, our backs pressed close together.

"What the Helheim are those?" I asked.

"*Ikkedød.* Hel's undead minions." Henrik held his sword at eye level. We shifted our feet in small steps, turning a slow circle while assessing the threat.

"Why aren't they attacking us?" I chanced a brief glance away from the gnarled figures, whose bandages dangled from bones protruding through decaying flesh. The odor in the room was ghastly, but the room itself was kind of beautiful. We seemed to be inside an ice castle, its crystallized walls coated with a faint frost. Purple and gold silky fabric circled thin columns spaced along the perimeter, and the place seemed to be lit by tiny candles flickering just outside the clear walls. The whole effect was light, and airy, and really quite beautiful.

If you forgot it was Hel's inner sanctum.

"I think they're waiting on a command from her." Tyr jutted his chin at the far end of the icy corridor, where a figure sat atop an ivory throne with indigo cushions.

"Hel," I said, keeping one eye on the *ikkedød*. They hovered menacingly in front of us, but didn't strike. They alternately snarled at us and turned their soulless eyes on their master.

I followed their sightlines and did a double take. We'd been taught Hel was a halfling; that physically she'd taken on the worst traits of her giantess mother and demi-god father. But the demon resting regally on the throne was far more beautiful than the textbooks made her out to be. The right half of her body was tinted a deep cerulean, while the left was the powdery blue of the Asgardian sky. Silver eyes stared impassively from above high cheekbones, and a shock of glossy black hair fell in soft waves around her angular face. She was as unique as the stories promised, but in a far more striking way.

Hel was beautiful.

But even more beautiful was the enormous winged dragon seated to her right. Its emerald scales glistened along its muscular frame, giving way to dark purple wings at its midsection and ending in a spiked mallet not unlike a mace at its tail. In its oversized talons it clutched a glowing red crystal. Each time it stroked the crystal, the stone emitted a pulse of light, like it was communicating with some far away receiver.

Oh, crud.

"We were right, the dragon's got the dwarves' gemstone," I murmured. "The transmutation one Berry told us about. Destroy it, and we disable the super soldiers. Let the dragon keep it, and we can start the countdown to the apocalypse."

An *ikkedød* lurched forward and Henrik lunged with his sword. The creature withdrew, melding back into the horrible horde. My stomach clenched. We needed to *never come back here.*

Tyr drew a breath. "Henrik. Stats."

"Hel, my twelve o'clock. Crystal-hoarding dragon at one. A half-dozen *ikkedød* at ten and another at two, and I do believe that's our lovely Freya in the cage next to Hel's… is the ice queen sitting on a throne made of human bones?" Henrik spoke quietly.

Oh, ew.

"First wave, now." Hel's voice rang out. A grating screech followed, as two of the *ikkedød* flew at us. With Asgardian speed, Tyr and Henrik raised their broadswords, angled them toward the demons, and swiped. The *ikkedød* snapped in half, fell to the ground, and disappeared in twin clouds of smoke.

"Oh gods." I gagged. "What is that horrible smell?"

"When eliminated, *ikkedød* leave behind a certain scent," Tyr explained.

"Stench," Henrik corrected.

"It's awful," I grumbled.

"Yeah, well, that's just the beginning. You've read

about them, *ja?*" Tyr pointed his sword at an approaching demon, and it backed off.

I ticked off what I'd learned in school. "*Ikkedød* are Hel's undead guards. They're shape-shifters, mood influencers, and they're capable of stealing their victims' souls by sucking out their energy."

"Right." Tyr nudged me with his elbow. "And that dagger's not going to do much. I suggest you pull out that vacuum thing or the one that makes everything implode."

"We can't use the particle accelerator. It's too risky." Henrik shook his head. "Nobody's ever studied an *ikkedød*, and we don't know their molecular composition. What if the bullet shot through and hit the ice wall? The whole place would go down, and we'd lose Freya... and possibly release the slew of dark souls Hel's got cooped up in here."

"Plus we'd be dead," I pointed out. "It's hard to stage a coup when you're dead."

"That too." Henrik continued the slow circular shuffle. When we'd completed our rotation, we formed a loose triangle. Tyr faced one horde of the *ikkedød*, Henrik the other, and I stood in the middle, poised to charge Hel.

It wasn't entirely clear which of us had drawn the short straw.

"They've let us stand here an awful long time," I whispered. "Why hasn't Hel sent a second wave to attack?"

"Because I know what you did to Nidhogg's shadow

guards in the forest, and I'm not in the mood to lose any more guardians today. Now you may turn yourselves over to me. Starting with you, blondie." The ruler of the underworld sat coolly on her throne, staring me down.

"Uh, yeah. I don't think so." I reached around and extracted the vacuum from my backpack. I passed it to Henrik, who slid it into his pocket while I spoke. "How about you hand over our friend, and we'll let your creepy minions live? Or stay dead? Or... whatever."

A throaty laugh echoed down the icy hall.

"Something funny?" I asked.

Hel placed her palms on the arms of her throne. "I just thought the God of War would be more... imposing. Your father made you sound *much* more intimidating when he offered your... services."

Tyr kept his voice level. "My *father* was Ragnar Fredriksen, and he wanted nothing to do with you. You must be referring to Hymir. I should have known he was behind this."

"Hymir didn't ask me to kidnap your little love goddess, if that's what you're thinking. He put my brother up to snacking on those simpering adopted Asgardian parents of yours, and by all accounts I hear they were *delicious*." Hel grinned, revealing rows of blindingly white teeth. "But I took your friend on my own. I was hoping to procure that pretty mortal girlfriend of yours, but the coward stayed in your ridiculously protected little house. So I got the next best thing."

Hel swung her hand to the left, and I got my first good look at Freya. She was hunched in a ball, in an ice cage cloaked with dark magic. Her normally slender frame looked positively emaciated, and she trembled in the corner of her jail, her pale strawberry-blond hair laced with dirt, leaves, and blood.

"Let her go, Hel," Tyr growled.

"Oh, that's not going to happen." Hel laughed. She pushed herself to her feet and squared her shoulders. "But this is. Your father promised you to *me*, not that simpering human you call a girlfriend. Your darkness is destined to unite with mine to create an unstoppable force. The realms will bow beneath our combined power, and you and I will rule the cosmos." Hel stretched her arm in front of her, turning her palm up to Tyr. "Join me, and I let your friends live. Turn down the offer of a lifetime, and everyone you love, including your precious little mortal, comes to spend an eternity with me. You wouldn't want to be responsible for all of their deaths, would you? After your loyalty to my *dog* of a brother killed your own parents." Hel clucked her tongue. "How *do* you live with yourself, Tyr?"

Tyr bristled, and I reached over to put a hand on his arm. "Don't bite. She's trying to goad you."

"Oh, am I?" Hel took a step toward us. Nidhogg shifted his weight as she moved. His eyes darted between the crystal and his mistress. No doubt he'd been ordered to protect them both.

Hel flicked a finger and a group of *ikkedød* flew from their horde. Most descended on Tyr, who lunged with his broadsword and made violent jabs at his attackers, but one flung itself at me. I dove out of the way, drawing my dagger from my boot as I rolled away from Tyr. When the demon passed over me again I jabbed at its decaying thigh, but it was too fast. It whirled in a tight circle, creating a vortex above my forehead that felt kind of like the Bifrost, but a *lot* more uncomfortable. Instead of feeling like my bones were being sucked out of my body, I felt like my very essence was trying to escape. The thing was stealing the life right out of me.

Oh, *skit*.

"Arugh!" I let out a cry as I rolled again. My blade swiped blindly at my attacker as I flipped my body over and over.

"Brynn, move back toward Tyr," Henrik called out. My eyes flew open. The *ikkedød* continued to swirl above me, and I had the horrible feeling it was going to win.

But I didn't feel like dying today. And I knew Henrik had a plan.

Despite the overwhelming suction pulling me back, I used my fingertips to claw across the icy floor. In my haze I saw Tyr swinging at the horde closing in on him. Moving *closer* to a group of the soul-suckers seemed like a bad idea, but Henrik had never let me down.

I really hoped he'd keep that streak running.

"Now drop!" Henrik shouted.

I watched Tyr fall to the ground in front of me, just before something large and heavy flew at me from behind. The smell of sunshine overpowered the stench of decay as Henrik covered my body with his. A whoosh of air gusted overhead and deafening shrieks filled my head. I pressed my cheek to the ice, looking up just in time to see the remaining *ikkedød* sucked into a tiny black box. The vacuum rattled in protest, then fell neatly into Henrik's outstretched palm.

"Very nice." I panted. I felt dizzy from lack of oxygen. Henrik pushed himself off me, holding out a hand to help me up. But before I could take it I was wrenched away, pulled by an invisible force along the length of the hallway to Hel's side. She slid one long fingernail under my chin and let out a quiet laugh.

"So young." Hel sighed. "You'll make a lovely handmaiden."

"I don't think so, sister." I raised my dagger to gauge her creepy silver eyes out, but the blade dropped from my grip and my hand froze over my head. My other hand flew up to meet it, so my wrists were stuck together. "What the Helheim?"

"Precisely." Hel waved her hand and my ankles slammed together, the shock of bone on bone sending a wave of pain through me. My wrists and ankles burned, as if they were being seared by an invisible rope.

"Arugh!" I cried out as Hel flung me against the wall, binding me to the stone with another unseen tie across my forehead. It burned, but I'd felt worse. I assessed the room from my new vantage point as I attempted to breathe through the pain. Freya was right

252

in front of me, seemingly catatonic in her icy prison. Hel stood to my left, entirely too pleased with the howl of fury coming from Tyr as he battled another wave of *ikkedød*. The dragon was on her other side, stroking the glowing crystal like it was his firstborn. And at the end of the hall, Henrik charged. His eyes seethed fury as he bore down on Hel like an enraged bull.

Gods, I loved his angry face.

"You killed my favorite guard. I think I'll kill you myself." Hel tilted her head to study Henrik's approach, then shifted her gaze when Tyr let out another roar. The war god eliminated the last of his attackers, and turned on Hel with tight eyes and bared teeth. "Nidhogg, handle the halfling for me, won't you?"

I fought against the ties that actually bound me... in Helheim... behind a dragon. Things were *so* not looking good.

Nidhogg gave the crystal a longing look as he flapped his enormous wings and took to the air. He soared down the hall, passing over Tyr as he ran behind Henrik, then doubling back to attack from behind. His claws raked the icy floor, which trembled at the violent contact. A fissure formed where his talon scraped, traveling along the length of the hall until it reached Tyr. With a snap, the fissure became a full-on crack, forcing the war god to fling himself to one side to avoid falling in. As my friend slid across the slick surface, Nidhogg dove again, clutching the god in his talons and chucking him against the wall. Tyr slid to the ground, blood seeping from his cheek.

So, *so* not good.

Henrik bore down on Hel, taking advantage of her momentary distraction to drive the blade of his dagger through her chest. She pulled her eyes away from Nidhogg in surprise before wrapping bony fingers around Henrik's arms and throwing him off. She withdrew the blade from her chest and threw it at the wall like she was playing a game of darts. She looked down and frowned.

"You tore my favorite shirt." She pouted. She wasn't even bleeding.

"Son of a—"

Hel let out a giddy laugh. "Darlings, I rule the underworld. Did you think you could *kill* me?"

I tugged at my bindings again, but the movement did nothing but intensify the burning sensation. Frustration bubbled in my chest as I realized my position. Henrik and I were supposed to be a team. And at the moment I was of absolutely *no* use to him.

This place seriously sucked.

"So blades won't hurt you." Henrik countered Hel's predatory circle. "I'm guessing fire's not a big deal either."

"No." Hel's lips stretched into a cruel smile.

"Hmm. Then I guess the only thing I've got up my sleeve is this." Henrik whipped Barney out of his pocket.

"And that is?" Hel studied her fingernails in apparent boredom. Behind her, an extremely angry dragon hovered over a semi-conscious Tyr.

"A little something that levels the playing field." Henrik gave me a wink. Then pulled the satchel of breakdown powder from his pocket with one hand and fired Barney with the other. The room rippled as the device emitted the wave we'd programmed to freeze time. Henrik leapt at Hel, preparing to apply the powder to her time-frozen body. It would only disable those protective enchantments she'd cast on herself—it wouldn't extinguish the spells she'd cast on me and Freya. But it was our best shot... and the only one we had left.

Gods, I hoped this worked.

CHAPTER 19

I HELD MY BREATH as the ripple moved toward me and time froze. The next instant, Henrik stood at my side, a grin as wide as the chasm in the floor across his face.

"Point, Asgard." He chuckled. "I'd high five you, but you're still stuck to the wall. Sorry about that; apparently Barney has a shorter functionality time in the field than we planned for. I'll just cut you down—"

He was interrupted by an angry monster flinging herself onto his back.

"What. Did. You. Do?" Hel shrieked, turning a palm on Henrik in a vain attempt to shoot a spell.

"The breakdown powder did its job. You're incapable of producing new magic. It looks like you have to fight hand to hand. And sorry, sweetheart, but that's my strength. Not yours." Henrik reached around and flung Hel to the ground. She scrambled to her feet, then launched herself at Henrik's ankles. He landed on the ice with a sickening crack. My stomach clenched as blood seeped from his head.

"No," I whispered. I fought against my bindings with every ounce of strength I had, but it wasn't enough. Hel's entrapment was too strong. I'd spent my life training for this very moment—to protect Asgard, Midgard, and all the realms in between from the unspeakable horrors Hel's dominion would bring. To ensure Freya's all-encompassing love was always available for those beings that chose to embrace it. To make sure nobody ever suffered the pain of losing someone they loved to the darkness.

Nobody like *me*.

As if sensing my thoughts, Henrik lifted himself from the pool of blood. As he launched himself at Hel, he spoke directly to me. "Come on, *sötnos*. Do it for Anja."

And though the words were barely more than a whisper, they traveled through my ear and pierced my heart, unleashing emotions I'd fought so hard to check. Henrik, more than anyone, understood the pain of losing my sister. After the ninth day of Freya's first disappearance, the mortals had turned on each other. History wrote it off as another war, but it was so much worse than that. The mortals hadn't been able to help themselves. An energy vacuum just wasn't sustainable, and a realm void of love must necessarily fill itself with energy of another kind.

The darkness was only too happy to take over.

I whipped my head from side to side, fighting Hel's

invisible restraints. Dark magic was powerful; I knew that. But hers was stronger than anything I'd encountered. It burned at my forehead, wrists and ankles— each spot the evil ties touched. My movement loosened the ties enough that I could shift my head to see Freya's crumpled form. She lay crouched, shaking under the weight of her curse. Her shoulders were hunched and her normally glossy hair was stringy with sweat and tears. The sight of the powerful Goddess of Love beaten into submission was heartbreaking. Freya's gift was the most powerful thing in all the realms. My sister had known that. And she'd chosen to give her life fighting for it.

On the ground, Freya whimpered, a sound of hopelessness that pelted my already bruised heart. I closed my eyes and for the first time in a long time, I allowed myself to remember.

Anja was sent to Midgard as a young Norn. Because she was kind and pure and knew the importance of love in shaping a realm, she was tasked early on with prophesying the fates of human babies and setting them on the path to finding their *perfekt* match. When Freya was kidnapped, most of the Norns fled their posts and returned to the safety of Asgard. Not Anja. Although she knew the mortals were taken with darkness, Anja chose to stay behind. She was alone and largely defenseless as she traveled from home to home, laying blessings on the human newborns and imbedding the choices that would lead them to their true loves deep within their subconscious. She believed humans' innate goodness would overcome the darkness, and that one day the world would again be beautiful; full of hope; full of love. Just as she was.

Freya was rescued on the eleventh day. A bomb killed my sister on the tenth.

I squeezed my eyes harder to stop the moisture seeping out. The mortals hadn't known some of their bombs were infused with dark magic, just as my parents hadn't known my sister had stayed behind—they'd believed she was on lockdown in the Norns' Asgardian compound, enhancing the protection of Yggdrasil, the world tree that linked all nine realms. But I'd known where Anja was. She'd sent me a message and asked me not to tell my parents she'd stayed behind to serve the mortals. I could have betrayed her confidence—told them where she was and made them evacuate her. But I trusted Anja knew what she was doing. In her message, she told me she was aware of the risks of remaining on Midgard, and chose to stay for the good of humankind. That was love. That was *ære*. And *that* was what we fought for.

My eyelids flew open as I let out a wail. The trickle of emotions within lapped at my heart, and for the first time in years I did the unthinkable.

I released my *perfekt* control, and with it the shackles of fear. In that moment, I chose love.

I hoped it would be enough.

Asgardians are taught there are two choices in life—act from fear, or act from love. Since my sister's death, all of my decisions had come from fear—fear of physically or emotionally losing someone I loved; fear of losing myself; fear of letting my family down; fear of losing control. Every choice, no matter how minute, was made based on fear. And where had it gotten me? Shackled in Hel's lair, watching the love of my existence bleed out in the icy underworld, while the realms' chance at survival wept in a cage.

Fear wasn't exactly working out for me.

But love... love offered the world. As I closed my eyes and purged the years of fear into the bowels of Hel's inner sanctum, I shed layers of agony that weighed so heavily it was a wonder I'd ever withstood their weight. The fear left in layers, and I felt the magnitude of each as it passed through my consciousness—the pain at losing my sister mixed with the humiliation at Henrik's rebuff, the frustration at the restraints of the valkyrie structure, and the loneliness I felt knowing it could be years before I truly experienced the love my kind fought daily to protect. But as the negative emotions ebbed from my heart, I released them from my body and opened myself to love. And I was filled with an overwhelming lightness that made my skin vibrate and my hands shake. I clung to the sensation, zeroing in on the first love I'd ever known— my love for my parents, my brother, and Anja. The golden memories of my beautiful childhood glowed inside of me like a pristine sunrise. Then I opened my mind to the love that graced my life in the years that had followed; my love for Elsa, Freya, and later Mia— the friends who blessed my heart in the simplest ways;

my love for Tyr, Forse, Gunnar—guys whose gentle heckling reminded me someone was always looking out for me. As I thought of each drop of love that had touched my life, the fire inside burned brighter so my heart felt it had erupted in a flame equal in strength to a star's glow.

With my power at an all-time high, I wrenched my hands apart, knowing I'd break the ropes. Surely Hel's dark magic couldn't bind all the love had Odin gifted to me. But the ropes didn't move. It wasn't enough.

My heart constricted, reminding me that I hadn't unleashed the most powerful tool in my arsenal.

Oh, gods.

Henrik represented my biggest fear—the fear that after all the years of friendship, of knowing all my hopes and dreams, my secrets and flaws, that he would reject me. And a rejection by the god who knew me better than anyone was something I didn't think even my abundantly blessed heart could take. But as I watched him bleeding, his bare hands turning blue with Hel's icy enchantment as he tried to choke the underworld's leader to save the nine realms, I realized there was nothing to gain by holding myself back.

There was only everything to lose.

I opened the hermetically sealed black box and unleashed the love I felt for Henrik. For the child who'd stood up for me on the playground, the adolescent who took the high road when so many of his friends chose the easy way out, for the warrior who dedicated his life to protecting the gods he loved, and the realms he was sworn to defend. With no effort at all, I let the waves of love wash over me, and I pushed the feeling through my torso, out my extremities, and directed it at Henrik.

It was probably coincidence, or maybe Hel was distracted by the change in my energy—Elsa swore energetic shifts were palpable, and maybe she was right. But as I opened myself up to the unfettered love I could no longer restrain, the power shifted from Hel to Henrik. Suddenly he had the upper hand, and it was Hel who looked on him with fear. The blue ebbed from Henrik's fingers as he tightened his grip around Hel's neck. He pushed her to the ground, driving his knee into her chest with a glorious crack. She lay pinned beneath him, her mouth opening and closing like a fish as she struggled for breath. And Henrik drew his dagger, holding it high above his head.

"Checkmate." Henrik grinned down at his conquest. "Tyr, what's the order?"

Tyr exhaled loudly. My gaze shifted to where he was locked in a stand down with Nidhogg. The dragon had its feet wrapped protectively around its thick red crystal, while Tyr had his hands wrapped comfortably around the helm of his broadsword. He held the sword high, ready to deflect a flame or impale a lizard. Or maybe both.

"Tyr," Henrik urged. I could see the desire to remove the threat written across his beautiful features. It was what he did. And I loved him for it.

Gods, I loved him *so very much*. If I had to wait two

hundred more years to act on that love, I'd do it. He was worth it.

"Now we play let's make a deal." Tyr kept his sword aloft. "I want the crystal, Freya, Brynn, and the promise these monsters never again attempt to harm our love goddess *in any way*. I also want you to release the dwarves I know you're keeping somewhere in here, and send them back to their home realm. That's right— I know about your weird science experiment. In exchange, we free the trapped dragons and let you live. Do we have a bargain?"

Hel's mouth opened and closed. Now, more than just her left side had turned dark blue.

"I said, do we have a bargain?" Tyr's calm voice echoed off the smooth icy walls.

Henrik loosened his grip just enough for Hel to squeak her consent. The dragon king narrowed its eyes, but gave a regal nod.

"The words are binding. Let it be done." Tyr lowered his sword and Nidhogg nudged the crystal forward with one giant toe. Henrik looked disappointed, but removed his hand from Hel's throat and stepped off her chest. She curled into the fetal position, gasping and clawing at her throat.

"Release them," Tyr growled.

Hel glared, but she waved a hand in my direction. Freya's cage disappeared at the same time the searing pain left my head, ankles and wrists. I ran to Freya's side, and wrapped my arms around her shoulders, helping her stand. Her eyes were foggy and unrecognizing. She felt cold and weak in my arms. No doubt she'd experienced horrors she wouldn't want to relive.

"It's okay," I murmured as I pulled her to me. Her teeth chattered against my shoulder. "We've got you. And we have their word this will never happen again."

"*Takk*," Freya rasped into my chest. Her body shook from head to toe.

"We've got to get her out of here." I turned to Hel, ignoring the way her eyes shot icy venom. "What's the fastest way back to the cavern room?"

"The cavern room?" she asked.

"You know; the place you drop into when you jump from the outlands—the spot where all the dragons are. The first space this side of the black abyss of Hel's gate. If you want us to uphold our bargain and free the dragons, tell us the fastest way to get there. Then we can get out of here, and Odin willing, *never* come back."

"Maybe you won't, *valkyrie,* but he will," Hel rasped. "I *will* possess you, War. The powers of my soldiers have grown, and I promise, we'll ensure that you belong to me."

"We'll see about that," Henrik interjected. "What did our source tell us, Brynn? Something along the lines of, *when a subterranean-based Nidavellir crystal is shattered, its power returns to the earth and it becomes just another rock.* Does that ring a bell?"

"It does," I nodded. "It really does."

"No!" Hel gasped.

"Yes." Tyr took the crystal and threw it on the ground. It shattered into tiny pieces, the red seeping out of the shards as they slipped down the ravine in the center of the room. Nidhogg let out a harrowing wail, clamoring to the edge of the crevice as the crystal's remains disappeared in the abyss.

Tyr wiped his hands. "I trust the super soldiers will no longer be an issue. And I trust the dwarves will be returned to Nidavellir within the hour. I'll send an Elite Team member to confirm their arrival, and if they aren't back then I will personally see to your punishment. Now I do believe my companion asked about an exit?"

Hel rubbed her throat. "The only way out is the way you came. When your Alfödr sentenced me to an eternity in Nifhel, he disabled the use of portals."

"Disabled portals? But you've got a link to Muspelheim. It's how you're accessing the super soldiers... isn't it?" I asked.

"Yes. But that portal exists in the outlands—in Niflheim. Inside the inner eight levels of Helheim, there are no shortcuts. Odin designed it that way." Hel's disgust was tempered with another emotion. Fear? Could it be that she was afraid of Odin? I filed that nugget away for future use.

"Fair enough. We've got a sample to collect in the outlands anyway, *ja*?" Henrik met my eye with a wink.

To be honest, I'd totally forgotten, what with the burning bindings and kidnapping rescue and near death by dragon and all. But the prospect of experimenting on the irid crystals with Henrik gave my brain a buzz, and before I knew it, I brimmed with excitement.

"Yes. Yes, we do. Okay. Let's get out of here. Wait." I turned to Hel and let my gaze pierce her evil soul. The minute I saw her empty eyes, the hollowness of her life filled me with sadness. She would never know the love we fought to protect. She was too filled with hatred and bitterness, too locked into the wounds of her past to appreciate the hopes of the future. My threat fell mute on my lips. Nothing I could say would make her life any more torturous than it already was. Her darkness kept her trapped in her own personal Helheim.

I tightened my grip on Freya and marched her to Tyr. "She's too weak to walk the whole way on her own. You fly her to the outlands. Henrik and I will free the dragons and meet you there."

Tyr nodded. He lifted Freya in his arms and pressed his forehead to hers. "Don't scare me again, okay, battle axe? I'm not sure the black parts of my heart can hold out next time."

Freya smiled thinly as she wrapped her arms around Tyr's neck and spoke in a weak voice. "If they haven't turned you yet, halfling, I doubt there's anything that can. Take me home. There's some *business* I need to talk to Brynn about."

What? Had Brynhild somehow gotten to her? I shot a panicked look at Henrik but he just gave a sanguine smile. His refusal to be a stress case like me was infuriating.

"Deal. Henrik, Brynn, finish out our business here

and meet us in the Niflheim forest. We'll catch the Bifrost from there." Tyr rose from the ground, carrying Freya as he flew through the entry of Hel's sanctuary, en route to the outlands.

"We're on it." Henrik crossed to my side and gripped my hand. My pulse skyrocketed as he took off running, pulling me with him. We raced through the levels of Helheim, fully expecting Hel to go back on her word, but the *ikkedød* and souls of the mortals let us pass, so that we reached the door to the cavern room in a quarter of the time it had taken us to descend. I put my hand on the door to open it, but Henrik pulled me back.

I turned, the question in my eyes, and Henrik tapped his ear. *Oh, right.* I forgot we'd be paralyzed by the sound wave the minute we opened the door.

"I'll call Tyr; he can send the muffling spell through the phone. But before I do, there's something I need you to know." Henrik cupped my face in his hands, and rested his forehead against mine. My breathing became very shallow.

"Yes?" I squeaked.

"What you did back there," he began, "I felt it."

"I don't know what you're talking about," I lied.

"Yes, you do." Henrik's lips turned up in a smile. Gods, they were beautiful lips. Perfect lips. Pale pink, with just a touch of fullness. They were really soft too, if my mortifying memory served correctly. But also hard when he wanted them to be. And probably demanding. And—*stop it Brynn!*

"Nope. Don't." I clamped my mouth shut.

"Well, before we go back up there and deal with whatever Freya's going to dish out, I just need you to know." Henrik rubbed his thumb across my cheek. My knees turned to the consistency of Jell-O.

"Hmm?" I whimpered. *Immortal battle goddess and you whimper? Seriously, get it together, Brynn.*

"I need you to know that I feel the same way."

Back the Bifrost up. Henrik felt the same way? My heart soared right out of my chest, through the pit of Helheim, and so high into the cosmos Heimdall probably mistook it for a shooting star. Henrik. Andersson. Was. Into. Me?!

"Ohmygod, you do?" I squeaked. Did I have to squeak right now? And giggle? Oh, oh, this was the greatest moment ever. Like my birthday and Saint Lucia's all rolled into one. *Brynn, stop giggling!*

"Of course I do." Henrik rubbed the back of his finger against my cheek, and I giggled again. *Seriously, stop it!* "I have since the night I took you to your Fall Ball."

I toed the ground with my boot. "Seriously. No joke. You're actually into me?"

"How could I not be?" Henrik brushed my chin with one finger. "You live a no-holds-barred life, *sötnos*. Always have. It's sexy as Helheim, when you're not on a course to self-destruct the very thing I've been working toward for the past century."

Henrik's hand moved down my cheek. He ran the pad of his thumb over my lips, which had formed a small O. He used his finger to lift my chin, closing my mouth and forcing me to meet his eyes.

"I—" I stammered.

"Don't look surprised. You've always been it for me. And we can talk all about it over my *delicious* Swedish pancakes when we get home. But right now, we've got some business to take care of, *ja?*" He nodded at the door.

Well, sure. Right. The deal with the dragon king needed to be honored. And the Goddess of Love needed to be returned to a friendly realm before the cosmos fell to total chaos. But couldn't we have this teensy epic moment for just a few more minutes? Maybe a real kiss? Like, one where Henrik *kissed me back?*

Henrik chuckled. "Not yet, *sötnos*. First I'm calling in the spell."

My cheeks flamed. "How did you..."

"You're picking up Mia's lousy poker face." He touched my cheek again. "You haven't broken your oath yet, and I don't intend to make you ineligible when Freya promotes you. I've got a horse in this race." He pulled his phone out of his pocket and dialed. When Tyr picked up, Henrik said two words. "Muffling spell." Then he nodded and turned to me with a grin. *Shall we?* he mouthed.

Yes. I turned and reached for the handle of the door.

Henrik wrapped his fingers around my upper arm and spun me around. I looked at him quizzically. The faster we got out of here, the better for all of us, right?

But he put a finger to his lips, and tilted his head. Then he mouthed the three words I'd been waiting an eternity for.

I love you.

My grin stretched so wide, it hurt my cheeks. Henrik Andersson, unquestionably the most outstanding specimen to come out of Asgard since, well, since *ever*, loved me. *Me!* Gods, this was amazing. Phenomenal. Beyond a doubt the greatest moment in the history of—wait, where was he going?

Henrik wrenched the door open and stepped to the other side. He turned and motioned for me to follow, and I did, skipping giddily after him toward the maze of frozen dragons. When we reached the other side of the bridge, Henrik bent and picked up the sound box. He held out his hand, and I gleefully laced my fingers through his, doing a mental fist bump at the way our hands fit perfectly together. Then I followed him to the area directly beneath the drop spot. He stopped and sent a text to Tyr, and the next moment a beam shot down into the cavern. It wasn't the Bifrost—if Hel's explanation was true, we wouldn't be able to port out until we'd reached the outlands of Helheim—the region we called Niflheim. Instead, the beam was one of the innumerable magic tools in Tyr's metaphorical pocket. A sort of Asgardian chairlift.

Ready? Henrik mouthed. Then he stepped right next to the beam of light.

I nodded, my ponytail bouncing up and down in my enthusiasm. *Get me out of here.*

Henrik counted down. *One. Two.* On three, he pulled me tightly against him and pressed the button on the sound box. At the same time as the dragons burst into motion, he leapt into the beam. I wrapped my arms around his neck, giddy with excitement, and he grinned back at me. Our audio restored, I could hear his beautiful voice as he said, "Let's go home."

We flew, shooting out of the cavern and back to the edge of the ravine that bordered the icy forest of Niflheim. Our landing was abrupt, but I didn't mind the jarring sensation that radiated from the soles of my boots all the way up my legs. Henrik's arm was still wrapped around my waist, and I clung to his neck like a heroine in one of Elsa's cheesy romance novels. If the ache in my cheeks was any indication, I was still grinning like a kid in a candy shop. And if the look on Freya's face as we approached was any indication, my glee hadn't escaped her notice.

"I didn't kiss him," I blurted as I leapt from Henrik's embrace. "I know the rules." Then I buried my face in Henrik's chest. Gods, why couldn't I act cool for once?

"I know you didn't." Freya didn't sound mad. When I worked up my courage to peek, she was still cradled in Tyr's arms, and she was smiling. Actually smiling. "Come on, we need to talk. Heimdall? Would you please open the Bifrost?"

The rainbow bridge shot down and the four of us moved inside.

"Wait." Henrik stepped out of the light, scooped a

sample of ice into a baggie, and tucked it into his pocket before returning to the Bifrost with a nod.

"To the safe house," Tyr ordered. And, after an endless moment of bone suckage and stomach lurching, we were back in Midgard, combat boots steady on the soft sand of the northwest compound.

Finally.

"Is it really over?" Freya asked as Tyr set her on her feet. She looked pale and drawn, and not at all the radiant love goddess we knew her to be.

"It's really over." Tyr offered his arm and she took it, walking unsteadily up the steps to the lawn.

"They're back!" Mia's voice rang from inside the beach house as Fang swooped joyfully overhead. My pegasus landed on the sand and pounded across the beach, stopping to nuzzle my cheek as I performed my standard post-Bifrost heave.

"Sorry, Fang," I murmured. "I promise I'll get the hang of it one of these days."

Henrik kept a steady hand on my lower back until I could stand. When I did, Fang let out a joyful whinny. "Told you I'd bring her back." Henrik grinned.

"Hey. I brought *you*," I challenged. "And you still owe me a pie for beating your kill count in Muspelheim."

"That I do, Brynnie. That I do."

While we spoke, the French doors flung open, and Mia, Elsa, and Forse spilled out onto the porch. They raced down to the lawn, skidding to a stop when they caught sight of Freya's gaunt cheeks. They each offered a ginger hug, being careful not to jostle our frail friend.

"Oh, Freya," Mia tutted. "You must be exhausted. And starving. Can I make you something to eat?"

Freya clasped Mia's hands in hers. "I would love something. Hel didn't have much by way of food. Did you know she really does eat with a utensil she calls Famine? Our teachers didn't make that up."

"She's really strange," I replied. Freya's eyes fell on my hand, once again entwined with Henrik's. I quickly pulled it away and avoided her gaze.

"Would you guys give me a moment alone with Brynn and Henrik, please?" Freya asked softly. My insides froze. What was she going to say? Was I in trouble for what I did in Alfheim? Had Brynhild somehow gotten to her? Was I about to get fired? Or worse, reassigned and ordered to stay away from Henrik? I didn't think I could handle being away from him now that I knew I had a fighting chance of actually having him in my life in the way I'd always wanted him.

"Of course," Elsa murmured. She touched my shoulder as she walked by, her warm hand offering reassurance that promptly dissipated when I found myself alone on the grass with Henrik and the goddess who held the keys to my happiness in her extremely slender hands.

We had to get Freya a sandwich.

I sucked in a breath, preparing to receive my sentence, but Henrik spoke first.

"Before you say anything, I need you to know something, Freya. Brynn hasn't broken her oath. Yes, she tried to kiss me in Alfheim, but it was one-sided. I stood down, just like you asked me to, and didn't engage."

Wait. What? I whirled on Freya. "You knew I was going to kiss Henrik?"

"Of course I did." She rolled her eyes. "I'm the Goddess of Love. I know everything. But before we talk, Brynn, you need to go see Elsa. It's time you underwent that *full* healing." She raised her eyebrows at me, and I gulped. Was I ready? Could I handle revisiting Anja's death?

I knew without hesitating the answer to both questions was *yes*. If I wanted to be with Henrik now or in two centuries from now, or whenever Freya finally lifted my endless chastity, I knew I needed to fully release my fear. And as High Healer, Elsa was the only goddess in the realm who could facilitate a full embracing of love. *Here we go.*

I squeezed Henrik's hand and followed Elsa back to the house. As I walked away, I heard Freya's soft voice behind me. "Henrik, I need you to take a walk with me."

Oh. Gods.

CHAPTER 20

"**YOU'RE SURE YOU'RE READY?**" Elsa scooted her chair so our knees were a few feet apart.

"I'm ready. I still feel guilty about Anja's death—I probably always will. If I'd just told my parents she was still on Midgard, they could have forced her to evacuate like the rest of the Norns, and she'd still be with us. But I know that was her choice to make. And I know she wouldn't want me to carry the guilt with me forever."

"And you know you can't move forward with love unless you release your fear." Elsa beamed. "I can see that in your energy. Brynn, you *are* ready!"

"I know." I inhaled slowly. "And I'm ready to accept whatever fate Freya's going to dole out because of my decision to kiss Henrik. Because even if it takes another six centuries, I know we'll find a way back to each other. We always do."

Elsa's eyes twinkled. "You sure you need a healing? It sounds like you've got this figured out."

"I want the healing," I confirmed. "I've put this off too long."

"Fair enough. Let's get started." Elsa scooted back in her chair and closed her eyes. "Is there anything you want to ask before we start? You know I won't probe where you don't want me to."

"Same rules as always, right?" I asked.

"Correct. Everything you share with me is confidential. Everything I do is to help you understand your relation to your world in the clearest possible light. I won't push in an area you want to remain closed, so don't worry about letting me too far in; I'll only see what you want me to. I won't tell you which choices you should make, though the best option is probably going to be pretty obvious to you. And at the end of the session, if there's anything we haven't addressed, just tell me and we'll make sure we cover it. You ready?"

"Let's do this." I leaned back in my chair and waited.

"Okay." Elsa took a slow breath, and I did the same. I knew from experience we were tying our energies to the earth—grounding ourselves so our individual charges had an anchor to this realm. "First, let's get you back in control of your own energy. You know you can't control anyone's choices. But you can control how presently you walk your path. Remember, when you are truly present, there can be no fear."

The clairvoyant might have sung a different tune if she'd been truly present with the guardians of Hel.

"That's not what I mean and you know it," Elsa corrected. *Oops.* Sometimes I forgot she could hear me in these little sessions. "I know I say it all the time, but I want you to really understand. Fear is the absence of presence. It exists in the past, or the future. But in this moment, this reality, there is only presence. There is only being. There can be no fear. Lock that into your memory, Brynn. It's important."

I nodded.

"Now let's get all of that beautiful golden energy back inside you. Do you feel grounded?" Elsa asked.

"*Ja.*"

"Good. Now hold your arms out and draw a circle around your body. It's *your* space—nobody else's. We're going to bring all of that gorgeous golden energy within this space. Now hold up your arms, like you're holding a big ball, and place your palms to the sky. Call back your energy from all the places you've left it over the past few days. You've got so much, it's very easy for you to leave pieces of yourself behind."

I closed my eyes and held up my arms. Then I pictured my room in Arcata, and the kitchen in our little cabin. I pictured Redwood State University's engineering lab where I'd been working on Barney with Mia and Henrik. I pulled my energy back from the nightmare in the man cave, from watching our friends under attack, from the nausea-inducing trips on the Bifrost, and the mortifying moment in Alfheim. I recalled my energy from our romp in the forest of Muspelheim, and I pulled back the sadness I left behind with Hyro in her cave of solitude. I pulled every last ounce of my energy out of Helheim, including the pity I felt for the goddess trapped within. With each retraction, I felt a prick in my palms, weighing my hands down one memory at a time until it actually felt like I carried the weight of the world in my hands.

"How does it feel?" Elsa asked.

"Heavy," I admitted.

"I know it does." Her voice sounded soft. "Now I want you to bring your hands together over your head so they're almost touching. And I want you to turn them around so your palms are face down, and I want you to push all of that energy straight down into the ground. Right into your circle." Elsa waited until I'd finished and took another slow breath. I did the same. "Good. How do you feel?"

"Anchored."

"That's my girl. Now bring your hands to your right foot and draw up the energy of the earth like this." Elsa waved her hands around her feet. I waved at my right foot, then my left, and mimicked Elsa as I drew my hands up my legs and to my waist. I really did feel more present. We rested with our hands in our laps, breathing slowly together.

"You ready?" Elsa asked.

"Absolutely."

"Draw on energy," Elsa ordered.

"I just did."

"No, that was calling back your excess energy. Now I want you to draw on all the good energy available to you in our worlds. Your parents, your experiments, your physical training. Draw on what Mia's brought to our lives, her unifying energy and that beautiful gift that is mentoring her. Draw on the love we share as friends—the peace we take from this beach house. Draw on your love for Henrik. Take it all in."

I nodded. And then I opened my palms and pictured everything Elsa had described shooting into my open hands. I lapped the positive energy greedily, devouring every bit until my chest puffed and my heart felt like it might burst. It was humbling; I hadn't realized the *absolut* excess of positive energy available to me. How did I ever feel like I was alone?

"Okay. I want you to think your name, and picture a circle that is uniquely yours on one side of a gorge, or a river, or a tree—whatever image feels right to you. Are you doing it?"

"Yes." I frowned. This was the part I liked least of all —the part where I had to *feel*.

"Good. Now I want you to think of Anja, and picture a circle that's uniquely hers on the other side of that obstacle. Are you doing it?"

"Yes," I whispered. My mind sifted through memories of the beautiful childhood we shared playing together in our backyard, picking flowers for our mom in the summer, and having snowball fights with our dad in the winter. I recalled holding Anja's hand on my first day of school, pulling strength from my brave big sister. I remembered hours spent sitting on our beds, talking about boys and friends and dreams. Warm tears pooled quickly and rolled down my cheeks. I didn't bother to wipe them away; I knew what came next.

"Good girl, Brynnie. You're doing great," Elsa encouraged. "Now I want you to say to yourself, 'I forgive myself for any hurts my actions or inactions may have caused her.'"

"But I don't," I whispered, as the tears fell harder.

"But you can," Elsa said softly. "Forgiveness, even self-forgiveness, is yours to give. It's a choice. One you deserve more than anyone."

I choked back a sob. "I for-for-forgive myself," I stammered, "f-f-f-or any hurts my ac-ac-ac-actions or inactions may have caused her."

The enormity of my words settled on my chest, nearly crushing me under their weight.

"Good. We're almost through the hard part," Elsa said. "Now I want you to say to yourself, 'I forgive her for any hurts her actions or inactions may have caused me.'"

I repeated the words, my voice cracking as I spoke. The heaviness in my chest pressed against me, making it nearly impossibly to breathe.

Since my eyes were squeezed firmly shut, I couldn't see what Elsa was doing, but I heard the flicking of her nails, and I knew the minute she'd unleashed her energy on me. The weight flew off my chest like someone drew a curtain, and my shoulders pulled back in gratitude. Breath filled my lungs in deep gasps, and my chest heaved up and down as I sucked in air. The whole effect was instant, and dizzying, and more than a little overwhelming. It was the buzzing that surprised me the most. Elsa had done minor healings before, but we'd never tackled an issue of this magnitude; I'd never been ready. But now, as she sat there doing whatever it was she was doing with her magical energy powers, my cells begin to vibrate. The tingling started in my face and hands, leaving my skin feeling as if it were on pins and needles in the most pleasant possible way. Then the muscles underneath my skin picked up the vibrations, buzzing with the fervor of a Golden Retriever on Red Bull. And finally, my organs picked up the sensation so that my entire being, from head to toe, was filled with a radiant energy. My breath came in deep gasps, my stomach pushing out with each inhale as a new wave of tears poured down my face. In that moment there was no guilt, no remorse, and not a hint of fear. There was just me. My energy, called fully into my being in the present.

I might have been one of Freya's warrior goddesses. But until that moment, I'd had no idea how much power I possessed.

The magnitude was too much for my little black box; tears flowed freely down my face as I was washed in wave after wave of pure energetic power. "Oh my gods, Elsa." I wept.

"I know," she soothed. Soft flicks sounded around my face, but I didn't open my eyes to see what Elsa was doing. I couldn't believe I was finally free.

I must have cried for a good minute, the cathartic tears of realizing the guilt I'd carried for years wasn't mine to own. And when I opened my eyes, Elsa sat across from me, lowering her hands from my head to my waist, as if pushing my energy down to my anchor. She opened her eyes with a gentle smile.

"Thank you." I sobbed.

"I'm a facilitator. That was all you," she said in earnest. "You grounded yourself firmly in your own circle, and any time you feel those undeserved thoughts of guilt or what ifs, you push them into that stream, or ravine, or tree, and know they're not yours. This energy, everything you're feeling—*this* is what's yours. You can call on it at any time. You know that, right?"

"Our healings have never been this... this powerful before," I said. "Why is that?"

"Because *you've* never been this powerful before. Think about it, Brynn; the last time I healed you— really healed you, not the surface wound stuff we do around here—was right after Freya's last disappearance. You weren't anywhere near ready to process this stuff then. But now you are. Now you know that none of what happened before is your fault. And you don't have to lose *anyone*"—Elsa raised an eyebrow—"who's important to you, for *any* reason, unless you choose to let them go. Do you hear what I'm telling you?"

I nodded, still high on vibrating cells.

"Now if I'm not mistaken, I believe your commanding officer is waiting for you on the beach." Elsa pulled a clear crystal from her pocket, rubbing it between her hands as she spoke.

"Thank you, Elsa," I whispered. "I never thought I'd be free of that guilt."

Elsa hugged me back. "There will still be sorrow. But you don't need to carry any more than that. Not if you plan to walk your path."

I squeezed her again. "I owe you big time."

"I accept payment in waffles. Or pancakes." Elsa opened the office door and pointed down the stairs.

"How about both?"

"Quit stalling." Elsa gave me a gentle nudge. "Freya and Henrik are waiting for you."

I took a grounding breath and walked outside. *Here goes nothing.*

CHAPTER 21

"AH, HERE SHE IS." Freya smiled from the beach. I walked carefully down the wooden steps and across the damp sand until I reached her side. I raised a brow at Henrik, who gave an infuriatingly calm smile before holding out his hand.

"Here she is," he echoed. "Let's take a walk." When I didn't move, he wrapped his fingers around mine and gave a gentle tug. The three of us began a slow amble toward the pine trees at the edge of the cove.

"Brynn," Freya began, when we'd put some distance between the houses and us. "I've known you the better part of your life. I've been your friend, your boss, and by the grace of Odin, I get to be your matchmaker."

"Just tell me if I'm fired," I pleaded.

Freya raised an eyebrow. "Why would you be fired?"

"Because... um..." I hemmed, waiting for the bad news.

Freya smiled. "No. You're not fired. In fact, it's just the opposite."

What was the opposite of fired?

Freya gave a sanguine smile as she continued. "Brynn, I've always appreciated your warmth and kindness—you're one of the most open spirits I've had the pleasure of knowing, and I knew that a soul as sensitive as yours would need its other half to be strong and dominant, but yielding when necessary, and ruled by compassion always. I also knew you'd need a counterpart who would challenge you, both intellectually and emotionally. You're one of the smartest goddesses I've ever worked with. Luckily." Freya's eyes twinkled. "The two of you and your genius technology saved my life back there."

"Yeah, well, that was mostly Mia's conception. She mapped out the schematics so all I had to do was—"

"Not true." Henrik shook his head. "Remember that day when we were all in the lab talking about 'what ifs,' and you said 'what if we'd been able to stop time right before Fenrir bit Tyr?' That's when we mocked up our original prototype and that's the—"

"You're a team," Freya interrupted. "And the *perfekt* one at that. To answer your question from earlier, Brynn, yes, I knew you'd give in at some point and try to kiss Henrik. You're smart as a whip, but you're ruled by your emotions. It was only a matter of time before they shattered your *perfekt* control. I'm just grateful it was love, and not fear, that you chose. For a long time after Anja's passing, I watched your heart battle itself. I was afraid the wrong side would win out."

"I miss her every day," I admitted. "But even on my saddest days, Henrik's always been right there. I've cried on his shoulder more times than I want to admit."

"I know." Freya smiled. "Who do you think told him to comfort you?"

I blinked at Henrik. He grinned down at me. "It didn't take too much convincing, *sötnos*. Nobody wants to see someone they love in pain."

There it was again. *Love.* My heart flew somewhere high in the clouds and beamed down on me.

"But we can't be together until I make captain, right, Freya?" My heart dive-bombed back into my chest. "Oh, gods. If I'm not fired for trying to kiss Henrik in Alfheim, then when I make captain someday you're going to present me with my *perfekt* match. But if he's not Henrik, I don't want him. I'll pass." My eyes pleaded with Freya. "I can pass, can't I? I do have a choice in this."

Freya laughed, the tinkling sound bouncing across the shore. "Sorry, I'm still pretty out of it. I'm not doing a good job. Let me make this clearer. Brynn Aksel, for your role in hunting down my abductors, for assisting in the development of tools that enabled your team to track my whereabouts, and for embracing the light within your heart and thereby saving my life in Helheim, I hereby promote you to the rank of captain within Odin's High Order of the Battle Goddesses, the Valkyries."

I gasped. "But that's a jump of two full ranks!"

"Are you questioning my decision?" Freya raised an eyebrow.

"No, ma'am."

"You are now titled captain in good standing, with virtues fully honorable. And as Goddess of Love, and head of the valkyries, it is my deepest pleasure to present you with your *perfekt* match. Henrik Andersson, you may claim what I promised you." Freya winked at Henrik, and started toward the beach house. "I'll leave you to it."

Henrik touched Freya's arm and she turned around. "You should know Brynhild's getting a bit ahead of herself. She threatened Brynn while you were gone. You might want to speak with her about her role."

Freya arched one eyebrow. "I will deal with Brynhild personally. Maybe it's time her *talents* were focused elsewhere within my organization."

"Good call." Henrik released Freya's arm, then touched it again. "Oh, and Freya?" He broke into a grin. "Thank you."

"Treat her well, Andersson. I've got my eye on you." With that, Freya retreated, walking backwards with an impish grin.

My jaw fell open as I watched her leave. When I gained the muscle control to look at Henrik, he wore a smirk.

"I was... promised to you?" I gaped.

"Freya's surprisingly open to suggestion," he responded. "I told her I'd been in love with you since high school. Then I explained how your credentials would make you an exceptional lab partner, and I wanted her to put you on Tyr's team so she could see how well we fit together. She didn't have to observe for long to realize I was right."

"Henrik Andersson, you... you..." I shook my head. "That was really smart! It never occurred to me to just *ask* her if we could be together."

Henrik stepped so he stood directly in front of me. He slipped his hand around my waist so his fingertips rested lightly against my lower back. A beam of heat shot somewhere due south of my navel at the touch. *Oh, gods.*

"'You miss one hundred percent of the shots you don't take,'" he quoted.

"That a scientific fact?" I teased.

"Mmm." He hiked me closer, so my hips were pressed against his upper thigh. A small gasp escaped my lips, and he used the moment to dip his head to mine. His cool breath brushed my cheek as he spoke. "Something like that."

My heart beat a thunderous rhythm in my chest as I brought one hand up to his bicep. Gods, it felt good. With the other hand, I lightly touched his hair, fingering a strand that curled in a gentle wave behind his ear. "Am I allowed to kiss you now?" I whispered.

"No," he whispered back. And my hands dropped to my side in defeat. *Still?*

Henrik slid the hand not holding my waist up my back until he cradled my head in his palm. His eyes bore into mine with an intensity that left me breathless.

"Because Freya made me another promise," he murmured.

"What's that?" The question came out as a squeak. A *squeak*. What was wrong with me today?

Henrik ran the side of his nose along mine, and my eyes fluttered closed. "She promised me that *I* got to kiss *you*."

Before I could blink, soft lips pressed against mine. My hands flew back to Henrik's hair, and I laced my fingers through the waves and pulled him closer. I'd waited *my whole entire life* for this moment, and I didn't have a drop of patience left. Henrik's throaty chuckle reverberated against my mouth before his tongue lightly probed my lips. I parted them, all but begging him to enter, and tasted the indescribable sweetness that was all Henrik. Everything that was right in all the worlds.

Henrik shifted me so I was cradled in his arms. As he dipped me backward, he nipped at my bottom lip, sending a wave of pleasure coursing all the way through my body. I held on tightly as he kissed a trail down my neck, committing every touch to memory. I knew I'd be reliving this moment for the rest of my life.

"Woo-hoo!"

"About bloody time!"

"Finally! Pay up, Fredriksen, I totally won."

The claps and cheers interrupted my long-awaited bliss, and I reluctantly opened my eyes. Henrik stared back at me, his grey-blue orbs twinkling with laughter. "Guess we deserve that." He righted me, holding me close to his chest, and wrapped both arms possessively around my waist. "Leave us alone," he shouted to the small crowd of gods and a solitary mortal gathered on Tyr's back lawn.

"No way!" Tyr called back with a laugh. "Mia and I had a bet, and I owe her some nominal mortal thing."

Mia elbowed his side. "We shouldn't be watching this." She giggled.

"You're the one who told us to look outside," he pointed out. I couldn't help but laugh.

"What do you say, *sötnos*? It's been a few hundred years—can this wait a few more hours?" Henrik looked down at me, his eyes mirroring the adoration I beamed up at him.

No. I sighed. "We should probably let Tyr debrief everyone, and give him an update on which weapons worked on which species."

"Mmm. Work first. Smart call." Henrik bent down and nipped at my ear. *Oh, hello.* "But after, what do you say you and I steal a little alone time?" He shot a pointed glance at the grass, where Forse let out a catcall.

"It's a date." I stood on tiptoe and pulled his head down so I could give him one more lingering kiss. Tyr's wolf whistle broke the spell. "All right!" I yelled across the sand. "We're coming!"

As we crossed the beach to the stairs, the only thing keeping me from floating to the heavens was Henrik's steadying hand holding tightly to mine. And though I was told I gave a thorough debriefing about the effect of the sound box on the dragons, about the properties of the ice on Helheim, and about what I suspected to be the inherent flaws in the worm hole of doom, the only thing I remembered about the meeting was the moment it ended, and Henrik whispered in my ear, "Let's get out of here." He scooped me in his arms, ignoring the catcalls of our friends and grinning the entire way to his house. He set me on my feet and backed me against the wall, pinning my arms to my sides and kissing me with such fervor, I lost all sense of time.

"Brynn Aksel," he murmured as I fought to stay standing.

"Mmm?" I murmured.

"Now that there's no muffling spell blocking your hearing, there's something I need to tell you." He pulled back and rested his forehead against mine. I grinned, knowing exactly what he was going to say. "I love you, *sötnos*."

"I love you, too. Now kiss me again." I pulled his head to mine and lost myself in the absolute joy that was *finally* kissing Henrik Andersson.

"I might never stop," he warned.

"I hope you never do," I vowed. Henrik covered my lips with his, finally claiming the *perfekt* match he'd been promised by the Goddess of Love.

And I realized something I think I knew all along.

Perfekt control was *way* overrated.

CHAPTER 22

"WE'VE GOT EVERYTHING UNDER control back at the house. Don't worry, we'll save you a sample to play with after you finish your last exam. It stinks that you have one the day before vacation—I had all of mine on the first two days, which sucked at the time, but—" I tilted my head to anchor my phone to my shoulder while Mia clucked her sympathy. As she moved on to listing her own academic-induced anxieties, I adjusted the lens on my microscope. "It's okay. I already know you passed Calc II; Henrik graded our tests this morning and said we both got an A. Just ace your Literature final so we don't have to hear what a bad influence we are during Christmas break. Okay. You too. Bye."

I hung up and slipped my phone in the back pocket of my jeans before glancing around our upstairs lab. The in-house workspace was small, occupying just half of the Arcata cabin's man cave, but it was considerably warmer than the bigger setup we kept downstairs in the garage. We would have preferred to use the engineering lab on campus, but due to the unpredictability of the irid crystal, we'd decided it would be safer for the student body if we tested this one at home.

"Mia stressed out about her test?" Henrik looked up from his own microscope.

"Yup." I removed my slide and passed it over to Henrik. "Even though she brought her books with her, she's convinced the few days she spent at the beach house impeded her study schedule. I don't think she's left the library in thirty-six hours, except to take an exam."

"It must be really hard to live inside that head." Henrik swapped slides, and adjusted the focus on the one I'd just passed him.

"Do you see how the cells in this sample look identical to the other one?" I asked.

Henrik leaned in. "I do."

"Okay. Now watch." I crossed to his side and turned the dial on a Bunsen burner. I held the flame a few inches from the microscope, and waited.

"Did they just mutate?" Henrik asked.

"They did," I confirmed, jotting a quick sentence in my notebook. "The irid crystals reconfigure at a cellular level—but don't dissolve—when they're exposed to an increase in temperature. If we track the pattern of the change, we'll be able to predict transitive properties and draw up a schematic for a climate suit."

"Then it's Muspelheim volcano expedition, here we

come." Henrik pulled back from the lens with a grin. "This changes everything."

"You're telling me." I switched the burner to "off" and set it on a shelf, then leaned my back against the lab table and crossed one ankle over the other.

Henrik removed his goggles. He took two steps to his left and positioned himself so one leg was on either side of mine. He placed his hands on the counter and leaned down so I was boxed in. I lifted my head and feigned annoyance.

"Henrik Andersson, we haven't finished documenting our findings."

"No, we haven't." Henrik leaned down to run his nose along my jaw. He inhaled softly as he moved, and the cool air left goose bumps across my neck.

"You're breaking protocol," I reminded him.

"That I am." He reached my ear, his lips brushing against the lobe as he spoke.

"Henrik," I murmured, willing my knees to hold out. It would be beyond unprofessional to actually swoon in the middle of a lab.

"Brynnie," he murmured back, raking my earlobe between his teeth. *Oh gods, screw protocol.* I reached up and wrapped my fingers through his tousled waves. I tilted my head to the side and guided Henrik to my neck. He let out a growl and shifted, nudging his knee against my legs to force them apart. Then he stepped closer, pressing his thigh against my hips as he kissed a path from my chin down. My head dropped back when he reached the hollow of my neck, and Henrik reached up to tug my hair free of my ponytail. When he fisted my hair in his hands and crushed his lips against mine, I let out a moan.

And then my phone beeped.

"Ignore it," Henrik urged.

"What if it's Tyr?" My eyes rolled back in my head as Henrik sucked on my bottom lip.

"*Knull* Tyr," Henrik swore.

"I can't." I reluctantly slid my phone out of my pocket and checked the screen.

"Is it Tyr?" Henrik pressed his thigh against me again. *Mmm...*

"What? Uh, no. Text from Hyro. She says she loves her new place." I set my phone down on the counter and giggled. "Setting her up next door to Finnea was an inspired touch. Thanks for that."

Henrik chuckled. "I thought you'd appreciate that relocation. Turns out the meadow elves were happy to take in a lost soul. Especially one who was so willing to join in on their solar-based worship. Finnea can just deal."

My phone beeped again, and Henrik raised an eyebrow. "Am I going to need to confiscate that?"

"Technically we're on duty, so that'd be unsafe," I reminded him. I checked the phone again, and turned it face down on the counter. "Berry. He says the missing dwarves are all accounted for and back to their normal routines. Jeez, Forse must be handing out our updated communication devices like candy."

"Well, it is almost Christmas. Maybe he's feeling

generous." Henrik picked up my phone and switched it to 'off'. "Now before Elsa can call to complain Forse still hasn't asked her out, or Mia rings again with a question about the pros and cons of becoming a Unifier, or which kind of fowl she should cook for our Christmas dinner to try and beat my turkey—because we all know my turkey is going to crush whatever she cooks—"

"I so love that you're having dueling dinners." I sighed. "We all win in that scenario."

"The point is, before *anything else* interrupts us, can we *please* finish what we started?"

"You mean our lab?" I batted my eyelashes.

"Call it whatever you want." Henrik reached behind me and swept my notebook to the side, lifted me onto the counter and tugged my legs open so they could wrap around his waist.

"Henrik!" I giggled.

"Mmm. Much better." He pulled me against him and rested his forehead against mine. "I like you right here, Brynn Aksel."

"I like it, too." I smiled. "You were worth the wait."

Henrik winked. "I was, wasn't I?"

"I guess I owe Freya a thank you." I re-wrapped my fingers in Henrik's hair.

"We both do. I've got an idea. Let's give her a break from her matchmaking duties and take on one of her toughest cases."

I tilted my head to the side. "Elsa and Forse?"

"Bingo. Whoever bet on them getting together before us was a lousy judge of character."

"Forse is just scared." I fingered one of Henrik's soft waves. "He's been through a lot."

"*Ja*, well, life's scary. He needs to get over it."

"Mmm. You planning to use those *impressive* powers of persuasion to get him to ask Elsa out?" I teased.

"Something like that. I thought it could be a fun project for us—a way to give back to Freya, and all."

"Well, we do have a lot to be thankful for," I agreed.

"And a *lot* of lost time to make up for."

Henrik brought his mouth back to mine, and I sighed happily as I kissed him back. It might have taken centuries, but being with Henrik had been worth every tortuous minute of waiting. And now we had forever.

Sometimes life was just, well... *perfekt*.

HENRIK'S SWEDISH PANCAKES

#HENRIKSHOTCAKES

4 eggs
½ cup sugar
1 cup flour
1 cup milk

Whip 4 eggs and ½ cup sugar together until the
mixture is slightly stiff.
Add 1 cup of flour and 1 cup of milk. Mix well.
Set pan to low heat, add a pat of butter. Pour a thin
layer of batter into pan and flip when cooked.
Add your favorite toppings (the Ære crew likes lemon
and sugar, lingonberry jam, or Nutella).
Enjoy #HenriksHotcakes!

Take a picture and share it with me!

ACKNOWLEDGMENTS

An eternity of gratitude to my handsome husband, for being my *perfekt* teammate. *Jeg elsker deg. Tusen takk* to our biggest little blessings, whose brilliant hearts illuminate what truly matters each and every day. We thank God for you.

Takk to my editor Lauren McKellar, for keeping the *Ære* crew on the straight and narrow; to Stacey Nash and Kristie Cook, for always making my stories richer; and to my beta readers, technical advisors, production team, and the greatest street team in all the realms, for being all kinds of awesome.

Takk to my RagnaRockstars—Gunnar may be funner, but you give him a run for his money. *Tusen takk* to every single reader who's taken a chance on these stories. You are the reason I get to continue dreaming across the realms, and I am so very grateful for the privilege. Thank you for sharing your reading time with me.

And to MorMorMa, for sharing your pancake recipe and your world. *Tusen takk*, from the bottom of my heart.

ABOUT THE AUTHOR

Before finding domestic bliss in suburbia, internation-ally bestselling author S.T. Bende lived in Manhattan Beach (became overly fond of Peet's Coffee) and Europe...where she became overly fond of McVitie's cookies. Her love of Scandinavian culture and a very patient Norwegian teacher inspired her YA Norse fantasy books. And her love of a galaxy far, far away inspired her to write children's books for Star Wars. She hopes her characters make you smile, and she dreams of skiing on Jotunheim and Hoth.

Learn more about the world of S.T. Bende at www.stbende.com.

See what happens when Asgard's High Healer
unleashes the full force of her powers on Justice, in

THE ÆRE SAGA: PERFEKT BALANCE

Become what you believe.

Elsa Fredriksen knows there's a thin line between love
and fear. As High Healer, she rights the wrongs
committed by those who choose the darkness. But
even Asgard's secret weapon can't undo every injury—
especially when her fate is completely entwined with
the god she's trying to save.

Elsa's in love with the Norse God of Justice. But Forse's

heart is ruled by fear—fear that the past will repeat itself; fear that opening his heart will compromise his ability to do his job; fear that he'll hurt the one girl he desperately wants to protect. *Again.*

When Elsa faces off against the very monster she once swore to protect, her survival depends on a power she isn't sure she can control. And when Forse's worst nightmare unfolds in front of him, Elsa has to decide whether it's more important to hold the realms in *perfekt* balance... or hold on to the guy she can't imagine existing without.

And now, a sneak peek at the next chapter in *The Ære Saga...*

PERFEKT BALANCE -SNEAK PEEK

"**I**'LL SHOW YOU MINE if you show me yours."
Forse Styrke lifted one corner of his mouth in a
lazy smile. My heart thudded before tumbling headfirst
into a familiar abyss.

"It doesn't work like that, and you know it," I
reminded him.

Forse shrugged. "Fair's fair."

"And if the God of Justice says it, it must be true."

Forse just winked.

"Are you going to let me do this or not? Odin
knows I need the practice." I planted my hands on my
hips and blinked at my longtime crush and longer-time
friend. It didn't take him long to break.

"All right, all right." Forse held up his hands. "The
big, blue deal-closers win."

I batted my eyelashes with a smile.

Forse reached up and brushed my temple with the

back of one finger. A wave of goose bumps broke out across my neck as I leaned into the touch. Seconds after his knuckles grazed my cheek, Forse pulled his hand back and took a step to the side. "All right, Miss Unifier, give me your best shot."

I pressed my lips together and extinguished the feeling of disappointment. Forse and I had danced this dance for a few months—longer, if I counted the time before I was stuck in the coma. Forse liked me...or I thought he did, but he pulled back every time we started to get close. And even though Odin had gifted me with the ability to read feelings, auras, and the occasional mind, I couldn't get a grasp on *why* Forse wouldn't let himself fall for me. My normally intuitive brain picked up on an inkling of fear flashing from somewhere in Forse's emotional center, but I couldn't for the life of me determine its source.

The God of Justice was proving to be one irritating wall of hard-headedness. And my supposed *gift* was completely letting me down.

"Elsa?" Forse waved his hand, and I snapped back to the present.

"Mmm?" A gust of wind pulled my attention to the redwood grove outside the window of my tiny house. Another storm was blowing in—the second one this month, and the sixth since December. A March shower in Northern California wasn't unusual...but a winter of snowfalls this close to the ocean sure was. *Better keep an eye on that.*

Forse furrowed his brow in concern. "I lost you. Do you still want to practice your energy analysis, or do you need to lie down for a while?"

"I'm good. Let's get started."

"It's only been a few months since you came out of the coma, and you know there can be residual effects. Maybe we should—"

"I'm fine, Forse, I swear. I just got distracted. There's a lot riding on me getting this right, so pretty please stand there and let me practice."

"I would, but—"

"But nothing. You and I both know that if I don't get a grip on this ability soon, the realms will be in serious trouble. Asgard needs a proper Unifier. My mom held the light realms in balance so well, they've kept it together since she died. But that can't last much longer, and I don't even want to think of how powerful the dark worlds will become if I don't make this work."

Forse shook his head. "I still think it's too soon. Fenrir nearly killed you. You—"

I placed my hand on his arm and kept my voice soft. "I've got this."

Forse and I stared at each other for a seemingly endless beat. He was the first to blink. "You'll let me know if you need a break?"

I ran my fingers along the throw that rested on my tan sofa. The soft blue fibers matched my new curtains perfectly. "You have my word. Now let's go over what we've learned since the Norns named me interim

Unifier. Maybe we can avoid repeating some of our earlier, uh, mistakes."

"Like the time you accidentally filled my energy with so much love I very nearly kissed Brynn?" Forse raised one eyebrow, and my cheeks grew hot. That hadn't been an accident. Right after my parents' deaths, the Norns had named me my mom's replacement, and Forse had volunteered to help me practice unifying—bringing opposing factions together. On my first attempt, I'd pushed an overwhelming amount of adoring energy into Forse's love center, thinking it would make him own up to his feelings for me. Brynn had walked in at just the wrong moment and almost reaped the benefit of my misguided work. *Right place, wrong goddess. Lesson learned.*

"Um, yes. Like that." I stared at the recessed lights in my living room, willing the blood to drain from my cheeks. "So we won't try that one again. Just like we won't try to override your consciousness—sorry I ended up making you think you were a fairy."

Forse glared at me.

"And we won't try to mute your sense of self-preservation—seriously, I did not see the whole 'handing over your broadsword and kneeling before my brother' thing coming." I giggled.

Forse glared harder.

"Right." I covered my mouth. "And we definitely won't invoke the guardian spirits from Valhalla. That did not end well."

"Thanks for pulling me out before the inebriated ones tried to decapitate me. Remember, they train during the *daytime*. Off hours, it's one giant mead-fest." Forse folded his arms across his perfectly sculpted chest. His grey T-shirt strained against a set of flexed biceps, and his profile was backlit by the lamp beside the three-quarter-length window, giving him an almost ethereal glow. *Oh dear gods, he is beautiful. So beautiful. It's completely unfair that Odin would—*

"Are you sticking your tongue out at me?" Forse asked.

Oops! I hadn't realized I was licking my lips. Thank Odin Forse was as dense as a forest. "Erm, just giving you a hard time. I promise I won't make those mistakes again. But you'd think with all the research we've done, all the books we've read and the subjects we've interviewed, we'd be closer to understanding *how* my mom did what she did. She made it look so easy. And it's just...not."

"That's the thing about this particular job." Forse shrugged. "Unifying's an intuitive skill. It's not like Tyr's job, where he can look at old war strategies to assess an enemy's weakness, or my job, where I can study the legal systems of the realms to get a handle on how they operate. What you're trying to do is a mystery. All of the subjects we interviewed had no idea how your mom helped them; they just knew that she did. We really don't have much of a choice—it's trial and error or bust here."

"Fair enough. So today we're going to . . ." I blew air out of my lips in a frustrated stream. "Odin's beard, what haven't we tried? We've been at this for ages."

Forse smiled, pale pink lips curving up to reveal a glimpse at two rows of blinding white teeth. Everything about him was *perfekt*. "Why don't we stick with what you know? You're an epic High Healer; try scanning my energy centers for blocks like you would with a regular healing, and if you find something pull it out. A removed block should make me more open to befriending thine enemy, *ja*?"

"Something like that." I smiled back, trying not to get lost in the beautiful green vortexes of his eyes. "And if that doesn't work, I'll just bang my head against your chest and cry."

Ooh, if I cry, maybe he'll comfort me. Wrap his arms around me and pull me close so I can—

Not helping!

Forse chuckled, oblivious to my inner turmoil. "My chest can take the head-butt," he pointed out. "You crying, on the other hand, might just break me."

My cheeks flamed again. "Okay, here we go. Unifying 101, take nine hundred." I was going to learn how to bring spirits together if it was the last thing I did. Not only was it my Odin-given destiny, at least until I could pass the torch to my brother's mortal girlfriend, Mia, but it was a key function of Asgardian security, therefore vital to the survival of our race and the realms as we knew them. Plus, there was a smidgeon of a chance my using Forse as a practice buddy might just open his heart to the possibility of *finally* dating me. Which, of course, would just be a pleasant side effect of my education, and not at all the reason I was working so hard.

I wasn't *totally* selfish, after all.

"Let's do this," Forse said. He closed his eyes, and I followed suit, drawing a deep breath. I exhaled and pressed my palms toward the ground, expelling all foreign energy from my body. Calling my energy back to me was second nature, and as I expanded my energetic bubble to nudge against Forse's space, I sent a prayer of thanks to my mom for passing on this extremely useful, albeit highly confusing, gift.

"You're in now, aren't you?" Forse sounded uncomfortable.

"What's the matter, Justice? Don't trust me?"

"I trust you. It's just . . ."

"It's okay; I know it's weird. You can push me out at any time. You know the drill, just intend to eject my energy from your space. Your energy will follow your intention."

"I'm not going to push you out," Forse said. "We've got to be getting close to cracking this."

"It would have been a lot easier if we'd known I got Mom's unifying gene," I whispered. "She could have explained everything to me before Fenrir...well, before."

Forse's energy flickered, and an air of remorse

passed through his aura, dimming it a notch. "I'm so sorry we lost your parents."

"It's not your fault. You didn't sic Fenrir on them." I sent a wave of love at him—just enough to be the equivalent of an energetic hug, definitely *not* enough to send him off trying to kiss the first girl who walked by. Again. *Lucky Brynn.*

"Yeah, but—"

"But nothing. They're gone; it's nobody's fault but Fenrir's...well, Fenrir's and *hers.*" I forced the image of Fenrir's accomplice out of my head. "And that devil woman fled Asgard the day of the attack, so let's move forward and give Mom a legacy to be proud of."

Forse nodded. I knew it was hard for him to put his worry aside, but he stayed very still and his energy started to calm. "I'm all yours."

Gods, I wish.

"I'm going back in," I declared. "Let's see if I can get it right this time."

Forse nodded again. With the path to his energy centers clear, I began my assessment. *Analyze each location. Identify any blocks. Isolate and remove the barrier.* It seemed simple enough. Odin willing, this approach worked. Between Fenrir's attacks, Hel's abduction of our love goddess, Freya, and this bizarre cold spell in a realm plagued by global warming, I sensed the *perfekt* balance of our realms was starting to tip toward the dark side. If I could just hold it together until my brother got around to marrying his girlfriend, Mia, then under Asgardian law she'd assume the role of Unifier. I had every confidence she'd be brilliant at the job. She had an innate knack for smoothing out emotionally charged situations, and she somehow managed to make my normally uptight brother calm enough to see the big picture. Once Mia could take over as Asgard's Unifier, I'd get to go back to my *other* full-time job, High Healer —a calling I was considerably less bad at.

For all our sakes, I hoped Tyr proposed soon. Like, yesterday, soon.

"Elsa? Are we still doing this?" Forse interrupted my derailed train of thought.

"Yes. Sorry. I'm really distracted today."

Forse chuckled. "Am I that boring on the inside?"

"Quite the opposite. You're positively brilliant on the inside." He was. His entire being was filled with a striking golden light. It was a testament to a life lived with *ære*—honor.

"You flatter me, *hjärtat*. Now get to work."

"Yes, sir." I zeroed in on the glowing light at the base of Forse's spine. Mortals called the pulsing markers along the spine chakras, but Asgardians knew them as energy centers. These tiny orbs contained a blueprint of Forse's past, and predicted the choices of his future. Each represented a different function—for example, Forse's first center, the one at the base of his spine, permeated a clear white light. It made sense that the center reflecting his family of origin would be so pure —Forse's dad, Balder, was the God of Light, and his mom, Nanna, was the Goddess of Warmth—the immortal embodiment of maternal love. Forse's childhood had been uncharacteristically secure for an Asgardian, and he'd maintained a close relationship with his parents and his brother once he took his own title.

"Your first center's clear—no blocks there. How are your parents?" I asked.

"They're good. Mom wants you to come for dinner the next time we're in Asgard. She looked at those pictures I sent her of you with Mia—she's convinced you're not eating enough, and she wants to fatten you up." I could hear Forse's smile, even with my eyes closed.

"I love your mom." I grinned back, then furrowed my brow as I analyzed the next two orbs. "Your second center's clear, and your third center is gorgeous—you really know where you fit in the world, don't you?"

Forse sighed. "It's the blessing and the curse of being of Asgard—when Odin gifts you a title, you kind of have to stick with it."

"Tell me about it," I murmured. "Fourth center is...hmm."

"What?" Forse asked.

"There's something in your love center—a little speck that's popping against the gold. Would you mind if I went in deeper?" Asking permission was a requisite of healing; I assumed the rules were the same for unifying. A god's spirit was uniquely theirs, after all.

"You do what you have to do," Forse agreed. But the speck grew bigger as he spoke. *Interesting.*

"Okay." I took a breath and pushed my energy against Forse's, making my way through the waves of gold surrounding his heart until I neared the speck. This close to the core of the love center, the energy was a muddied brown. *That's strange.* I pressed closer, and for the first time I felt a resistance. With another breath, I ploughed forward. Forse's energy pushed back, rejecting my advances. I squared my shoulders and tried again, and this time the energy parted to let me though. The moment I caught sight of the iron wall surrounding the center's core, the brown energy closed ranks and pushed me back, forcibly ejecting me from the justice god's energy field.

"Elsa? Are you all right?" Forse's hand reached out to steady me. My eyes flew open. The sudden transition had thrown me off balance. Forse's fingers squeezed my shoulder, and I fixated on the way the thick muscles of his forearms flexed as he pulled me back up. "Why don't you lie down for a bit?"

"I'm fine." I tore my eyes away from Forse's arms and studied his face. "What happened? You pushed me out."

"I...uh . . ."

Forse's body language spoke volumes. His shoulders were tense, his fists clenched. Everything about him screamed *run.*

"Hey." I reached up and placed my hand over his heart. It pounded against my palm in a frenetic rhythm, its anxious beat a stark contrast to the soothing snowfall outside the window. "I'm sorry. I shouldn't have pressured you. You don't have to talk about it, what-ever it is."

"I want to help, Elsa, it's just—"

A whirl of violet-blue eyes and vanilla perfume interrupted Forse's explanation. My brother's girl-friend threw open the front door and burst into my living room, her normally sleek hair frizzing beneath a light layer of snowflakes.

"*Hei,* Mia. Is everything okay?" My hand fell from Forse's heart as I moved to her side.

"Not exactly." She finger-combed her hair into submission.

"What's going on?" Forse asked.

"Well, first of all, it's snowing again. We live in Arcata, for Pete's sake. If I'd wanted to walk to class in the snow, I would have stayed on the East Coast for college." Mia shook her head. "But more importantly, Tyr wants to see Forse back at his place right away. I figured I'd find him here."

"Am I that predictable?" Forse asked.

"Yes." Mia nodded. "Elsa, you'd better come, too. Tyr was doing the jaw-clench thing. Whatever it is that's got his boxer-briefs in a twist, it's probably not good."

Forse raised an eyebrow at me, and I shrugged. We'd had a string of calm months since we got Freya back from Helheim. We were about due for a crisis.

"Let's go." Forse crossed to the hooks by the entry and helped me into my jacket. He tugged his sweater over his head and opened the front door. Mia filed through, and I followed suit. As we walked across the forest to my brother's house, I snuck a glance at the god clenching his fists beside me.

Something told me it wasn't Tyr's summons that had him on edge. What was Forse Styrke hiding behind that iron wall?